THE LAST TRAIL

Zane Grey

DOVER PUBLICATIONS, INC.
MINEOLA, NEW YORK

DOVER THRIFT EDITIONS

GENERAL EDITOR: SUSAN L. RATTINER
EDITOR OF THIS VOLUME: JANET B. KOPITO

Bibliographical Note

This Dover edition, first published in 2018, is an unabridged republication of a standard edition of the work published by Grosset and Dunlap, New York, in 1909. A new Note has been specially prepared for the Dover edition. The work contains language and attitudes of the period during which it is set, which, regrettably, may offend the modern reader.

Library of Congress Cataloging-in-Publication Data

Names: Grey, Zane, 1872–1939, author.
Title: The last trail / Zane Grey.
Description: Mineola, New York : Dover Publications, 2018. | Series: Dover thrift editions
Identifiers: LCCN 2018027184| ISBN 9780486827698 (paperback) | ISBN 0486827690 (paperback)
Subjects: LCSH: Zane, Betty—Fiction. | Wetzel, Lewis, 1763–1808—Fiction. | Frontier and pioneer life—Fiction. | Scouting (Reconnaissance)—Fiction. | Women pioneers—Fiction. | Ohio River Valley—Fiction. | Biographical fiction. | Western stories. | BISAC: FICTION / Westerns. | FICTION / Action & Adventure.
Classification: LCC PS3513.R6545 L3 2018 | DDC 813/.52—dc23
LC record available at https://lccn.loc.gov/2018027184

Manufactured in the United States by LSC Communications
82769002   2019
www.doverpublications.com

Note

The author of dozens of novels set in the American West, Zane Grey was born Pearl Zane Gray in Zanesville, Ohio, a town founded by his ancestors. After playing baseball on a college scholarship and then at the amateur level, he chose to open a dental practice in New York City (his father was a dentist as well). Lina Elise Roth, whom he met in Pennsylvania and married in 1905, suggested that he try his hand at writing, and Grey abandoned dentistry to pursue novel writing. Mrs. Grey, known as "Dolly," was prescient: Zane Grey found great success as an author; in fact, he was the first American writer to become a millionaire from the sale of his books.

Grey first visited the western states in 1906 on his honeymoon. Several years later, he wrote *The Last of the Plainsmen*, an account of his travels with Buffalo Jones, an outdoorsman who preferred taming buffalo to killing them. A highlight of the book is an encounter between the travelers' dogs and a pack of white wolves that leaves some of the dogs infected with rabies, and the travelers exposed to the rabid, charging beasts. Illustrated by Grey with his own photographs and drawings, the book conveys the excitement of wilderness travel and the author's growing fascination with the vivid colors and land formations of the western landscape. Rejected by a publisher, the work was picked up by *Outing* magazine. *Riders of the Purple Sage,* his best-known and bestselling work, was published in 1912; its sequel, *Rainbow Trial,* appeared in 1915. These novels of the Old West established Grey's literary reputation once and for all.

After moving to California in 1918 with his wife and children, Grey formed a production company to make silent movies of his novels; he sold the company and continued to write Westerns and novels. He still found time for his athletic and outdoor pursuits and achieved renown as an award-winning ocean fisherman. Wandering far from the United States, he visited Australia, New Zealand, and Tahiti, following his passion for deep-sea fishing. In addition to his many articles on sport fishing, Grey wrote about this all-consuming aspect of his life in *An American Angler in Australia*.

Zane Grey died in 1939 in California. Many of his manuscripts, hitherto unpublished, were brought out to an enthusiastic public after his death. The dozens of Hollywood movies based on his Westerns helped preserve his vision of the American West; they also brought to the screen actors such as Randolph Scott, Gary Cooper, Shirley Temple, and Robert Young, as well as drawing upon the talents of the directors John Ford, Fritz Lang, and Victor Fleming. The *Zane Grey Theatre* presented to an eager television-viewing public adaptations of Grey's work (as well as some original material) for a run of five years (1956–61).

The Last Trail, published in 1909, takes place during a time of westward expansion in the United States, with confrontations between the settlers and the native populations. Set in the late 1700s, the plot concerns a party of settlers near Fort Henry in the Ohio Valley as they face the uncertainties of life amid constant dangers, including their "hazardous journey through the wilderness" as they sought land and new lives. The complicated romantic relationship between Helen Sheppard, a "splendid specimen of womanhood," and Jonathan Zane, a "borderman" who patrols the region to protect the pioneers from both outlaws and local Native Americans, is set against this background. The "hot, young love" experienced by Helen leads her into the "depths of despair," as she pins her hopes on the valiant but conflicted, stoic Jonathan, a man who is wedded to his job; in his words: "My life is the border's: my sweetheart is the North Star!" The abduction of Helen spurs Jonathan forward on the borderman's "last trail."

THE LAST TRAIL

CHAPTER I

TWILIGHT OF A certain summer day, many years ago, shaded softly down over the wild Ohio valley bringing keen anxiety to a traveler on the lonely river trail. He had expected to reach Fort Henry with his party on this night, thus putting a welcome end to the long, rough, hazardous journey through the wilderness; but the swift, on-coming dusk made it imperative to halt. The narrow, forest-skirted trail, difficult to follow in broad daylight, apparently led into gloomy aisles in the woods. His guide had abandoned him that morning, making excuse that his services were no longer needed; his teamster was new to the frontier, and, altogether, the situation caused him much uneasiness.

"I wouldn't so much mind another night in camp, if the guide had not left us," he said in a low tone to the teamster.

That worthy shook his shaggy head, and growled while he began unhitching the horses.

"Uncle," said a young man, who had clambered out from the wagon, "we must be within a few miles of Fort Henry."

"How d'ye know we're near the fort?" interrupted the teamster, "or safe, either, fer thet matter? I don't know this country."

"The guide assured me we could easily make Fort Henry by sundown."

"Thet guide! I tell ye, Mr. Sheppard——"

"Not so loud. Do not alarm my daughter," cautioned the man who had been called Sheppard.

"Did ye notice anythin' queer about thet guide?" asked the teamster, lowering his voice. "Did ye see how oneasy he was last night? Did it strike ye he left us in a hurry, kind of excited like, in spite of his offhand manner?"

1

"Yes, he acted odd, or so it seemed to me," replied Sheppard. "How about you, Will?"

"Now that I think of it, I believe he was queer. He behaved like a man who expected somebody, or feared something might happen. I fancied, however, that it was simply the manner of a woodsman."

"Wal, I hev my opinion," said the teamster, in a gruff whisper. "Ye was in a hurry to be a-goin', an' wouldn't take no advice. The fur-trader at Fort Pitt didn't give this guide Jenks no good send off. Said he wasn't well-known round Pitt, 'cept he could handle a knife some."

"What is your opinion?" asked Sheppard, as the teamster paused.

"Wal, the valley below Pitt is full of renegades, outlaws an' hoss-thieves. The redskins ain't so bad as they used to be, but these white fellers are wusser'n ever. This guide Jenks might be in with them, that's all. Mebbe I'm wrong. I hope so. The way he left us looks bad."

"We won't borrow trouble. If we have come all this way without seeing either Indian or outlaw—in fact, without incident—I feel certain we can perform the remainder of the journey in safety." Then Mr. Sheppard raised his voice. "Here, Helen, you lazy girl, come out of that wagon. We want some supper. Will, you gather some firewood, and we'll soon give this gloomy little glen a more cheerful aspect."

As Mr. Sheppard turned toward the canvas-covered wagon a girl leaped lightly down beside him. She was nearly as tall as he.

"Is this Fort Henry?" she asked, cheerily, beginning to dance around him. "Where's the inn? I'm *so* hungry. How glad I am to get out of that wagon! I'd like to run. Isn't this a lonesome, lovely spot?"

A camp-fire soon crackled with hiss and sputter, and fragrant wood-smoke filled the air. Steaming kettle, and savory steaks of venison cheered the hungry travelers, making them forget for the time the desertion of their guide and the fact that they might be lost. The last glow faded entirely out of the western sky. Night enveloped the forest, and the little glade was a bright spot in the gloom.

The flickering light showed Mr. Sheppard to be a well-preserved old man with gray hair and ruddy, kindly face. The nephew had a boyish, frank expression. The girl was a spendid specimen of womanhood. Her large, laughing eyes were as dark as the shadows beneath the trees.

Suddenly a quick start on Helen's part interrupted the merry flow of conversation. She sat bolt upright with half-averted face.

"Cousin, what is the matter?" asked Will, quickly.

Helen remained motionless.

"My dear," said Mr. Sheppard sharply.

"I heard a footstep," she whispered, pointing with trembling finger toward the impenetrable blackness beyond the camp-fire.

All could hear a soft patter on the leaves. Then distinct footfalls broke the silence.

The tired teamster raised his shaggy head and glanced fearfully around the glade. Mr. Sheppard and Will gazed doubtfully toward the foliage; but Helen did not change her position. The travelers appeared stricken by the silence and solitude of the place. The faint hum of insects, and the low moan of the night wind, seemed accentuated by the almost painful stillness.

"A panther, most likely," suggested Sheppard, in a voice which he intended should be reassuring. "I saw one to-day slinking along the trail."

"I'd better get my gun from the wagon," said Will.

"How dark and wild it is here!" exclaimed Helen nervously. "I believe I was frightened. Perhaps I fancied it—there! Again—listen. Ah!"

Two tall figures emerged from the darkness into the circle of light, and with swift, supple steps gained the camp-fire before any of the travelers had time to move. They were Indians, and the brandishing of their tomahawks proclaimed that they were hostile.

"Ugh!" grunted the taller savage, as he looked down upon the defenseless, frightened group.

As the menacing figures stood in the glare of the fire gazing at the party with shifty eyes, they presented a frightful appearance. Fierce lineaments, all the more so because of bars of paint, the hideous, shaven heads adorned with tufts of hair holding a single feather, sinewy, copper-colored limbs suggestive of action and endurance, the general aspect of untamed ferocity, appalled the travelers and chilled their blood.

Grunts and chuckles manifested the satisfaction with which the Indians fell upon the half-finished supper. They caused it to vanish with astonishing celerity, and resembled wolves rather than human beings in their greediness.

Helen looked timidly around as if hoping to see those who would aid, and the savages regarded her with ill humor. A movement on the part of any member of the group caused muscular hands to steal toward the tomahawks.

Suddenly the larger savage clutched his companion's knee. Then lifting his hatchet, shook it with a significant gesture in Sheppard's face, at the same time putting a finger on his lips to enjoin silence. Both Indians became statuesque in their immobility. They crouched in an attitude of listening, with heads bent on one side, nostrils dilated, and mouths open.

One, two, three moments passed. The silence of the forest appeared to be unbroken; but ears as keen as those of a deer had detected some sound. The larger savage dropped noiselessly to the ground, where he lay stretched out with his ear to the ground. The other remained immovable; only his beady eyes gave signs of life, and these covered every point.

Finally the big savage rose silently, pointed down the dark trail, and strode out of the circle of light. His companion followed close at his heels. The two disappeared in the black shadows like specters, as silently as they had come.

"Well!" breathed Helen.

"I am immensely relieved!" exclaimed Will.

"What do you make of such strange behavior?" Sheppard asked of the teamster.

"I 'spect they got wind of somebody; most likely thet guide, an 'll be back again. If they ain't, it's because they got switched off by some signs or tokens, skeered, perhaps, by the scent of the wind."

Hardly had he ceased speaking when again the circle of light was invaded by stalking forms.

"I thought so! Here comes the skulkin' varmints," whispered the teamster.

But he was wrong. A deep, calm voice spoke the single word: "Friends."

Two men in the brown garb of woodsmen approached. One approached the travelers; the other remained in the background, leaning upon a long, black rifle.

Thus exposed to the glare of the flames, the foremost woodsman presented a singularly picturesque figure. His costume was the fringed buckskins of the border. Fully six feet tall, this lithe-limbed young giant had something of the wild, free grace of the Indian in his posture.

He surveyed the wondering travelers with dark, grave eyes.

"Did the reddys do any mischief?" he asked.

"No, they didn't harm us," replied Sheppard. "They ate our supper, and slipped off into the woods without so much as touching one of us. But, indeed, sir, we are mighty glad to see you."

Will echoed this sentiment, and Helen's big eyes were fastened upon the stranger in welcome and wonder.

"We saw your fire blazin' through the twilight, an' came up just in time to see the Injuns make off."

"Might they not hide in the bushes and shoot us?" asked Will, who had listened to many a border story at Fort Pitt. "It seems as if we'd make good targets in this light."

The gravity of the woodsman's face relaxed.

"You wills pursue them?" asked Helen.

"They've melted into the night-shadows long ago," he replied. "Who was your guide?"

"I hired him at Fort Pitt. He left us suddenly this morning. A big man, with black beard and bushy eyebrows. A bit of his ear had been shot or cut out," Sheppard replied.

"Jenks, one of Bing Legget's border-hawks."

"You have his name right. And who may Bing Legget be?"

"He's an outlaw. Jenks has been tryin' to lead you into a trap. Likely he expected those Injuns to show up a day or two ago. Somethin' went wrong with the plan, I reckon. Mebbe he was waitin' for five Shawnees, an' mebbe he'll never see three of 'em again."

Something suggestive, cold, and grim, in the last words did not escape the listeners.

"How far are we from Fort Henry?" asked Sheppard.

"Eighteen miles as a crow flies; longer by trail."

"Treachery!" exclaimed the old man. "We were no more than that this morning. It is indeed fortunate that you found us. I take it you are from Fort Henry, and will guide us there? I am an old friend of Colonel Zane's. He will appreciate any kindness you may show us. Of course you know him?"

"I am Jonathan Zane."

Sheppard suddenly realized that he was facing the most celebrated scout on the border. In Revolutionary times Zane's fame had extended even to the far Atlantic Colonies.

"And your companion?" asked Sheppard with keen interest. He guessed what might be told. Border lore coupled Jonathan Zane with a strange and terrible character, a border Nemesis, a mysterious, shadowy, elusive man, whom few pioneers ever saw, but of whom all knew.

"Wetzel," answered Zane.

With one accord the travelers gazed curiously at Zane's silent companion. In the dim background of the glow cast by the fire, he stood a gigantic figure, dark, quiet, and yet with something intangible in his shadowy outline.

Suddenly he appeared to merge into the gloom as if he really were a phantom. A warning, "Hist!" came from the bushes.

With one swift kick Zane scattered the camp-fire.

The travelers waited with bated breaths. They could hear nothing save the beating of their own hearts; they could not even see each other.

"Better go to sleep," came in Zane's calm voice. What a relief it was! "We'll keep watch, an' at daybreak guide you to Fort Henry."

CHAPTER II

COLONEL ZANE, A rugged, stalwart pioneer, with a strong, dark face, sat listening to his old friend's dramatic story. At its close a genial smile twinkled in his fine dark eyes.

"Well, well, Sheppard, no doubt it was a thrilling adventure to you," he said. "It might have been a little more interesting, and doubtless would, had I not sent Wetzel and Jonathan to look you up."

"You did? How on earth did you know I was on the border? I counted much on the surprise I should give you."

"My Indian runners leave Fort Pitt ahead of any travelers, and acquaint me with particulars."

"I remembered a fleet-looking Indian who seemed to be asking for information about us, when we arrived at Fort Pitt. I am sorry I did not take the fur-trader's advice in regard to the guide. But I was in such a hurry to come, and didn't feel able to bear the expense of a raft or boat that we might come by river. My nephew brought considerable gold, and I all my earthly possessions."

"All's well that ends well," replied Colonel Zane cheerily. "But we must thank Providence that Wetzel and Jonathan came up in the nick of time."

"Indeed, yes. I'm not likely to forget those fierce savages. How they slipped off into the darkness! I wonder if Wetzel pursued them? He disappeared last night, and we did not see him again. In fact we hardly had a fair look at him. I question if I should recognize him now, unless by his great stature."

"He was ahead of Jonathan on the trail. That is Wetzel's way. In times of danger he is seldom seen, yet is always near. But come, let us go out and look around. I am running up a log cabin which will come in handy for you."

They passed out into the shade of pine and maples. A winding path led down a gentle slope. On the hillside under a spreading tree a throng of bearded pioneers, clad in faded buckskins and wearing white-ringed coonskin caps, were erecting a log cabin.

"Life here on the border is keen, hard, invigorating," said Colonel Zane. "I tell you, George Sheppard, in spite of your gray hair and your pretty daughter, you have come out West because you want to live among men who do things."

"Colonel, I won't gainsay I've still got hot blood," replied Sheppard; "but I came to Fort Henry for land. My old home in Williamsburg has fallen into ruin together with the fortunes of my family. I brought my daughter and my nephew because I wanted them to take root in new soil."

"Well, George, right glad we are to have you. Where are your sons? I remember them, though 'tis sixteen long years since I left old Williamsburg."

"Gone. The Revolution took my sons. Helen is the last of the family."

"Well, well, indeed that's hard. Independence has cost you colonists as big a price as border-freedom has us pioneers. Come, old friend, forget the past. A new life begins for you here, and it will be one which gives you much. See, up goes a cabin; that will soon be your home."

Sheppard's eye marked the sturdy pioneers and a fast diminishing pile of white-oak logs.

"Ho-heave!" cried a brawny foreman.

A dozen stout shoulders sagged beneath a well-trimmed log.

"Ho-heave!" yelled the foreman.

"See, up she goes," cried the colonel, "and to-morrow night she'll shed rain."

They walked down a sandy lane bounded on the right by a wide, green clearing, and on the left by a line of chestnuts and maples, outposts of the thick forests beyond.

"Yours is a fine site for a house," observed Sheppard, taking in the clean-trimmed field that extended up the hillside, a brook that splashed clear and noisy over the stones to tarry in a little grass-bound lake which forced water through half-hollowed logs into a spring house.

"I think so; this is the fourth time I've put up a cabin on this land," replied the colonel.

"How's that?"

"The redskins are keen to burn things."

Sheppard laughed at the pioneer's reply. "It's not difficult, Colonel Zane, to understand why Fort Henry has stood all these years, with you as its leader. Certainly the location for your cabin is the finest in the settlement. What a view!"

High upon a bluff overhanging the majestic, slow-winding Ohio, the colonel's cabin afforded a commanding position from which to view the picturesque valley. Sheppard's eye first caught the outline of the huge, bold, time-blackened fort which frowned protectingly over surrounding log-cabins; then he saw the wide-sweeping river with its verdant islands, golden, sandy bars, and willow-bordered shores, while beyond, rolling pastures of wavy grass merging into green forests that swept upward with slow swell until lost in the dim purple of distant mountains.

"Sixteen years ago I came out of the thicket upon yonder bluff, and saw this valley. I was deeply impressed by its beauty, but more by its wonderful promise."

"Were you alone?"

"I and my dog. There had been a few white men before me on the river; but I was the first to see this glorious valley from the bluff. Now, George, I'll let you have a hundred acres of well-cleared land. The soil is so rich you can raise two crops in one season. With some stock, and a few good hands, you'll soon be a busy man."

"I didn't expect so much land; I can't well afford to pay for it."

"Talk to me of payment when the farm yields an income. Is this young nephew of yours strong and willing?"

"He is, and has gold enough to buy a big farm."

"Let him keep his money, and make a comfortable home for some good lass. We marry our young people early out here. And your daughter, George, is she fitted for this hard border life?"

"Never fear for Helen."

"The brunt of this pioneer work falls on our women. God bless them, how heroic they've been! The life here is rough for a man, let alone a woman. But it is a man's game. We need girls, girls who will bear strong men. Yet I am always saddened when I see one come out on the border."

"I think I knew what I was bringing Helen to, and she didn't flinch," said Sheppard, somewhat surprised at the tone in which the colonel spoke.

"No one knows until he has lived on the border. Well, well, all this is discouraging to you. Ah! here is Miss Helen with my sister."

The colonel's fine, dark face lost its sternness, and brightened with a smile.

"I hope you rested well after your long ride."

"I am seldom tired, and I have been made most comfortable. I thank you and your sister," replied the girl, giving Colonel Zane her hand, and including both him and his sister in her grateful glance.

The colonel's sister was a slender, handsome young woman, whose dark beauty showed to most effective advantage by the contrast with her companion's fair skin, golden hair, and blue eyes.

Beautiful as was Helen Sheppard, it was her eyes that held Colonel Zane irresistibly. They were unusually large, of a dark purple-blue that changed, shaded, shadowed with her every thought.

"Come, let us walk," Colonel Zane said abruptly, and, with Mr. Sheppard, followed the girls down the path. He escorted them to the fort, showed a long room with little squares cut in the rough-hewn logs, many bullet holes, fire-charred timbers, and dark stains, terribly suggestive of the pain and heroism which the defense of that rude structure had cost.

Under Helen's eager questioning Colonel Zane yielded to his weakness for story-telling, and recited the history of the last siege of Fort Henry; how the renegade Girty swooped down upon the settlement with hundreds of Indians and British soldiers; how for three days of whistling bullets, flaming arrows, screeching demons, fire, smoke, and attack following attack, the brave defenders stood at their posts, there to die before yielding.

"Grand!" breathed Helen, and her eyes glowed. "It was then Betty Zane ran with the powder? Oh! I've heard the story."

"Let my sister tell you of that," said the colonel, smiling.

"You! Was it you?" And Helen's eyes glowed brighter with the light of youth's glory in great deeds.

"My sister has been wedded and widowed since then," said Colonel Zane, reading in Helen's earnest scrutiny of his sister's calm, sad face a wonder if this quiet woman could be the fearless and famed Elizabeth Zane.

Impulsively Helen's hand closed softly over her companion's. Out of the girlish sympathetic action a warm friendship was born.

"I imagine things do happen here," said Mr. Sheppard, hoping to hear more from Colonel Zane.

The colonel smiled grimly.

"Every summer during fifteen years has been a bloody one on the border. The sieges of Fort Henry, and Crawford's defeat, the biggest things we ever knew out here, are matters of history; of course you are familiar with them. But the numberless Indian forays and attacks, the women who have been carried into captivity by renegades, the murdered farmers, in fact, ceaseless war never long directed at any point, but carried on the entire length of the river, are matters known only to the pioneers. Within five miles of Fort Henry I can show you where the laurel bushes grow three feet high over the ashes of two settlements, and many a clearing where some unfortunate pioneer had staked his claim and thrown up a log cabin, only to die fighting for his wife and children. Between here and Fort Pitt there is only one settlement, Yellow Creek, and most of its inhabitants are survivors of abandoned villages farther up the river. Last summer we had the Moravian Massacre, the blackest, most inhuman deed ever committeed. Since then Simon Girty and his bloody redskins have lain low."

"You must always have had a big force," said Sheppard.

"We've managed always to be strong enough, though there never were a large number of men here. During the last siege I had only forty in the fort, counting men, women and boys. But I had pioneers and women who could handle a rifle, and the best border-men on the frontier."

"Do you make a distinction between pioneers and bordermen?" asked Sheppard.

"Indeed, yes. I am a pioneer; a borderman is an Indian hunter, or scout. For years my cabins housed Andrew Zane, Sam and John McCollock, Bill Metzar, and John and Martin Wetzel, all of whom are dead. Not one saved his scalp. Fort Henry is growing; it has pioneers, rivermen, soldiers, but only two bordermen. Wetzel and Jonathan are the only ones we have left of those great men."

"They must be old," mused Helen, with a dreamy glow still in her eyes.

"Well, Miss Helen, not in years, as you mean. Life here is old in experience; few pioneers, and no bordermen, live to a great age. Wetzel is about forty, and my brother Jonathan still a young man; but both are old in border lore."

Earnestly, as a man who loves his subject, Colonel Zane told his listeners of these two most prominent characters of the border. Sixteen years previously, when but boys in years, they had cast in their lot with his, and journeyed over the Virginian Mountains, Wetzel to devote his life to the vengeful calling he had chosen, and Jonathan to give rein to an adventurous spirit and love of the wilds. By some wonderful chance, by cunning, woodcraft, or daring, both men had lived through the years of border warfare which had brought to a close the careers of all their contemporaries.

For many years Wetzel preferred solitude to companionship; he roamed the wilderness in pursuit of Indians, his life-long foes, and seldom appeared at the settlement except to bring news of an intended raid of the savages. Jonathan also spent much time alone in the woods, or scouting along the river. But of late years a friendship had ripened between the two bordermen. Mutual interest had brought them together on the trail of a noted renegade, and when, after many long days of patient watching and persistent tracking, the outlaw paid an awful penalty for his bloody deeds, these lone and silent men were friends.

Powerful in build, fleet as deer, fearless and tireless, Wetzel's peculiar bloodhound sagacity, ferocity, and implacability, balanced by Jonathan's keen intelligence and judgment caused these bordermen to become the bane of redmen and renegades. Their fame increased with each succeeding summer, until now the people of the settlement looked upon wonderful deeds of strength and of woodcraft as a matter of course, rejoicing in the power and skill with which these men were endowed.

By common consent the pioneers attributed any mysterious deed, from the finding of a fat turkey on a cabin doorstep, to the discovery of a savage scalped and pulled from his ambush near a settler's spring, to Wetzel and Jonathan. All the more did they feel sure of this conclusion because the bordermen never spoke of their deeds. Sometimes a pioneer living on the outskirts of the settlement would be awakened in the morning by a single rifle shot, and on peering out would see a dead Indian lying almost across his doorstep, while beyond, in the dim, gray mist, a tall figure stealing away. Often in the twilight on a summer evening, while fondling his children and enjoying his smoke after a hard day's labor in the fields, this same settler would see the tall, dark figure of Jonathan

Zane step noiselessly out of a thicket, and learn that he must take his family and flee at once to the fort for safety. When a settler was murdered, his children carried into captivity by Indians, and the wife given over to the power of some brutal renegade, tragedies wofully frequent on the border, Wetzel and Jonathan took the trail alone. Many a white woman was returned alive and, sometimes, unharmed to her relatives; more than one maiden lived to be captured, rescued, and returned to her lover, while almost numberless were the bones of brutal redmen lying in the deep and gloomy woods, or bleaching on the plains, silent, ghastly reminders of the stern justice meted out by these two heroes.

"Such are my two bordermen, Miss Sheppard. The fort there, and all these cabins, would be only black ashes, save for them, and as for us, our wives and children—God only knows."

"Haven't they wives and children, too?" asked Helen.

"No," answered Colonel Zane, with his genial smile. "Such joys are not for bordermen."

"Why not? Fine men like them deserve happiness," declared Helen.

"It is necessary we have such," said the colonel simply, "and they cannot be bordermen unless free as the air blows. Wetzel and Jonathan have never had sweethearts. I believe Wetzel loved a lass once; but he was an Indian-killer whose hands were red with blood. He silenced his heart, and kept to his chosen, lonely life. Jonathan does not seem to realize that women exist to charm, to please, to be loved and married. Once we twitted him about his brothers doing their duty by the border, whereupon he flashed out: 'My life is the border's: my sweetheart is the North Star!'"

Helen dreamily watched the dancing, dimpling waves that broke on the stones of the river shore. All unconscious of the powerful impression the colonel's recital had made upon her, she was feeling the greatness of the lives of these bordermen, and the glory it would now be for her to share with others the pride in their protection.

"Say, Sheppard, look here," said Colonel Zane, on the return to his cabin, "that girl of yours has a pair of eyes. I can't forget the way they flashed! They'll cause more trouble here among my garrison than would a swarm of redskins."

"No! You don't mean it! Out here in this wilderness?" queried Sheppard doubtfully.

"Well, I do."

"O Lord! What a time I've had with that girl! There was one man especially, back home, who made our lives miserable. He was rich and well born; but Helen would have none of him. He got around me, old fool that I am! Practically stole what was left of my estate, and gambled it away when Helen said she'd die before giving herself to him. It was partly on his account that I brought her away. Then there were a lot of moon-eyed beggars after her all the time, and she's young and full of fire. I hoped I'd marry her to some farmer out here, and end my days in peace."

"Peace? With eyes like those? Never on this green earth," and Colonel Zane laughed as he slapped his friend on the shoulder. "Don't worry, old fellow. You can't help her having those changing dark-blue eyes any more than you can help being proud of them. They have won me, already, susceptible old backwoodsman! I'll help you with this spirited young lady. I've had experience, Sheppard, and don't you forget it. First, my sister, a Zane all through, which is saying enough. Then as sweet and fiery a little Indian princess as ever stepped in a beaded moccasin, and since, more than one beautiful, impulsive creature. Being in authority, I suppose it's natural that all the work, from keeping the garrison ready against an attack, to straightening out love affairs, should fall upon me. I'll take the care off your shoulders; I'll keep these young dare-devils from killing each other over Miss Helen's favors. I certainly—Hello! There are strangers at the gate. Something's up."

Half a dozen rough-looking men had appeared from round the corner of the cabin, and halted at the gate.

"Bill Elsing, and some of his men from Yellow Creek," said Colonel Zane, as he went toward the group.

"Hullo, Kurnel," was the greeting of the foremost, evidently the leader. "We've lost six head of hosses over our way, an' are out lookin' 'em up."

"The deuce you have! Say, this horse-stealing business is getting interesting. What did you come in for?"

"Wal, we meets Jonathan on the ridge about sunup, an' he sent us back lickety-cut. Said he had two of the hosses corralled, an' mebbe Wetzel could git the others."

"That's strange," replied Colonel Zane thoughtfully.

"'Pears to me Jack and Wetzel hev some redskins treed, an' didn't want us to spile the fun. Mebbe there wasn't scalps enough to go round. Anyway, we come in, an' we'll hang up here to-day."

"Bill, who's doing this horse-stealing?"

"Damn if I know. It's a mighty pert piece of work. I've a mind it's some slick white fellar, with Injuns backin' him."

Helen noted, when she was once more indoors, that Colonel Zane's wife appeared worried. Her usual placid expression was gone. She put off the playful overtures of her two bright boys with unusual indifference, and turned to her husband with anxious questioning as to whether the strangers brought news of Indians. Upon being assured that such was not the case, she looked relieved, and explained to Helen that she had seen armed men come so often to consult the colonel regarding dangerous missions and expeditions, that the sight of a stranger caused her unspeakable dread.

"I am accustomed to danger, yet I can never control my fears for my husband and children," said Mrs. Zane. "The older I grow the more of a coward I am. Oh! this border life is sad for women. Only a little while ago my brother Samuel McColloch was shot and scalped right here on the river bank. He was going to the spring for a bucket of water. I lost another brother in almost the same way. Every day during the summer a husband and a father fall victim to some murderous Indian. My husband will go in the same way some day. The border claims them all."

"Bessie, you must not show your fears to our new friend. And, Miss Helen, don't believe she's the coward she would make out," said the colonel's sister smilingly.

"Betty is right, Bess, don't frighten her," said Colonel Zane. "I'm afraid I talked too much to-day. But, Miss Helen, you were so interested, and are such a good listener, that I couldn't refrain. Once for all let me say that you will no doubt see stirring life here; but there is little danger of its affecting you. To be sure I think you'll have troubles; but not with Indians or outlaws."

He winked at his wife and sister. At first Helen did not understand his sally, but then she blushed red all over her fair face.

Some time after that, while unpacking her belongings, she heard the clatter of horses' hoofs on the rocky road, accompanied by loud voices. Running to the window, she saw a group of men at the gate.

"Miss Sheppard, will you come out?" called Colonel Zane's sister from the door. "My brother Jonathan has returned."

Helen joined Betty at the door, and looked over her shoulder.

"Wal, Jack, ye got two on 'em, anyways," drawled a voice which she recognized as that of Elsing's.

A man, lithe and supple, slipped from the back of one of the horses, and, giving the halter to Elsing with a single word, turned and entered the gate. Colonel Zane met him there.

"Well, Jonathan, what's up?"

"There's hell to pay," was the reply, and the speaker's voice rang clear and sharp.

Colonel Zane laid his hand on his brother's shoulder, and thus they stood for a moment, singularly alike, and yet the sturdy pioneer was, somehow, far different from the dark-haired borderman.

"I thought we'd trouble in store from the look on your face," said the colonel calmly. "I hope you haven't very bad news on the first day, for our old friends from Virginia."

"Jonathan," cried Betty when he did not answer the colonel. At her call he half turned, and his dark eyes, steady, strained like those of a watching deer, sought his sister's face.

"Betty, old Jake Lane was murdered by horse thieves yesterday, and Mabel Lane is gone."

"Oh!" gasped Betty; but she said nothing more.

Colonel Zane cursed inaudibly.

"You know, Eb, I tried to keep Lane in the settlement for Mabel's sake. But he wanted to work that farm. I believe horse-stealing wasn't as much of an object as the girl. Pretty women are bad for the border, or any other place, I guess. Wetzel has taken the trail, and I came in because I've serious suspicions—I'll explain to you alone."

The borderman bowed gravely to Helen, with a natural grace, and yet a manner that sat awkwardly upon him. The girl, slightly flushed, and somewhat confused by this meeting with the man around whom her romantic imagination had already woven a story, stood in the doorway after giving him a fleeting glance, the fairest, sweetest picture of girlish beauty ever seen.

The men went into the house; but their voices came distinctly through the door.

"Eb, if Bing Legget or Girty ever see that big-eyed lass, they'll have her even if Fort Henry has to be burned, an' in case they do get her, Wetzel an' I'll have taken our last trail."

CHAPTER III

Supper over, Colonel Zane led his guests to a side porch, where they were soon joined by Mrs. Zane and Betty. The host's two boys, Noah and Sammy, who had preceded them, were now astride the porch-rail and, to judge by their antics, were riding wild Indian mustangs.

"It's quite cool," said Colonel Zane; "but I want you to see the sunset in the valley. A good many of your future neighbors may come over to-night for a word of welcome. It's the border custom."

He was about to seat himself by the side of Mr. Sheppard, on a rustic bench, when a Negro maid appeared in the doorway carrying a smiling, black-eyed baby. Colonel Zane took the child and, holding it aloft, said with fatherly pride:

"This is Rebecca Zane, the first girl baby born to the Zanes, and destined to be the belle of the border."

"May I have her?" asked Helen softly, holding out her arms. She took the child, and placed it upon her knee where its look of solemnity soon changed to one of infantile delight.

"Here come Nell and Jim," said Mrs. Zane, pointing toward the fort.

"Yes, and there comes my brother Silas with his wife, too," added Colonel Zane. "The first couple are James Douns, our young minister, and Nell, his wife. They came out here a year or so ago. James had a brother Joe, the finest young fellow who ever caught the border fever. He was killed by one of the Girtys. His was a wonderful story, and some day you shall hear about the parson and his wife."

"What's the border fever?" asked Mr. Sheppard.

"It's what brought you out here," replied Colonel Zane with a hearty laugh.

17

Helen gazed with interest at the couple now coming into the yard, and when they gained the porch she saw that the man was big and tall, with a frank, manly bearing, while his wife was a slender little woman with bright, sunny hair, and a sweet, smiling face. They greeted Helen and her father cordially.

Next came Silas Zane, a typical bronzed and bearded pioneer, with his buxom wife. Presently a little group of villagers joined the party. They were rugged men, clad in faded buckskins, and sober-faced women who wore dresses of plain gray linsey. They welcomed the newcomers with simple, homely courtesy. Then six young frontiersmen appeared from around a corner of the cabin, advancing hesitatingly. To Helen they all looked alike, tall, awkward, with brown faces and big hands. When Colonel Zane cheerily cried out to them, they stumbled forward with evident embarrassment, each literally crushing Helen's hand in his horny palm. Afterward they leaned on the rail and stole glances at her.

Soon a large number of villagers were on the porch or in the yard. After paying their respects to Helen and her father they took part in a general conversation. Two or three girls, the latest callers, were surrounded by half a dozen young fellows, and their laughter sounded high above the hum of voices.

Helen gazed upon this company with mingled feelings of relief and pleasure. She had been more concerned regarding the young people with whom her lot might be cast, than the dangers of which others had told. She knew that on the border there was no distinction of rank. Though she came of an old family, and, during her girlhood, had been surrounded by refinement, even luxury, she had accepted cheerfully the reverses of fortune, and was determined to curb the pride which had been hers. It was necessary she should have friends. Warm-hearted, impulsive and loving, she needed to have around her those in whom she could confide. Therefore it was with sincere pleasure she understood how groundless were her fears and knew that if she did not find good, true friends the fault would be her own. She saw at a glance that the colonel's widowed sister was her equal, perhaps her superior, in education and breeding, while Nellie Douns was as well-bred and gracious a little lady as she had ever met. Then, the other girls, too, were charming, with frank wholesomeness and freedom.

Concerning the young men, of whom there were about a dozen, Helen had hardly arrived at a conclusion. She liked the ruggedness, the signs of honest worth which clung to them. Despite her youth, she had been much sought after because of her personal attractions, and had thus added experience to the natural keen intuition all women possess. The glances of several of the men, particularly the bold regard of one Roger Brandt, whom Colonel Zane introduced, she had seen before, and learned to dislike. On the whole, however, she was delighted with the prospect of new friends and future prosperity, and she felt even greater pleasure in the certainty that her father shared her gratification.

Suddenly she became aware that the conversation had ceased. She looked up to see the tall, lithe form of Jonathan Zane as he strode across the porch. She could see that a certain constraint had momentarily fallen upon the company. It was an involuntary acknowledgment of the borderman's presence, of a presence that worked on all alike with a subtle, strong magnetism.

"Ah, Jonathan, come out to see the sunset? It's unusually fine to-night," said Colonel Zane.

With hardly more than a perceptible bow to those present, the borderman took a seat near the rail, and, leaning upon it, directed his gaze westward.

Helen sat so near she could have touched him. She was conscious of the same strange feeling, and impelling sense of power, which had come upon her so strongly at first sight of him. More than that, a lively interest had been aroused in her. This borderman was to her a new and novel character. She was amused at learning that here was a young man absolutely indifferent to the charms of the opposite sex, and although hardly admitting such a thing, she believed it would be possible to win him from his indifference. On raising her eyelids, it was with the unconcern which a woman feigns when suspecting she is being regarded with admiring eyes. But Jonathan Zane might not have known of her presence, for all the attention he paid her. Therefore, having a good opportunity to gaze at this borderman of daring deeds, Helen regarded him closely.

He was clad from head to foot in smooth, soft buckskin which fitted well his powerful frame. Beaded moccasins, leggings bound high above the knees, hunting coat laced and fringed, all had the neat, tidy appearance due to good care. He wore no weapons. His hair fell in a raven mass over his shoulders. His profile was regular, with a long, straight nose, strong chin, and eyes black as night.

They were now fixed intently on the valley. The whole face gave an impression of serenity, of calmness.

Helen was wondering if the sad, almost stern, tranquillity of that face ever changed, when the baby cooed and held out its chubby little hands. Jonathan's smile, which came quickly, accompanied by a warm light in the eyes, relieved Helen of an unaccountable repugnance she had begun to feel toward the borderman. That smile, brief as a flash, showed his gentle kindness and told that he was not a creature who had set himself apart from human life and love.

As he took little Rebecca, one of his hands touched Helen's. If he had taken heed of the contact, as any ordinary man might well have, she would, perhaps, have thought nothing about it, but because he did not appear to realize that her hand had been almost inclosed in his, she could not help again feeling his singular personality. She saw that this man had absolutely no thought of her. At the moment this did not awaken resentment, for with all her fire and pride she was not vain; but amusement gave place to a respect which came involuntarily.

Little Rebecca presently manifested the faithlessness peculiar to her sex, and had no sooner been taken upon Jonathan's knee than she cried out to go back to Helen.

"Girls are uncommon coy critters," said he, with a grave smile in his eyes. He handed back the child, and once more was absorbed in the setting sun.

Helen looked down the valley to behold the most beautiful spectacle she had ever seen. Between the hills far to the west, the sky flamed with a red and gold light. The sun was poised above the river, and the shimmering waters merged into a ruddy horizon. Long rays of crimson fire crossed the smooth waters. A few purple clouds above caught the refulgence, until aided by the delicate rose and blue space beyond, they became many hued ships sailing on a rainbow sea. Each second saw a gorgeous transformation. Slowly the sun dipped into the golden flood; one by one the clouds changed from crimson to gold, from gold to rose, and then to gray; slowly all the tints faded until, as the sun slipped out of sight, the brilliance gave way to the soft afterglow of warm lights. These in turn slowly toned down into gray twilight.

Helen retired to her room soon afterward, and, being unusually thoughtful, sat down by the window. She reviewed the events of this first day of her new life on the border. Her impressions had been so many, so varied, that she wanted to distinguish them. First she felt glad, with a sweet, warm thankfulness, that her father seemed so happy, so encouraged by the outlook. Breaking old ties had been, she knew, no child's play for him. She realized also that it had been done solely because there had been nothing left to offer her in the old home, and in a new one were hope and possibilities. Then she was relieved at getting away from the attentions of a man whose persistence had been most annoying to her. From thoughts of her father, and the old life, she came to her new friends of the present. She was so grateful for their kindness. She certainly would do all in her power to win and keep their esteem.

Somewhat of a surprise was it to her, that she reserved for Jonathan Zane the last and most prominent place in her meditations. She suddenly asked herself how she regarded this fighting borderman. She recalled her unbounded enthusiasm for the man as Colonel Zane had told of him; then her first glimpse, and her surprise and admiration at the lithe-limbed young giant; then incredulity, amusement, and respect followed in swift order, after which an unaccountable coldness that was almost resentment. Helen was forced to admit that she did not know how to regard him, but surely he was a man, throughout every inch of his superb frame, and one who took life seriously, with neither thought nor time for the opposite sex. And this last brought a blush to her cheek, for she distinctly remembered she had expected, if not admiration, more than passing notice from this hero of the border.

Presently she took a little mirror from a table near where she sat. Holding it to catch the fast-fading light, she studied her face seriously.

"Helen Sheppard, I think on the occasion of your arrival in a new country a little plain talk will be wholesome. Somehow or other, perhaps because of a crowd of idle men back there in the colonies, possibly from your own misguided fancy, you imagined you were fair to look at. It is well to be undeceived."

Scorn spoke in Helen's voice. She was angry because of having been interested in a man, and allowed that interest to betray her into a girlish expectation that he would treat her as all other men had. The mirror, even in the dim light, spoke more truly than she, for it caught the golden tints of her luxuriant hair, the thousand beautiful shadows in her great, dark eyes, the white glory of a face fair as a star, and the swelling outline of neck and shoulders.

With a sudden fiery impetuosity she flung the glass to the floor, where it was broken into several pieces.

"How foolish of me! What a temper I have!" she exclaimed repentantly. "I'm glad I have another glass. Wouldn't Mr. Jonathan Zane, borderman, Indian fighter, hero of a hundred battles and never a sweetheart, be flattered? No, most decidedly he wouldn't. He never looked at me. I don't think I expected that; I'm sure I didn't want it; but still he might have—Oh! what am I thinking, and he a stranger?"

Before Helen lost herself in slumber on that eventful evening, she vowed to ignore the borderman; assured herself that she did not want to see him again, and, rather inconsistently, that she would cure him of his indifference.

* * * * * *

When Colonel Zane's guests had retired, and the villagers were gone to their homes, he was free to consult with Jonathan.

"Well, Jack," he said, "I'm ready to hear about the horse thieves."

"Wetzel makes it out the man who's runnin' this hoss-stealin' is located right here in Fort Henry," answered the borderman.

The colonel had lived too long on the frontier to show surprise; he hummed a tune while the genial expression faded slowly from his face.

"Last count there were one hundred and ten men at the fort," he replied thoughtfully. "I know over a hundred, and can trust them. There are some new fellows on the boats, and several strangers hanging round Metzar's."

"'Pears to Lew an' me that this fellar is a slick customer, an' one who's been here long enough to know our hosses an' where we keep them."

"I see. Like Miller, who fooled us all, even Betty, when he stole our powder and then sold us to Girty," rejoined Colonel Zane grimly.

"Exactly, only this fellar is slicker an' more desperate than Miller."

"Right you are, Jack, for the man who is trusted and betrays us, must be desperate. Does he realize what he'll get if we ever find out, or is he underrating us?"

"He knows all right, an' is matchin' his cunnin' against our'n."

"Tell me what you and Wetzel learned."

The borderman proceeded to relate the events that had occurred during a recent tramp in the forest with Wetzel. While returning from a hunt in a swamp several miles over the ridge, back of Fort Henry, they ran across the trail of three Indians. They followed this until darkness set in, when both laid down to rest and wait for the early dawn, that time most propitious for taking the savage by surprise. On resuming the trail they found that other Indians had joined the party they were tracking. To the bordermen this was significant of some unusual activity directed toward the settlement. Unable to learn anything definite from the moccasin traces, they hurried up on the trail to find that the Indians had halted.

Wetzel and Jonathan saw from their covert that the savages had a woman prisoner. A singular feature about it all was that the Indians remained in the same place all day, did not light a campfire, and kept a sharp lookout. The bordermen crept up as close as safe, and remained on watch during the day and night.

Early next morning, when the air was fading from black to gray, the silence was broken by the snapping of twigs and a tremor of the ground. The bordermen believed another company of Indians was approaching; but they soon saw it was a single white man leading a number of horses. He departed before daybreak. Wetzel and Jonathan could not get a clear view of him owing to the dim light; but they heard his voice, and afterwards found the imprint of his moccasins. They did, however, recognize the six horses as belonging to settlers in Yellow Creek.

While Jonathan and Wetzel were consulting as to what it was best to do, the party of Indians divided, four going directly west, and the others north. Wetzel immediately took the trail of the larger party with the prisoner and four of the horses. Jonathan caught two of the animals which the Indians had turned loose, and tied them in the forest. He then started after the three Indians who had gone northward.

"Well?" Colonel Zane said impatiently, when Jonathan hesitated in his story.

"One got away," he said reluctantly. "I barked him as he was runnin' like a streak through the bushes, an' judged that he was hard hit. I got the hosses, an' turned back on the trail of the white man."

"Where did it end?"

"In that hard-packed path near the blacksmith shop. An' the fellar steps as light as an Injun."

"He's here, then, sure as you're born. We've lost no horses yet, but last week old Sam heard a noise in the barn, and on going there found Betty's mare out of her stall."

"Some one as knows the lay of the land had been after her," suggested Jonathan.

"You can bet on that. We've got to find him before we lose all the fine horse-flesh we own. Where do these stolen animals go? Indians would steal any kind; but this thief takes only the best."

"I'm to meet Wetzel on the ridge soon, an' then we'll know, for he's goin' to find out where the hosses are taken."

"That'll help some. On the way back you found where the white girl had been taken from. Murdered father, burned cabin, the usual deviltry."

"Exactly."

"Poor Mabel! Do you think this white thief had anything to do with carrying her away?"

"No. Wetzel says that's Bing Legget's work. The Shawnees were members of his gang."

"Well, Jack, what'll I do?"

"Keep quiet an' wait," was the borderman's answer.

Colonel Zane, old pioneer and frontiersman though he was, shuddered as he went to his room. His brother's dark look, and his deadly calmness, were significant.

CHAPTER IV

To THOSE FEW who saw Jonathan Zane in the village, it seemed as if he was in his usual quiet and dreamy state. The people were accustomed to his silence, and long since learned that what little time he spent in the settlement was not given to sociability. In the morning he sometimes lay with Colonel Zane's dog, Chief, by the side of a spring under an elm tree, and in the afternoon strolled aimlessly along the river bluff, or on the hillside. At night he sat on his brother's porch smoking a long Indian pipe. Since that day, now a week past, when he had returned with the stolen horses, his movements and habits were precisely what would have been expected of an unsuspicious borderman.

In reality, however, Jonathan was not what he seemed. He knew all that was going on in the settlement. Hardly a bird could have entered the clearing unobserved.

At night, after all the villagers were in bed, he stole cautiously about the stockade, silencing with familiar word the bristling watch-hounds, and went from barn to barn, ending his stealthy tramp at the corral where Colonel Zane kept his thoroughbreds.

But all this scouting by night availed nothing. No unusual event occurred, not even the barking of a dog, a suspicious rustling among the thickets, or whistling of a night-hawk had been heard.

Vainly the borderman strained ears to catch some low night-signal given by waiting Indians to the white traitor within the settlement. By day there was even less to attract the sharp-eyed watcher. The clumsy river boats, half raft, half sawn lumber, drifted down the Ohio on their first and last voyage, discharged their cargoes of grain, liquor, or merchandise, and were broken up. Their crews came back on the long overland journey to Fort Pitt, there to man another craft. The garrison at the fort performed their

25

customary duties; the pioneers tilled the fields; the blacksmith scattered sparks, the wheelwright worked industriously at his bench, and the housewives attended to their many cares. No strangers arrived at Fort Henry. The quiet life of the village was uninterrupted.

Near sunset of a long day Jonathan strolled down the sandy, well-trodden path toward Metzar's inn. He did not drink, and consequently seldom visited the rude, dark, ill-smelling bar-room. When occasion demanded his presence there, he was evidently not welcome. The original owner, a sturdy soldier and pioneer, came to Fort Henry when Colonel Zane founded the settlement, and had been killed during Girty's last attack. His successor, another Metzar, was, according to Jonathan's belief, as bad as the whiskey he dispensed. More than one murder had been committed at the inn; countless fatal knife and tomahawk fights had stained red the hard clay floor; and more than one desperate character had been harbored there. Once Colonel Zane sent Wetzel there to invite a thief and outlaw to quit the settlement, with the not unexpected result that it became necessary the robber be carried out.

Jonathan thought of the bad name the place bore all over the frontier, and wondered if Metzar could tell anything about the horse-thieves. When the borderman bent his tall frame to enter the low-studded door he fancied he saw a dark figure disappear into a room just behind the bar. A roughly-clad, heavily-bearded man turned hastily at the same moment.

"Hullo," he said gruffly.

"H' are you, Metzar. I just dropped in to see if I could make a trade for your sorrel mare," replied Jonathan. Being well aware that the innkeeper would not part with his horse, the borderman had made this announcement as his reason for entering the bar-room.

"Nope, I'll allow you can't," replied Metzar.

As he turned to go, Jonathan's eyes roamed around the bar-room. Several strangers of shiftless aspect bleared at him.

"They wouldn't steal a pumpkin," muttered Jonathan to himself as he left the inn. Then he added suspiciously, "Metzar was talkin' to some one, an' 'peared uneasy. I never liked Metzar. He'll bear watchin'."

The borderman passed on down the path thinking of what he had heard against Metzar. The colonel had said that the man was prosperous for an innkeeper who took pelts, grain or meat in exchange for rum. The village gossips disliked him because he was unmarried, taciturn, and did not care for their company. Jonathan reflected also on the fact that Indians were frequently coming to the inn, and this made him distrustful of the proprietor. It was true that Colonel Zane had red-skinned visitors, but there was always good reason for their coming. Jonathan had seen, during the Revolution, more than one trusted man proven to be a traitor, and the conviction settled upon him that some quiet scouting would show up the innkeeper as aiding the horse-thieves if not actually in league with them.

"Good evening, Jonathan Zane."

This greeting in a woman's clear voice brought Jonathan out from his reveries. He glanced up to see Helen Sheppard standing in the doorway of her father's cabin.

"Evenin', miss," he said with a bow, and would have passed on.

"Wait," she cried, and stepped out of the door.

He waited by the gate with a manner which showed that such a summons was novel to him.

Helen, piqued at his curt greeting, had asked him to wait without any idea of what she would say. Coming slowly down the path she felt again a subtle awe of this borderman. Regretting her impulsiveness, she lost confidence.

Gaining the gate she looked up intending to speak; but was unable to do so as she saw how cold and grave was his face, and how piercing were his eyes. She flushed slightly, and then, conscious of an embarrassment new and strange to her, blushed rosy red, making, as it seemed to her, a stupid remark about the sunset. When he took her words literally, and said the sunset was fine, she felt guilty of deceitfulness. Whatever Helen's faults, and they were many, she was honest, and because of not having looked at the sunset, but only wanting him to see her as did other men, the innocent ruse suddenly appeared mean and trifling.

Then, with a woman's quick intuition, she understood that coquetries were lost on this borderman, and, with a smile, got the better of her embarrassment and humiliation by telling the truth.

"I wanted to ask a favor of you, and I'm a little afraid."

She spoke with girlish shyness, which increased as he stared at her.

"Why—why do you look at me so?"

"There's a lake over yonder which the Shawnees say is haunted by a woman they killed," he replied quietly. "You'd do for her spirit, so white an' beautiful in the silver moonlight."

"So my white dress makes me look ghostly," she answered lightly, though deeply conscious of surprise and pleasure at such an unexpected reply from him. This borderman might be full of surprises. "Such a time as I had bringing my dresses out here! I don't know when I can wear them. This is the simplest one."

"An' it's mighty new an' bewilderin' for the border," he replied with a smile in his eyes.

"When these are gone I'll get no more except linsey ones," she said brightly, yet her eyes shone with a wistful uncertainty of the future.

"Will you be happy here?"

"I am happy. I have always wanted to be of some use in the world. I assure you, Master Zane, I am not the butterfly I seem. I have worked hard all day, that is, until your sister Betty came over. All the girls have helped me fix up the cabin until it's more comfortable than I ever dreamed one could be on the frontier. Father is well content here, and that makes me happy. I haven't had time for forebodings. The young men of Fort Henry have been—well, attentive; in fact, they've been here all the time."

She laughed a little at this last remark, and looked demurely at him.

"It's a frontier custom," he said.

"Oh, indeed? Do all the young men call often and stay late?"

"They do."

"You didn't," she retorted. "You're the only one who hasn't been to see me."

"I do not wait on the girls," he replied with a grave smile.

"Oh, you don't? Do you expect them to wait on you?" she asked, feeling, now she had made this silent man talk, once more at her ease.

"I am a borderman," replied Jonathan. There was a certain dignity or sadness in his answer which reminded Helen of Colonel Zane's portrayal of a borderman's life. It struck her keenly. Here was this young giant standing erect and handsome before her, as rugged as one of the ash trees of his beloved forest. Who could tell when his strong life might be ended by an Indian's hatchet?

"For you, then, is there no such thing as friendship?" she asked. "On the border men are serious."

This recalled his sister's conversation regarding the attentions of the young men, that they would follow her, fight for her, and give her absolutely no peace until one of them had carried her to his cabin a bride.

She could not carry on the usual conventional conversation with this borderman, but remained silent for a time. She realized more keenly than ever before how different he was from other men, and watched closely as he stood gazing out over the river. Perhaps something she had said caused him to think of the many pleasures and joys he missed. But she could not be certain what was in his mind. She was not accustomed to impassive faces and cold eyes with unlit fires in their dark depths. More likely he was thinking of matters nearer to his wild, free life; of his companion Wetzel somewhere out beyond those frowning hills. Then she remembered that the colonel had told her of his brother's love for nature in all its forms; how he watched the shades of evening fall; lost himself in contemplation of the last copper glow flushing the western sky, or became absorbed in the bright stars. Possibly he had forgotten her presence. Darkness was rapidly stealing down upon them. The evening, tranquil and gray, crept over them with all its mystery. He was a part of it. She could not hope to understand him; but saw clearly that his was no common personality. She wanted to speak, to voice a sympathy strong within her; but she did not know what to say to this borderman.

"If what your sister tells me of the border is true, I may soon need a friend," she said, after weighing well her words. She faced him modestly yet bravely, and looked him straight in the eyes. Because he did not reply she spoke again.

"I mean such a friend as you or Wetzel."

"You may count on both," he replied.

"Thank you," she said softly, giving him her hand. "I shall not forget. One more thing. Will you break a borderman's custom, for my sake?"

"How?"

"Come to see me when you are in the settlement?"

Helen said this in a low voice with just a sob in her breath; but she met his gaze fairly. Her big eyes were all aglow, alight with girlish appeal, and yet proud with a woman's honest demand for fair exchange. Promise was there, too, could he but read it, of wonderful possibilities.

"No," he answered gently.

Helen was not prepared for such a rebuff. She was interested in him, and not ashamed to show it. She feared only that he might misunderstand her; but to refuse her proffered friendship, that was indeed unexpected. Rude she thought it was, while from brow to curving throat her fair skin crimsoned. Then her face grew pale as the moonlight. Hard on her resentment had surged the swell of some new emotion strong and sweet. He refused her friendship because he did not dare accept it; because his life was not his own; because he was a borderman.

While they stood thus, Jonathan looking perplexed and troubled, feeling he had hurt her, but knowing not what to say, and Helen with a warm softness in her eyes, the stalwart figure of a man loomed out of the gathering darkness.

"Ah, Miss Helen! Good evening," he said.

"Is it you, Mr. Brandt?" asked Helen. "Of course you know Mr. Zane."

Brandt acknowledged Jonathan's bow with an awkwardness which had certainly been absent in his greeting to Helen. He started slightly when she spoke the borderman's name.

A brief pause ensued.

"Good night," said Jonathan, and left them.

He had noticed Brandt's gesture of surprise, slight though it was, and was thinking about it as he walked away. Brandt may have been astonished at finding a borderman talking to a girl, and certainly, as far as Jonathan was concerned, the incident was without precedent. But, on the other hand, Brandt may have had another reason, and Jonathan tried to study out what it might be.

He gave but little thought to Helen. That she might like him exceedingly well, did not come into his mind. He remembered his sister Betty's gossip regarding Helen and her admirers, and particularly Roger Brandt; but felt no great concern; he had no curiosity to know more of her. He admired Helen because she was beautiful, yet the feeling was much the same he might have experienced for a graceful deer, a full-foliaged tree, or a dark mossy-stoned bend in a murmuring brook. The girl's face and figure, perfect and alluring as they were, had not awakened him from his indifference.

On arriving at his brother's home, he found the colonel and Betty sitting on the porch.

"Eb, who is this Brandt?" he asked.

"Roger Brandt? He's a French-Canadian; came here from Detroit a year ago. Why do you ask?"

"I want to know more about him."

Colonel Zane reflected a moment, first as to this unusual request from Jonathan, and secondly in regard to what little he really did know of Roger Brandt.

"Well, Jack, I can't tell you much; nothing of him before he showed up here. He says he has been a pioneer, hunter, scout, soldier, trader—everything. When he came to the fort we needed men. It was just after Girty's siege, and all the cabins had been burned. Brandt seemed honest, and was a good fellow. Besides, he had gold. He started the river barges, which came from Fort Pitt. He has surely done the settlement good service, and has prospered. I never talked a dozen times to him, and even then, not for long. He appears to like the young people, which is only natural. That's all I know; Betty might tell you more, for he tried to be attentive to her."

"Did he, Betty?" Jonathan asked.

"He followed me until I showed him I didn't care for company," answered Betty.

"What kind of a man is he?"

"Jack, I know nothing against him, although I never fancied him. He's better educated than the majority of frontiersmen; he's good-natured and agreeable, and the people like him."

"Why don't you?"

Betty looked surprised at his blunt question, and then said with a laugh: "I never tried to reason why; but since you have spoken I believe my dislike was instinctive."

After Betty had retired to her room the brothers remained on the porch smoking.

"Betty's pretty keen, Jack. I never knew her to misjudge a man. Why this sudden interest in Roger Brandt?"

The borderman puffed his pipe in silence.

"Say, Jack," Colonel Zane said suddenly, "do you connect Brandt in any way with this horse-stealing?"

"No more than some, an' less than others," replied Jonathan curtly.

Nothing more was said for a time. To the brothers this hour of early dusk brought the same fullness of peace. From gray twilight to gloomy dusk quiet reigned. The insects of night chirped and chorused with low, incessant hum. From out the darkness came the peeping of frogs.

Suddenly the borderman straightened up, and, removing the pipe from his mouth, turned his ear to the faint breeze, while at the same time one hand closed on the colonel's knee with a warning clutch.

Colonel Zane knew what that clutch signified. Some faint noise, too low for ordinary ears, had roused the borderman. The colonel listened, but heard nothing save the familiar evening sounds.

"Jack, what'd you hear?" he whispered.

"Somethin' back of the barn," replied Jonathan, slipping noiselessly off the steps, lying at full length with his ear close to the ground. "Where's the dog?" he asked.

"Chief must have gone with Sam. The old nigger sometimes goes at this hour to see his daughter."

Jonathan lay on the grass several moments; then suddenly he arose much as a bent sapling springs to place.

"I hear footsteps. Get the rifles," he said in a fierce whisper.

"Damn! There is some one in the barn."

"No; they're outside. Hurry, but softly."

Colonel Zane had but just risen to his feet, when Mrs. Zane came to the door and called him by name.

Instantly from somewhere in the darkness overhanging the road, came a low, warning whistle.

"A signal!" exclaimed Colonel Zane.

"Quick, Eb! Look toward Metzar's light. One, two, three, shadows—Injuns!"

"By the Lord Harry! Now they're gone; but I couldn't mistake those round heads and bristling feathers."

"Shawnees!" said the borderman, and his teeth shut hard like steel on flint.

"Jack, they were after the horses, and some one was on the lookout! By God! right under our noses!"

"Hurry," cried Jonathan, pulling his brother off the porch.

Colonel Zane followed the borderman out of the yard, into the road, and across the grassy square.

"We might find the one who gave the signal," said the colonel. "He was near at hand, and couldn't have passed the house."

Colonel Zane was correct, for whoever had whistled would be forced to take one of two ways of escape; either down the straight road ahead, or over the high stockade fence of the fort.

"There he goes," whispered Jonathan.

"Where? I can't see a blamed thing."

"Go across the square, run around the fort, an' head him off on the road. Don't try to stop him for he'll have weapons, just find out who he is."

"I see him now," replied Colonel Zane, as he hurried off into the darkness.

During a few moments Jonathan kept in view the shadow he had seen first come out of the gloom by the stockade, and thence pass swiftly down the road. He followed swiftly, silently. Presently a light beyond threw a glare across the road. He thought he was approaching a yard where there was a fire, and the flames proved to be from pine cones burning in the yard of Helen Sheppard. He remembered then that she was entertaining some of the young people.

The figure he was pursuing did not pass the glare. Jonathan made certain it disappeared before reaching the light, and he knew his eyesight too well not to trust to it absolutely. Advancing nearer the yard, he heard the murmur of voices in gay conversation, and soon saw figures moving about under the trees.

No doubt was in his mind but that the man who gave the signal to warn the Indians, was one of Helen Sheppard's guests.

Jonathan had walked across the street then down the path, before he saw the colonel coming from the opposite direction. Halting under a maple he waited for his brother to approach.

"I didn't meet any one. Did you lose him?" whispered Colonel Zane breathlessly.

"No; he's in there."

"That's Sheppard's place. Do you mean he's hiding there?"

"No!"

Colonel Zane swore, as was his habit when exasperated. Kind and generous man that he was, it went hard with him to believe in the guilt of any of the young men he had trusted. But Jonathan had said there was a traitor among them, and Colonel Zane did not question this assertion. He knew the borderman. During years full of strife, and war, and blood had he lived beside this silent man who said little, but that little was the truth. Therefore Colonel Zane gave way to anger.

"Well, I'm not so damned surprised! What's to be done?"

"Find out what men are there?"

"That's easy. I'll go to see George and soon have the truth."

"Won't do," said the borderman decisively. "Go back to the barn, an' look after the hosses."

When Colonel Zane had obeyed Jonathan dropped to his hands and knees, and swiftly, with the agile movements of an Indian, gained a corner of the Sheppard yard. He crouched in the shade of a big plum tree. Then, at a favorable opportunity, vaulted the fence and disappeared under a clump of lilac bushes.

The evening wore away no more tediously to the borderman, than to those young frontiersmen who were whispering tender or playful words to their partners. Time and patience were the same to Jonathan Zane. He lay hidden under the fragrant lilacs, his eyes, accustomed to the dark from long practice, losing no movement of the guests. Finally it became evident that the party was at an end. One couple took the initiative, and said good night to their hostess.

"Tom Bennet, I hope it's not you," whispered the borderman to himself, as he recognized the young fellow.

A general movement followed, until the merry party were assembled about Helen near the front gate.

"Jim Morrison, I'll bet it's not you," was Jonathan's comment. "That soldier Williams is doubtful; Hart an' Johnson being strangers, are unknown quantities around here, an' then comes Brandt."

All departed except Brandt, who remained talking to Helen in low, earnest tones. Jonathan lay very quietly, trying to decide what should be his next move in the unraveling of the mystery. He paid little attention to the young couple, but could not help overhearing their conversation.

"Indeed, Mr. Brandt, you frontiersmen are not backward," Helen was saying in her clear voice. "I am surprised to learn that you love me upon such short acquaintance, and am sorry, too, for I hardly know whether I even so much as like you."

"I love you. We men of the border do things rapidly," he replied earnestly.

"So it seems," she said with a soft laugh.

"Won't you care for me?" he pleaded.

"Nothing is surer than that I never know what I am going to do," Helen replied lightly.

"All these fellows are in love with you. They can't help it any more than I. You are the most glorious creature. Please give me hope."

"Mr. Brandt, let go my hand. I'm afraid I don't like such impulsive men."

"Please let me hold your hand."

"Certainly not."

"But I will hold it, and if you look at me like that again I'll do more," he said.

"What, bold sir frontiersman?" she returned, lightly still, but in a voice which rang with a deeper note.

"I'll kiss you," he cried desperately.

"You wouldn't dare."

"Wouldn't I though? You don't know us border fellows yet. You come here with your wonderful beauty, and smile at us with that light in your eyes which makes men mad. Oh, you'll pay for it."

The borderman listened to all this love-making half disgusted, until he began to grow interested. Brandt's back was turned to him, and Helen stood so that the light from the pine cones shone on her face. Her eyes were brilliant, otherwise she seemed a woman perfectly self-possessed. Brandt held her hand despite the repeated efforts she made to free it. But she did not struggle violently, or make an outcry.

Suddenly Brandt grasped her other hand, pulling her toward him.

"These other fellows will kiss you, and I'm going to be the first!" he declared passionately.

Helen drew back, now thoroughly alarmed by the man's fierce energy. She had been warned against this very boldness in frontiersmen; but had felt secure in her own pride and dignity. Her blood boiled at the thought that she must exert strength to escape insult. She struggled violently when Brandt bent his head. Almost sick with fear, she had determined to call for help, when a violent wrench almost toppled her over. At the same instant her wrists were freed; she heard a fierce cry, a resounding blow, and then the sodden thud of a heavy body falling. Recovering her balance, she saw a tall figure beside her, and a man in the act of rising from the ground.

"You?" whispered Helen, recognizing the tall figure as Jonathan's.

The borderman did not answer. He stepped forward, slipping his hand inside his hunting frock. Brandt sprang nimbly to his feet, and with a face which, even in the dim light, could be seen distorted with fury, bent forward to look at the stranger. He, too, had his hand within his coat, as if grasping a weapon; but he did not draw it.

"Zane, a lighter blow would have been easier to forget," he cried, his voice clear and cutting. Then he turned to the girl. "Miss Helen, I got what I deserved. I crave your forgiveness, and ask you to understand a man who was once a gentleman. If I am one no longer, the frontier is to blame. I was mad to treat you as I did."

Thus speaking, he bowed low with the grace of a man sometimes used to the society of ladies, and then went out of the gate.

"Where did you come from?" asked Helen, looking up at Jonathan.

He pointed under the lilac bushes.

"Were you there?" she asked wonderingly. "Did you hear all?"

"I couldn't help hearin'."

"It was fortunate for me; but why—why were you there?"

Helen came a step nearer, and regarded him curiously with her great eyes now black with excitement.

The borderman was silent.

Helen's softened mood changed instantly. There was nothing in his cold face which might have betrayed in him a sentiment similar to that of her admirers.

"Did you spy on me?" she asked quickly, after a moment's thought.

"No," replied Jonathan calmly.

Helen gazed in perplexity at this strange man. She did not know how to explain it; she was irritated, but did her best to conceal it. He had no interest in her, yet had hidden under the lilacs in her yard. She was grateful because he had saved her from annoyance, yet could not fathom his reason for being so near.

"Did you come here to see me?" she asked, forgetting her vexation.

"No."

"What for, then?"

"I reckon I won't say," was the quiet, deliberate refusal.

Helen stamped her foot in exasperation.

"Be careful that I do not put a wrong construction on your strange action," said she coldly. "If you have reasons, you might trust me. If you are only—"

"Sh-s-sh!" he breathed, grasping her wrist, and holding it firmly in his powerful hand. The whole attitude of the man had altered swiftly, subtly. The listlessness was gone. His lithe body became rigid as he leaned forward, his head toward the ground, and turned slightly in a manner that betokened intent listening.

Helen trembled as she felt his powerful frame quiver. Whatever had thus changed him, gave her another glimpse of his complex personality. It seemed to her incredible that with one whispered exclamation this man could change from cold indifference to a fire and force so strong as to dominate her.

Statue-like she remained listening; but hearing no sound, and thrillingly conscious of the hand on her arm.

Far up on the hillside an owl hooted dismally, and an instant later, faint and far away, came an answer so low as to be almost indistinct.

The borderman raised himself erect as he released her.

"It's only an owl," she said in relief.

His eyes gleamed like stars.

"It's Wetzel, an' it means Injuns!"

Then he was gone into the darkness.

CHAPTER V

IN THE MISTY morning twilight Colonel Zane, fully armed, paced to and fro before his cabin, on guard. All night he had maintained a watch. He had not considered it necessary to send his family into the fort, to which they had often been compelled to flee. On the previous night Jonathan had come swiftly back to the cabin, and, speaking but two words, seized his weapons and vanished into the black night. The words were "Injuns! Wetzel!" and there were none others with more power to affect hearers on the border. The colonel believed that Wetzel had signaled to Jonathan.

On the west a deep gully with precipitous sides separated the settlement from a high, wooded bluff. Wetzel often returned from his journeying by this difficult route. He had no doubt seen Indian signs, and had communicated the intelligence to Jonathan by their system of night-bird calls. The nearness of the mighty hunter reassured Colonel Zane.

When the colonel returned from his chase of the previous night, he went directly to the stable, there to find that the Indians had made off with a thoroughbred, and Betty's pony. Colonel Zane was furious, not on account of the value of the horses, but because Bess was his favorite bay, and Betty loved nothing more than her pony Madcap. To have such a march stolen on him after he had heard and seen the thieves was indeed hard. High time it was that these horse thieves be run to earth. No Indian had planned these marauding expeditions. An intelligent white man was at the bottom of the thieving, and he should pay for his treachery.

The colonel's temper, however, soon cooled. He realized after thinking over the matter, that he was fortunate it passed off without bloodshed. Very likely the intent had been to get all his horses, perhaps his neighbor's as well, and it had been partly frustrated by

Jonathan's keen sagacity. These Shawnees, white leader or not, would never again run such risks.

"It's like a skulking Shawnee," muttered Colonel Zane, "to slip down here under cover of early dusk, when no one but an Indian hunter could detect him. I didn't look for trouble, especially so soon after the lesson we gave Girty and his damned English and redskins. It's lucky Jonathan was here. I'll go back to the old plan of stationing scouts at the outposts until snow flies."

While Colonel Zane talked to himself and paced the path he had selected to patrol, the white mists cleared, and a rosy hue followed the brightening in the east. The birds ceased twittering to break into gay songs, and the cock in the barnyard gave one final clarion-voiced salute to the dawn. The rose in the east deepened into rich red, and then the sun peeped over the eastern hilltops to drench the valley with glad golden light.

A blue smoke curling lazily from the stone chimney of his cabin, showed that Sam had made the kitchen fire, and a little later a rich, savory odor gave pleasing evidence that his wife was cooking breakfast.

"Any sign of Jack?" a voice called from the open door, and Betty appeared.

"Nary a sign."

"Of the Indians, then?"

"Well, Betts, they left you a token of their regard," and Colonel Zane smiled as he took a broken halter from the fence.

"Madcap?" cried Betty.

"Yes, they've taken Madcap and Bess."

"Oh, the villains! Poor pony," exclaimed Betty indignantly. "Eb, I'll coax Wetzel to fetch the pony home if he has to kill every Shawnee in the valley."

"Now you're talking, Betts," Colonel Zane replied. "If you could get Lew to do that much, you'd be blessed from one end of the border to the other."

He walked up the road; then back, keeping a sharp lookout on all sides, and bestowing a particularly keen glance at the hillside across the ravine, but could see no sign of the bordermen. As it was now broad daylight he felt convinced that further watch was unnecessary, and went in to breakfast. When he came out again the villagers were astir. The sharp strokes of axes rang out on the clear morning air, and a mellow anvil-clang pealed up from the blacksmith shop. Colonel Zane found his brother Silas and Jim Douns near the gate.

"Morning, boys," he cried cheerily.

"Any glimpse of Jack or Lew?" asked Silas.

"No; but I'm expecting one of 'em any moment."

"How about the Indians?" asked Douns. "Silas roused me out last night; but didn't stay long enough to say more than 'Indians.'"

"I don't know much more than Silas. I saw several of the red devils who stole the horses; but how many, where they've gone, or what we're to expect, I can't say. We've got to wait for Jack or Lew. Silas, keep the garrison in readiness at the fort, and don't allow a man, soldier or farmer, to leave the clearing until further orders. Perhaps there were only three of those Shawnees, and then again the woods might have been full of them. I take it something's amiss, or Jack and Lew would be in by now."

"Here come Sheppard and his girl," said Silas, pointing down the lane. "'Pears George is some excited."

Colonel Zane had much the same idea as he saw Sheppard and his daughter. The old man appeared in a hurry, which was sufficient reason to believe him anxious or alarmed, and Helen looked pale.

"Ebenezer, what's this I hear about Indians?" Sheppard asked excitedly. "What with Helen's story about the fort being besieged, and this brother of yours routing honest people from their beds, I haven't had a wink of sleep. What's up? Where are the redskins?"

"Now, George, be easy," said Colonel Zane calmly. "And you, Helen, mustn't be frightened. There's no danger. We did have a visit from Indians last night; but they hurt no one, and got only two horses."

"Oh, I'm so relieved that it's not worse," said Helen.

"It's bad enough, Helen," Betty cried, her black eyes flashing, "my pony Madcap is gone."

"Colonel Zane, come here quick!" cried Douns, who stood near the gate.

With one leap Colonel Zane was at the gate, and, following with his eyes the direction indicated by Douns' trembling finger, he saw two tall, brown figures striding down the lane. One carried two rifles, and the other a long bundle wrapped in a blanket.

"It's Jack and Wetzel," whispered Colonel Zane to Jim. "They've got the girl, and by God! from the way that bundle hangs,

I think she's dead. Here," he added, speaking loudly, "you women get into the house."

Mrs. Zane, Betty and Helen stared.

"Go into the house!" he cried authoritatively.

Without a protest the three women obeyed.

At that moment Nellie Douns came across the lane; Sam shuffled out from the backyard, and Sheppard arose from his seat on the steps. They joined Colonel Zane, Silas and Jim at the gate.

"I wondered what kept you so late," Colonel Zane said to Jonathan, as he and his companion came up. "You've fetched Mabel, and she's—" The good man could say no more. If he should live an hundred years on the border amid savage murderers, he would still be tender-hearted. Just now he believed the giant borderman by the side of Jonathan held a dead girl, one whom he had danced, when a child, upon his knee.

"Mabel, an' jest alive," replied Jonathan.

"By God! I'm glad!" exclaimed Colonel Zane. "Here, Lew, give her to me."

Wetzel relinquished his burden to the colonel.

"Lew, any bad Indian sign?" asked Colonel Zane as he turned to go into the house.

The borderman shook his head.

"Wait for me," added the colonel.

He carried the girl to that apartment in the cabin which served the purpose of a sitting-room, and laid her on a couch. He gently removed the folds of the blanket, disclosing to view a fragile, white-faced girl.

"Bess, hurry, hurry!" he screamed to his wife, and as she came running in, followed no less hurriedly by Betty, Helen and Nellie, he continued, "Here's Mabel Lane, alive, poor child; but in sore need of help. First see whether she has any bodily injury. If a bullet must be cut out, or a knife-wound sewed up, it's better she remained unconscious. Betty, run for Bess's instruments, and bring brandy and water. Lively now!" Then he gave vent to an oath and left the room.

Helen, her heart throbbing wildly, went to the side of Mrs. Zane, who was kneeling by the couch. She saw a delicate girl, not over eighteen years old, with a face that would have been beautiful but for the set lips, the closed eyelids, and an expression of intense pain.

"Oh! Oh!" breathed Helen.

"Nell, hand me the scissors," said Mrs. Zane, "and help me take off this dress. Why, it's wet, but, thank goodness! 'tis not with blood. I know that slippery touch too well. There, that's right. Betty, give me a spoonful of brandy. Now heat a blanket, and get one of your linsey gowns for this poor child."

Helen watched Mrs. Zane as if fascinated. The colonel's wife continued to talk while with deft fingers she forced a few drops of brandy between the girl's closed teeth. Then with the adroitness of a skilled surgeon, she made the examination. Helen had heard of this pioneer woman's skill in setting broken bones and treating injuries, and when she looked from the calm face to the steady fingers, she had no doubt as to the truth of what had been told.

"Neither bullet wound, cut, bruise, nor broken bone," said Mrs. Zane. "It's fear, starvation, and the terrible shock."

She rubbed Mabel's hands while gazing at her pale face. Then she forced more brandy between the tightly-closed lips. She was rewarded by ever so faint a color tinging the wan cheeks, to be followed by a fluttering of the eyelids. Then the eyes opened wide. They were large, soft, dark and humid with agony.

Helen could not bear their gaze. She saw the shadow of death, and of worse than death. She looked away, while in her heart rose a storm of passionate fury at the brutes who had made of this tender girl a wreck.

The room was full of women now, sober-faced matrons and grave-eyed girls, yet all wore the same expression, not alone of anger, nor fear, nor pity, but of all combined.

Helen instinctively felt that this was one of the trials of border endurance, and she knew from the sterner faces of the maturer women that such a trial was familiar. Despite all she had been told, the shock and pain were too great, and she went out of the room sobbing.

She almost fell over the broad back of Jonathan Zane who was sitting on the steps. Near him stood Colonel Zane talking with a tall man clad in faded buckskin.

"Lass, you shouldn't have stayed," said Colonel Zane kindly.

"It's—hurt—me—here," said Helen, placing her hand over her heart.

"Yes, I know, I know; of course it has," he replied, taking her hand. "But be brave, Helen, bear up, bear up. Oh! this border is a stern place! Do not think of that poor girl. Come, let me introduce Jonathan's friend, Wetzel!"

Helen looked up and held out her hand. She saw a very tall man with extremely broad shoulders, a mass of raven-black hair, and a white face. He stepped forward, and took her hand in his huge, horny palm, pressing it, he stepped back without speaking. Colonel Zane talked to her in a soothing voice; but she failed to hear what he said. This Wetzel, this Indian-hunter whom she had heard called "Deathwind of the Border," this companion, guide, teacher of Jonathan Zane, this borderman of wonderful deeds, stood before her.

Helen saw a cold face, deathly in its pallor, lighted by eyes sloe-black but like glinting steel. Striking as were these features, they failed to fascinate as did the strange tracings which apparently showed through the white, drawn skin. This first repelled, then drew her with wonderful force. Suffering, of fire, and frost, and iron was written there, and, stronger than all, so potent as to cause fear, could be read the terrible purpose of this man's tragic life.

"You avenged her! Oh! I know you did!" cried Helen, her whole heart leaping with a blaze to her eyes.

She was answered by a smile, but such a smile! Kindly it broke over the stern face, giving a glimpse of a heart still warm beneath that steely cold. Behind it, too, there was something fateful, something deadly.

Helen knew, though the borderman spoke not, that somewhere among the grasses of the broad plains, or on the moss of the wooded hills, lay dead the perpetrators of this outrage, their still faces bearing the ghastly stamp of Deathwind.

CHAPTER VI

HAPPIER days than she had hoped for, dawned upon Helen after the first touch of border sorrow. Mabel Lane did not die. Helen and Betty nursed the stricken girl tenderly, weeping for very joy when signs of improvement appeared. She had remained silent for several days, always with that haunting fear in her eyes, and then gradually came a change. Tender care and nursing had due effect in banishing the dark shadow. One morning after a long sleep she awakened with a bright smile, and from that time her improvement was rapid.

Helen wanted Mabel to live with her. The girl's position was pitiable. Homeless, fatherless, with not a relative on the border, yet so brave, so patient that she aroused all the sympathy in Helen's breast. Village gossip was in substance, that Mabel had given her love to a young frontiersman, by name Alex Bennet, who had an affection for her, so it was said, but as yet had made no choice between her and the other lasses of the settlement. What effect Mabel's terrible experience might have on this lukewarm lover, Helen could not even guess; but she was not hopeful as to the future. Colonel Zane and Betty approved of Helen's plan to persuade Mabel to live with her, and the latter's faint protestations they silenced by claiming she could be of great assistance in the management of the house, therefore it was settled.

Finally the day came when Mabel was ready to go with Helen. Betty had given her a generous supply of clothing, for all her belongings had been destroyed when the cabin was burned. With Helen's strong young arm around her she voiced her gratitude to Betty and Mrs. Zane and started toward the Sheppard home.

From the green square, where the ground was highest, an unobstructed view could be had of the valley. Mabel gazed down the river to where her home formerly stood. Only a faint, dark spot,

44

like a blur on the green landscape, could be seen. Her soft eyes filled with tears; but she spoke no word.

"She's game and that's why she didn't go under," Colonel Zane said to himself as he mused on the strength and spirit of border-women. To their heroism, more than any other thing, he attributed the establishing of homes in this wilderness.

In the days that ensued, as Mabel grew stronger, the girls became very fond of each other. Helen would have been happy at any time with such a sweet companion, but just then, when the poor girl's mind was so sorely disturbed she was doubly glad. For several days, after Mabel was out of danger, Helen's thoughts had dwelt on a subject which caused extreme vexation. She had begun to suspect that she encouraged too many admirers for whom she did not care, and thought too much of a man who did not reciprocate. She was gay and moody in turn. During the moody hours she suspected herself, and in her gay ones, scorned the idea that she might ever care for a man who was indifferent. But that thought once admitted, had a trick of returning at odd moments, clouding her cheerful moods.

One sunshiny morning while the May flowers smiled under the hedge, when dew sparkled on the leaves, and the locust-blossoms shone creamy-white amid the soft green of the trees, the girls set about their much-planned flower gardening. Helen was passionately fond of plants, and had brought a jar of seeds of her favorites all the way from her eastern home.

"We'll plant the morning-glories so they'll run up the porch, and the dahlias in this long row and the nasturtiums in this round bed," Helen said.

"You have some trailing arbutus," added Mabel, "and must have clematis, wild honeysuckle and golden-glow, for they are all sweet flowers."

"This arbutus is so fresh, so dewy, so fragrant," said Helen, bending aside a lilac bush to see the pale, creeping flowers. "I never saw anything so beautiful. I grow more and more in love with my new home and friends. I have such a pretty garden to look into, and I never tire of the view beyond."

Helen gazed with pleasure and pride at the garden with its fresh green and lavender-crested lilacs, at the white-blossomed trees, and the vine-covered log cabins with blue smoke curling from their stone chimneys. Beyond, the great bulk of the fort stood guard above the willow-skirted river, and far away over the winding stream the dark hills, defiant, kept their secrets.

"If it weren't for that threatening fort one could imagine this little hamlet, nestling under the great bluff, as quiet and secure as it is beautiful," said Helen. "But that charred stockade fence with its scarred bastions and these lowering port-holes, always keep me alive to the reality."

"It wasn't very quiet when Girty was here," Mabel replied thoughtfully.

"Were you in the fort then?" asked Helen breathlessly.

"Oh, yes, I cooled the rifles for the men," replied Mabel calmly.

"Tell me all about it."

Helen listened again to a story she had heard many times; but told by new lips it always gained in vivid interest. She never tired of hearing how the notorious renegade, Girty, rode around the fort on his white horse, giving the defenders an hour in which to surrender; she learned again of the attack, when the British soldiers remained silent on an adjoining hillside, while the Indians yelled exultantly and ran about in fiendish glee, when Wetzel began the battle by shooting an Indian chieftain who had ventured within range of his ever fatal rifle. And when it came to the heroic deeds of that memorable siege Helen could not contain her enthusiasm. She shed tears over little Harry Bennet's death at the south bastion where, though riddled with bullets, he stuck to his post until relieved. Clark's race across the roof of the fort to extinguish a burning arrow, she applauded with clapping hands. Her great eyes glowed and burned, but she was silent, when hearing how Wetzel ran alone to a break in the stockade, and there, with an ax, the terrible borderman held at bay the whole infuriated Indian mob until the breach was closed. Lastly Betty Zane's never-to-be-forgotten run with the powder to the relief of the garrison and the saving of the fort was something not to cry over or applaud; but to dream of and to glorify.

"Down that slope from Colonel Zane's cabin is where Betty ran with the powder," said Mabel, pointing.

"Did you see her?" asked Helen.

"Yes, I looked out of a port-hole. The Indians stopped firing at the fort in their eagerness to shoot Betty. Oh, the banging of guns and yelling of savages was one fearful, dreadful roar! Through all that hail of bullets Betty ran swift as the wind."

"I almost wish Girty would come again," said Helen.

"Don't; he might."

"How long has Betty's husband, Mr. Clarke, been dead?" inquired Helen.

"I don't remember exactly. He didn't live long after the siege. Some say he inhaled the flames while fighting fire inside the stockade."

"How sad!"

"Yes, it was. It nearly killed Betty. But we border girls do not give up easily; we must not," replied Mabel, an unquenchable spirit showing through the sadness of her eyes.

Merry voices interrupted them, and they turned to see Betty and Nell entering the gate. With Nell's bright chatter and Betty's wit, the conversation became indeed vivacious, running from gossip to gowns, and then to that old and ever new theme, love. Shortly afterward the colonel entered the gate, with swinging step and genial smile.

"Well, now, if here aren't four handsome lasses," he said with an admiring glance.

"Eb, I believe if you were single any girl might well suspect you of being a flirt," said Betty.

"No girl ever did. I tell you I was a lady-killer in my day," replied Colonel Zane, straightening his fine form. He was indeed handsome, with his stalwart frame, dark, bronzed face and rugged, manly bearing.

"Bess said you were; but that it didn't last long after you saw her," cried Betty, mischief gleaming in her dark eye.

"Well, that's so," replied the colonel, looking a trifle crest-fallen; "but you know every dog has his day." Then advancing to the porch, he looked at Mabel with a more serious gaze as he asked, "How are you to-day?"

"Thank you, Colonel Zane, I am getting quite strong."

"Look up the valley. There's a raft coming down the river," said he softly.

Far up the broad Ohio a square patch showed dark against the green water.

Colonel Zane saw Mabel start, and a dark red flush came over her pale face. For an instant she gazed with an expression of appeal, almost fear. He knew the reason. Alex Bennet was on that raft.

"I came over to ask if I can be of any service?"

"Tell him," she answered simply.

"I say, Betts," Colonel Zane cried, "has Helen's cousin cast any more such sheep eyes at you?"

"Oh, Eb, what nonsense!" exclaimed Betty, blushing furiously.

"Well, if he didn't look sweet at you I'm an old fool."

"You're one anyway, and you're horrid," said Betty, tears of anger glistening in her eyes.

Colonel Zane whistled softly as he walked down the lane. He went into the wheelwright's shop to see about some repairs he was having made on a wagon, and then strolled on down to the river. Two Indians were sitting on the rude log wharf, together with several frontiersmen and rivermen, all waiting for the raft. He conversed with the Indians, who were friendly Chippewas, until the raft was tied up. The first person to leap on shore was a sturdy young fellow with a shock of yellow hair, and a warm, ruddy skin.

"Hello, Alex, did you have a good trip?" asked Colonel Zane of the youth.

"H'are ye, Colonel Zane. Yes, first-rate trip," replied young Bennet. "Say, I've a word for you. Come aside," and drawing Colonel Zane out of earshot of the others, he continued, "I heard this by accident, not that I didn't spy a bit when I got interested, for I did; but the way it came about was all chance. Briefly, there's a man, evidently an Englishman, at Fort Pitt, whom I overheard say he was out on the border after a Sheppard girl. I happened to hear from one of Brandt's men, who rode into Pitt just before we left, that you had new friends here by that name. This fellow was a handsome chap, no common sort, but lordly, dissipated and reckless as the devil. He had a servant traveling with him, a sailor, by his gab, who was about the toughest customer I've met in many a day. He cut a fellow in bad shape at Pitt. These two will be on the next boat, due here in a day or so, according to river and weather conditions, an' I thought, considerin' how unusual the thing was, I'd better tell ye."

"Well, well," said Colonel Zane reflectively. He recalled Sheppard's talk about an Englishman. "Alex, you did well to tell me. Was the man drunk when he said he came west after a woman?"

"Sure he was," replied Alex. "But not when he spoke the name. Ye see I got suspicious, an' asked about him. It's this way: Jake Wentz, the trader, told me the fellow asked for the Sheppards when he got off the wagon-train. When I first seen him he was drunk, and I heard Jeff Lynn say as how the border was a bad place to come after a woman. That's what made me prick up my ears. Then the Englishman said: 'It is, eh? By God! I'd go to hell after a woman I wanted.' An' Colonel, he looked it, too."

Colonel Zane remained thoughtful while Alex made up a bundle and forced the haft of an ax under the string; but as the young man started away the colonel suddenly remembered his errand down to the wharf.

"Alex, come back here," he said, and wondered if the lad had good stuff in him. The boatman's face was plain, but not evil, and a close scrutiny of it rather prepossessed the colonel.

"Alex, I've some bad news for you," and then bluntly, with his keen gaze fastened on the young man's face, he told of old Lane's murder, of Mabel's abduction, and of her rescue by Wetzel.

Alex began to curse and swear vengeance.

"Stow all that," said the colonel sharply. "Wetzel followed four Indians who had Mabel and some stolen horses. The redskins quarreled over the girl, and two took the horses, leaving Mabel to the others. Wetzel went after these last, tomahawked them, and brought Mabel home. She was in a bad way, but is now getting over the shock."

"Say, what'd we do here without Wetzel?" Alex said huskily, unmindful of the tears that streamed from his eyes and ran over his brown cheeks. "Poor old Jake! Poor Mabel! Damn me! it's my fault. If I'd 'a done right an' married her as I should, as I wanted to, she wouldn't have had to suffer. But I'll marry her yet, if she'll have me. It was only because I had no farm, no stock, an' only that little cabin as is full now, that I waited."

"Alex, you know me," said Colonel Zane in kindly tones. "Look there, down the clearing half a mile. See that green strip of land along the river, with the big chestnut in the middle and a cabin beyond. There's as fine farming land as can be found on the border, eighty acres, well watered. The day you marry Mabel that farm is yours."

Alex grew red, stammered, and vainly tried to express his gratitude.

"Come along, the sooner you tell Mabel the better," said the colonel with glowing face. He was a good matchmaker. He derived more pleasure from a little charity bestowed upon a deserving person, than from a season's crops.

When they arrived at the Sheppard house the girls were still on the porch. Mabel rose when she saw Alex, standing white and still. He, poor fellow, was embarrassed by the others, who regarded him with steady eyes.

Colonel Zane pushed Alex up on the porch, and said in a low voice: "Mabel, I've just arranged something you're to give Alex. It's a nice little farm, and it'll be a wedding present."

Mabel looked in a bewildered manner from Colonel Zane's happy face to the girls, and then at the red, joyous features of her lover. Only then did she understand, and uttering a strange little cry, put her trembling hands to her bosom as she swayed to and fro.

But she did not fall, for Alex, quick at the last, leaped forward and caught her in his arms.

★　★　★　★　★　★

That evening Helen denied herself to Mr. Brandt and several other callers. She sat on the porch with her father while he smoked his pipe.

"Where's Will?" she asked.

"Gone after snipe, so he said," replied her father.

"Snipe? How funny! Imagine Will hunting! He's surely catching the wild fever Colonel Zane told us about."

"He surely is."

Then came a time of silence. Mr. Sheppard, accustomed to Helen's gladsome spirit and propensity to gay hatter, noted how quiet she was, and wondered.

"Why are you so still?"

"I'm a little homesick," Helen replied reluctantly.

"No? Well, I declare! This is a glorious country; but not for such as you, dear, who love music and gaiety. I often fear you'll not be happy here, and then I long for the old home, which reminds me of your mother."

"Dearest, forget what I said," cried Helen earnestly. "I'm only a little blue to-day; perhaps not at all homesick."

"Indeed, you always seemed happy."

"Father, I am happy. It's only—only a girl's foolish sentiment."

"I've got something to tell you, Helen, and it has bothered me since Colonel Zane spoke of it to-night. Mordaunt is coming to Fort Henry."

"Mordaunt? Oh, impossible! Who said so? How did you learn?"

"I fear 'tis true, my dear. Colonel Zane told me he had heard of an Englishman at Fort Pitt who asked after us. Moreover, the fellow answers the description of Mordaunt. I am afraid it is he, and come after you."

"Suppose he has—who cares? We owe him nothing. He cannot hurt us."

"But, Helen, he's a desperate man. Aren't you afraid of him?"

"Not I," cried Helen, laughing in scorn. "He'd better have a care. He can't run things with a high hand out here on the border. I told him I would have none of him, and that ended it."

"I'm much relieved. I didn't want to tell you; but it seemed necessary. Well, child, good night, I'll go to bed."

Long after Mr. Sheppard had retired Helen sat thinking. Memories of the past, and of the unwelcome suitor, Mordaunt, thronged upon her thick and fast. She could see him now with his pale, handsome face, and distinguished bearing. She had liked him, as she had other men, until he involved her father, with himself, in financial ruin, and had made his attention to her unpleasantly persistent. Then he had followed the fall of fortune with wild dissipation, and became a gambler and a drunkard. But he did not desist in his mad wooing. He became like her shadow, and life grew to be unendurable, until her father planned to emigrate west, when she hailed the news with joy. And now Mordaunt had tracked her to her new home. She was sick with disgust. Then her spirit, always strong, and now freer for this new, wild life of the frontier, rose within her, and she dismissed all thoughts of this man and his passion.

The old life was dead and buried. She was going to be happy here. As for the present, it was enough to think of the little border village, now her home; of her girl friends; of the quiet borderman: and, for the moment, that the twilight was somber and beautiful.

High up on the wooded bluff rising so gloomily over the village, she saw among the trees something silver-bright. She watched it rise slowly from behind the trees, now hidden, now white through rifts in the foliage, until it soared lovely and grand above the black horizon. The ebony shadows of night seemed to lift, as might a sable mantle moved by invisible hands. But dark shadows, safe from the moon-rays, lay under the trees, and a pale, misty vapor hung below the brow of the bluff.

Mysterious as had grown the night before darkness yielded to the moon, this pale, white light flooding the still valley, was even more soft and strange. To one of Helen's temperament no thought was needed; to see was enough. Yet her mind was active. She felt with haunting power the beauty of all before her; in fancy transporting herself far to those silver-tipped clouds, and peopling the dells and shady nooks under the hills with spirits and fairies, maidens and valiant knights. To her the day was as a far-off dream. The great watch stars grew wan before the radiant moon; it reigned alone. The immensity of the world with its glimmering rivers, pensive valleys and deep, gloomy forests lay revealed under the glory of the clear light.

Absorbed in this contemplation Helen remained a long time gazing with dreamy ecstasy at the moonlit valley until a slight chill disturbed her happy thoughts. She knew she was not alone. Trembling, she stood up to see, easily recognizable in the moonlight, the tall buckskin-garbed figure of Jonathan Zane.

"Well, sir," she called, sharply, yet with a tremor in her voice.

The borderman came forward and stood in front of her. Somehow he appeard changed. The long, black rifle, the dull, glinting weapons made her shudder. Wilder and more untamable he looked than ever. The very silence of the forest clung to him; the fragrance of the grassy plains came faintly from his buckskin garments.

"Evenin', lass," he said in his slow, cool manner.

"How did you get here?" asked Helen presently, because he made no effort to explain his presence at such a late hour.

"I was able to walk."

Helen observed, with a vaulting spirit, one ever ready to rise in arms, that Master Zane was disposed to add humor to his penetrating mysteriousness. She flushed hot and then paled. This borderman certainly possessed the power to vex her, and, reluctantly she admitted, to chill her soul and rouse her fear. She strove to keep back sharp words, because she had learned that this singular individual always gave good reason for his odd actions.

"I think in kindness to me," she said, choosing her words carefully, "you might tell me why you appear so suddenly, as if you had sprung out of the ground."

"Are you alone?"

"Yes. Father is in bed; so is Mabel, and Will has not yet come home. Why?"

"Has no one else been here?"

"Mr. Brandt came, as did some others; but wishing to be alone, I did not see them," replied Helen in perplexity.

"Have you seen Brandt since?"

"Since when?"

"The night I watched by the lilac bush."

"Yes, several times," replied Helen. Something in his tone made her ashamed. "I couldn't very well escape when he called. Are you surprised because after he insulted me I'd see him?"

"Yes."

Helen felt more ashamed.

"You don't love him?" he continued.

Helen was so surprised she could only look into the dark face above her. Then she dropped her gaze, abashed by his searching eyes. But, thinking of his question, she subdued the vague stirrings of pleasure in her breast, and answered coldly:

"No, I do not; but for the service you rendered me I should never have answered such a question."

"I'm glad, an' hope you care as little for the other five men who were here that night."

"I declare, Master Zane, you seem exceedingly interested in the affairs of a young woman whom you won't visit, except as you have come to-night."

He looked at her with his piercing eyes.

"You spied upon my guests," she said, in no wise abashed now that her temper was high. "Did you care so very much?"

"Care?" he asked slowly.

"Yes; you were interested to know how many of my admirers were here, what they did, and what they said. You even hint disparagingly of them."

"True, I wanted to know," he replied; "but I don't hint about any man."

"You are so interested you wouldn't call on me when I invited you," said Helen, with poorly veiled sarcasm. It was this that made her bitter; she could never forget that she had asked this man to come to see her, and he had refused.

"I reckon you've mistook me," he said calmly.

"Why did you come? Why do you shadow my friends? This is twice you have done it. Goodness knows how many times you've been here! Tell me."

The borderman remained silent.

"Answer me," commanded Helen, her eyes blazing. She actually stamped her foot. "Borderman or not, you have no right to pry into my affairs. If you are a gentleman, tell me why you came here?"

The eyes Jonathan turned on Helen stilled all the angry throbbing of her blood.

"I come here to learn which of your lovers is the dastard who plotted the abduction of Mabel Lane, an' the thief who stole our hosses. When I find the villain I reckon Wetzel an' I'll swing him to some tree."

The borderman's voice rang sharp and cold, and when he ceased speaking she sank back upon the step, shocked, speechless, to gaze up at him with staring eyes.

"Don't look so, lass; don't be frightened," he said, his voice gentle and kind as it had been hard. He took her hand in his. "You nettled me into replyin'. You have a sharp tongue, lass, and when I spoke I was thinkin' of him. I'm sorry."

"A horse-thief and worse than murderer among my friends!" murmured Helen, shuddering, yet she never thought to doubt his word.

"I followed him here the night of your company."

"Do you know which one?"

"No."

He still held her hand, unconsciously, but Helen knew it well. A sense of his strength came with the warm pressure, and comforted her. She would need that powerful hand, surely, in the evil days which seemed to darken the horizon.

"What shall I do?" she whispered, shuddering again.

"Keep this secret between you an' me."

"How can I? How can I?"

"You must," his voice was deep and low. "If you tell your father, or any one, I might lose the chance to find this man, for, lass, he's desperate cunnin'. Then he'd go free to rob others, an' mebbe help make off with other poor girls. Lass, keep my secret."

"But he might try to carry me away," said Helen in fearful perplexity.

"Most likely he might," replied the borderman with the smile that came so rarely.

"Oh! Knowing all this, how can I meet any of these men again? I'd betray myself."

"No; you've got too much pluck. It so happens you are the one to help me an' Wetzel rid the border of these hell-hounds, an' you won't fail. I know a woman when it comes to that."

"I—I help you and Wetzel?"

"Exactly."

"Gracious!" cried Helen, half-laughing, half-crying. "And poor me with more trouble coming on the next boat."

"Lass, the colonel told me about the Englishman. It'll be bad for him to annoy you."

Helen thrilled with the depth of meaning in the low voice. Fate surely was weaving a bond between her and this borderman. She felt it in his steady, piercing gaze; in her own tingling blood.

Then as her natural courage dispelled all girlish fears, she faced him, white, resolute, with a look in her eyes that matched his own.

"I will do what I can," she said.

CHAPTER VII

WESTWARD FROM FORT Henry, far above the eddying river, Jonathan Zane slowly climbed a narrow, hazel-bordered, mountain trail. From time to time he stopped in an open patch among the thickets and breathed deep of the fresh, wood-scented air, while his keen gaze swept over the glades near by, along the wooded hill-sides, and above at the timber-strewn woodland.

This June morning in the wild forest was significant of nature's brightness and joy. Broad-leaved poplars, dense foliaged oaks, and vine-covered maples shaded cool, mossy banks, while between the trees the sunshine streamed in bright spots. It shone silver on the glancing silver-leaf, and gold on the colored leaves of the butternut tree. Dewdrops glistened on the ferns; ripples sparkled in the brooks; spider-webs glowed with wondrous rainbow hues, and the flower of the forest, the sweet, pale-faced daisy, rose above the green like a white star.

Yellow birds flitted among the hazel bushes caroling joyously, and cat-birds sang gaily. Robins called; bluejays screeched in the tall, white oaks; wood-peckers hammered in the dead hard-woods, and crows cawed overhead. Squirrels chattered everywhere. Ruffed grouse rose with great bustle and a whirr, flitting like brown flakes through the leaves. From far above came the shrill cry of a hawk, followed by the wilder scream of an eagle.

Wilderness music such as all this fell harmoniously on the bor-derman's ear. It betokened the gladsome spirit of his wild friends, happy in the warm sunshine above, or in the cool depths beneath the fluttering leaves, and everywhere in those lonely haunts un-alarmed and free.

Familiar to Jonathan, almost as the footpath near his home, was this winding trail. On the height above was a safe rendezvous, much frequented by him and Wetzel. Every lichen-covered stone, mossy bank, noisy brook and giant oak on the way up this mountain-side, could have told, had they spoken their secrets, stories of the bordermen. The fragile ferns and slender-bladed grasses peeping from the gray and amber mosses, and the flowers that hung from craggy ledges, had wisdom to impart. A borderman lived under the green tree-tops, and, therefore, all the nodding branches of sassafras and laurel, the grassy slopes and rocky cliffs, the stately ash trees, kingly oaks and dark, mystic pines, together with the creatures that dwelt among them, save his deadly red-skinned foes, he loved. Other affection as close and true as this, he had not known. Hearkening thus with single heart to nature's teachings, he learned her secrets. Certain it was, therefore, that the many hours he passed in the woods apart from savage pursuits, were happy and fruitful.

Slowly he pressed on up the ascent, at length coming into open light upon a small plateau marked by huge, rugged, weather-chipped stones. On the eastern side was a rocky promontory, and close to the edge of this cliff, a hundred feet in sheer descent, rose a gnarled, time and tempest-twisted chestnut tree. Here the borderman laid down his rifle and knapsack, and, half-reclining against the tree, settled himself to rest and wait.

This craggy point was the lonely watch-tower of eagles. Here on the highest headland for miles around where the bordermen were wont to meet, the outlook was far-reaching and grand.

Below the gray, splintered cliffs sheered down to meet the waving tree-tops, and then hill after hill, slope after slope, waved and rolled far, far down to the green river. Open grassy patches, bright little islands in that ocean of dark green, shone on the hillsides. The rounded ridges ran straight, curved, or zigzag, but shaped their graceful lines in the descent to make the valley. Long, purple-hued, shadowy depressions in the wide expanse of foliage marked deep clefts between ridges where dark, cool streams bounded on to meet the river. Lower, where the land was level, in open spaces could be seen a broad trail, yellow in the sunlight, winding along with the curves of the water-course. On a swampy meadow, blue in the distance, a herd of buffalo browsed. Beyond the river, high over the green island, Fort Henry lay peaceful and solitary, the only token of the works of man in all that vast panorama.

Jonathan Zane was as much alone as if one thousand miles, instead of five, intervened between him and the settlement. Loneliness was to him a passion. Other men loved home, the light of woman's eyes, the rattle of dice or the lust of hoarding; but to him this wild, remote promontory, with its limitless view, stretching away to the dim hazy horizon, was more than all the aching joys of civilization.

Hours here, or in the shady valley, recompensed him for the loss of home comforts, the soft touch of woman's hands, the kiss of baby lips, and also for all he suffered in his pitiless pursuits, the hard fare, the steel and blood of a borderman's life.

Soon the sun shone straight overhead, dwarfing the shadow of the chestnut on the rock.

During such a time it was rare that any connected thought came into the borderman's mind. His dark eyes, now strangely luminous, strayed lingeringly over those purple, undulating slopes. This intense watchfulness had no object, neither had his listening. He watched nothing; he hearkened to the silence. Undoubtedly in this state of rapt absorption his perceptions were acutely alert; but without thought, as were those of the savage in the valley below, or the eagle in the sky above.

Yet so perfectly trained were these perceptions that the least unnatural sound or sight brought him wary and watchful from his dreamy trance.

The slight snapping of a twig in the thicket caused him to sit erect, and reach out toward his rifle. His eyes moved among the dark openings in the thicket. In another moment a tall figure pressed the bushes apart. Jonathan let fall his rifle, and sank back against the tree once more. Wetzel stepped over the rocks toward him.

"Come from Blue Pond?" asked Jonathan as the newcomer took a seat beside him.

Wetzel nodded as he carefully laid aside his long, black rifle.

"Any Injun sign?" continued Jonathan, pushing toward his companion the knapsack of eatables he had brought from the settlement.

"Nary Shawnee track west of this divide," answered Wetzel, helping himself to bread and cheese.

"Lew, we must go eastward, over Bing Legget's way, to find the trail of the stolen horses."

"Likely, an' it'll be a long, hard tramp."

"Who's in Legget's gang now beside Old Horse, the Chippewa, an' his Shawnee pard, Wildfire? I don't know Bing; but I've seen some of his Injuns an' they remember me."

"Never seen Legget but onct," replied Wetzel, "an' that time I shot half his face off. I've been told by them as have seen him since, that he's got a nasty scar on his temple an' cheek. He's a big man an' knows the woods. I don't know who all's in his gang, nor does anybody. He works in the dark, an' for cunnin' he's got some on Jim Girty, Deerin', an' several more renegades we know of lyin' quiet back here in the woods. We never tackled as bad a gang as his'n; they're all experienced woodsmen, old fighters, an' desperate, outlawed as they be by Injuns an' whites. It wouldn't surprise me to find that it's him an' his gang who are runnin' this hoss-thievin'; but bad or no, we're goin' after 'em."

Jonathan told of his movements since he had last seen his companion.

"An' the lass Helen is goin' to help us," said Wetzel, much interested. "It's a good move. Women are keen. Betty put Miller's schemin' in my eye long 'afore I noticed it. But girls have chances we men'd never get."

"Yes, an' she's like Betts, quicker'n lightnin'. She'll find out this hoss-thief in Fort Henry; but Lew, when we do get him we won't be much better off. Where do them hosses go? Who's disposin' of 'em for this fellar?"

"Where's Brandt from?" asked Wetzel.

"Detroit; he's a French-Canadian."

Wetzel swung sharply around, his eyes glowing like wakening furnaces.

"Bing Legget's a French-Canadian, an' from Detroit. Metzar was once thick with him down Fort Pitt way 'afore he murdered a man an' became an outlaw. We're on the trail, Jack."

"Brandt an' Metzar, with Legget backin' them, an' the horses go overland to Detroit?"

"I calkilate you've hit the mark."

"What'll we do?" asked Jonathan.

"Wait; that's best. We've no call to hurry. We must know the truth before makin' a move, an' as yet we're only suspicious. This lass'll find out more in a week than we could in a year. But Jack, have a care she don't fall into any snare. Brandt ain't any too honest a lookin' chap, an' them renegades is hell for women. The scars you wear prove that well enough. She's a rare, sweet, bloomin' lass, too. I never seen her equal. I remember how her eyes flashed when she said she knew I'd avenged Mabel. Jack, they're wonderful eyes; an' that girl, however sweet an' good as she must be, is chain-lightnin' wrapped up in a beautiful form. Aren't the boys at the fort runnin' arter her?"

"Like mad; it'd make you laugh to see 'em," replied Jonathan calmly.

"There'll be some fights before she's settled for, an' mebbe arter thet. Have a care for her, Jack, an' see that she don't ketch you."

"No more danger than for you."

"I was ketched onct," replied Wetzel.

Jonathan Zane looked up at his companion. Wetzel's head was bowed; but there was no merriment in the serious face exposed to the borderman's scrutiny.

"Lew, you're jokin'."

"Not me. Some day, when you're ketched good, an' I have to go back to the lonely trail, as I did afore you an' me become friends, mebbe then, when I'm the last borderman, I'll tell you."

"Lew, 'cordin' to the way settlers are comin', in a few more years there won't be any need for a borderman. When the Injuns are all gone where'll be our work?"

"'Tain't likely either of us'll ever see them times," said Wetzel, "an' I don't want to. Wal, Jack, I'm off now, an' I'll meet you here every other day."

Wetzel shouldered his long rifle, and soon passed out of sight down the mountain-side.

Jonathan arose, shook himself as a big dog might have done, and went down into the valley. Only once did he pause in his descent, and that was when a crackling twig warned him some heavy body was moving near. Silently he sank into the bushes bordering the trail. He listened with his ear close to the ground. Presently he heard a noise as of two hard substances striking together. He resumed his walk, having recognized the grating noise of a deer-hoof striking a rock. Farther down he espied a pair grazing. The buck ran into the thicket; but the doe eyed him curiously.

Less than an hour's rapid walking brought him to the river. Here he plunged into a thicket of willows, and emerged on a sandy strip of shore. He carefully surveyed the river bank, and then pulled a small birch-bark canoe from among the foliage. He launched the frail craft, paddled across the river and beached it under a reedy, over-hanging bank.

The distance from this point in a straight line to his destination was only a mile; but a rocky bluff and a ravine necessitated his making a wide detour. While lightly leaping over a brook his keen eye fell on an imprint in the sandy loam. Instantly he was on his knees. The footprint was small, evidently a woman's, and, what was more unusual, instead of the flat, round moccasin-track, it was pointed, with a sharp, square heel. Such shoes were not worn by border girls. True Betty and Nell had them; but they never went into the woods without moccasins.

Jonathan's experienced eye saw that this imprint was not an hour old. He gazed up at the light. The day was growing short. Already shadows lay in the glens. He would not long have light enough to follow the trail; but he hurried on hoping to find the person who made it before darkness came. He had not traveled many paces before learning that the one who made it was lost. The uncertainty in those hasty steps was as plain to the borderman's eyes, as if it had been written in words on the sand. The course led along the brook, avoiding the rough places, and leading into the open glades and glens; but it drew no nearer to the settlement. A quarter of an hour of rapid trailing enabled Jonathan to discern a dark figure moving among the trees. Abandoning the trail, he cut across a ridge to head off the lost woman. Stepping out of a sassafras thicket, he came face to face with Helen Sheppard.

"Oh!" she cried in alarm, and then the expression of terror gave place to one of extreme relief and gladness. "Oh! Thank goodness! You've found me. I'm lost!"

"I reckon," answered Jonathan grimly. "The settlement's only five hundred yards over that hill."

"I was going the wrong way. Oh! suppose you hadn't come!" exclaimed Helen, sinking on a log and looking up at him with warm, glad eyes.

"How did you lose your way?" Jonathan asked. He saw neither the warmth in her eyes nor the gladness.

"I went up the hillside, only a little way, after flowers, keeping the fort in sight all the time. Then I saw some lovely violets down a little hill, and thought I might venture. I found such loads of them I forgot everything else, and I must have walked on a little way. On turning to go back I couldn't find the little hill. I have hunted in vain for the clearing. It seems as if I have been wandering about for hours. I'm so glad you've found me!"

"Weren't you told to stay in the settlement, inside the clearing?" demanded Jonathan.

"Yes," replied Helen, with her head up.

"Why didn't you?"

"Because I didn't choose."

"You ought to have better sense."

"It seems I hadn't," Helen said quietly, but her eyes belied that calm voice.

"You're a headstrong child," Jonathan added curtly.

"Mr. Zane!" cried Helen with pale face.

"I suppose you've always had your own sweet will; but out here on the border you ought to think a little of others, if not of yourself."

Helen maintained a proud silence.

"You might have run right into prowlin' Shawnees."

"That dreadful disaster would not have caused you any sorrow," she flashed out.

"Of course it would. I might have lost my scalp tryin' to get you back home," said Jonathan, beginning to hesitate. Plainly he did not know what to make of this remarkable young woman.

"Such a pity to have lost all your fine hair," she answered with a touch of scorn.

Jonathan flushed, perhaps for the first time in his life. If there was anything he was proud of, it was his long, glossy hair.

"Miss Helen, I'm a poor hand at words," he said, with a pale, grave face. "I was only speakin' for your own good."

"You are exceedingly kind; but need not trouble yourself."

"Say," Jonathan hesitated, looking half-vexed at the lovely, angry face. Then an idea occurred to him. "Well, I won't trouble. Find your way home yourself."

Abruptly he turned and walked slowly away. He had no idea of allowing her to go home alone; but believed it might be well for her to think so. If she did not call him back he would remain near at hand, and when she showed signs of anxiety or fear he could go to her.

Helen determined she would die in the woods, or be captured by Shawnees, before calling him back. But she watched him. Slowly the tall, strong figure, with its graceful, springy stride, went down the glade. He would be lost to view in a moment, and then she would be alone. How dark it had suddenly become! The gray cloak of twilight was spread over the forest, and in the hollows night already had settled down. A breathless silence pervaded the woods. How lonely! thought Helen, with a shiver. Surely it would be dark before she could find the settlement. What hill hid the settlement from view? She did not know, could not remember which he had pointed out. Suddenly she began to tremble. She had been so frightened before he had found her, and so relieved afterward; and now he was going away.

"Mr. Zane," she cried with a great effort. "Come back."

Jonathan kept slowly on.

"Come back, Jonathan, please."

The borderman retraced his steps.

"Please take me home," she said, lifting a fair face all flushed, tear-stained, and marked with traces of storm. "I was foolish, and silly to come into the woods, and so glad to see you! But you spoke to me—in—in a way no one ever used before. I'm sure I deserved it. Please take me home. Papa will be worried."

Softer eyes and voice than hers never entreated man.

"Come," he said gently, and, taking her by the hand, he led her up the ridge.

Thus they passed through the darkening forest, hand in hand, like a dusky redman and his bride. He helped her over stones and logs, but still held her hand when there was no need of it. She looked up to see him walking, so dark and calm beside her, his eyes ever roving among the trees. Deepest remorse came upon her because of what she had said. There was no sentiment for him in this walk under the dark canopy of the leaves. He realized the responsibility. Any tree might hide a treacherous foe. She would atone for her sarcasm, she promised herself, while walking, ever conscious of her hand in his, her bosom heaving with the sweet, undeniable emotion which came knocking at her heart.

Soon they were out of the thicket, and on the dusty lane. A few moments of rapid walking brought them within sight of the twinkling lights of the village, and a moment later they were at the lane leading to Helen's home. Releasing her hand, she stopped him with a light touch and said:

"Please don't tell papa or Colonel Zane."

"Child, I ought. Some one should make you stay at home."

"I'll stay. Please don't tell. It will worry papa."

Jonathan Zane looked down into her great, dark, wonderful eyes with an unaccountable feeling. He really did not hear what she asked. Something about that upturned face brought to his mind a rare and perfect flower which grew in far-off rocky fastnesses. The feeling he had was intangible, like no more than a breath of fragrant western wind, faint with tidings of some beautiful field.

"Promise me you won't tell."

"Well, lass, have it your own way," replied Jonathan, wonderingly conscious that it was the first pledge ever asked of him by a woman.

"Thank you. Now we have two secrets, haven't we?" she laughed, with eyes like stars.

"Run home now, lass. Be careful hereafter. I do fear for you with such spirit an' temper. I'd rather be scalped by Shawnees than have Bing Legget so much as set eyes on you."

"You would? Why?" Her voice was like low, soft music.

"Why?" he mused. "It'd seem like a buzzard about to light on a doe."

"Good-night," said Helen abruptly, and, wheeling, she hurried down the lane.

CHAPTER VIII

"JACK," SAID COLONEL Zane to his brother next morning, "to-day is Saturday and all the men will be in. There was high jinks over at Metzar's place yesterday, and I'm looking for more today. The two fellows Alex Bennet told me about, came on day-before-yesterday's boat. Sure enough, one's a lordly Englishman, and the other, the cussedest-looking little chap I ever saw. They started trouble immediately. The Englishman, his name is Mordaunt, hunted up the Sheppards and as near as I can make out from George's story, Helen spoke her mind very plainly. Mordaunt and Case, that's his servant, the little cuss, got drunk and raised hell down at Metzar's where they're staying. Brandt and Williams are drinking hard, too, which is something unusual for Brandt. They got chummy at once with the Englishman, who seems to have plenty of gold and is fond of gambling. This Mordaunt is a gentleman, or I never saw one. I feel sorry for him. He appears to be a ruined man. If he lasts a week out here I'll be surprised. Case looks ugly, as if he were spoiling to cut somebody. I want you to keep your eye peeled. The day may pass off as many other days of drinking bouts have, without anything serious, and on the other hand there's liable to be trouble."

Jonathan's preparations were characteristic of the borderman. He laid aside his rifle, and, removing his short coat, buckled on a second belt containing a heavier tomahawk and knife than those he had been wearing. Then he put on his hunting frock, or shirt, and wore it loose with the belts underneath, instead of on the outside. Unfastened, the frock was rather full, and gave him the appearance of a man unarmed and careless.

Jonathan Zane was not so reckless as to court danger, nor, like many frontiersmen, fond of fighting for its own sake. Colonel Zane was commandant of the fort, and, in a land where there was no law, tried to maintain a semblance of it. For years he had kept thieves, renegades and outlaws away from his little settlement by dealing out stern justice. His word was law, and his bordermen executed it as such. Therefore Jonathan and Wetzel made it their duty to have a keen eye on all that was happening. They kept the colonel posted, and never interfered in any case without orders.

The morning passed quietly. Jonathan strolled here or loitered there; but saw none of the roisterers. He believed they were sleeping off the effects of their orgy on the previous evening. After dinner he smoked his pipe. Betty and Helen passed, and Helen smiled. It struck him suddenly that she had never looked at him in such a way before. There was meaning in that warm, radiant flash. A little sense of vexation, the source of which he did not understand, stirred in him against this girl; but with it came the realization that her white face and big, dark eyes had risen before him often since the night before. He wished, for the first time, that he could understand women better.

"Everything quiet?" asked Colonel Zane, coming out on the steps.

"All quiet," answered Jonathan.

"They'll open up later, I suspect. I'm going over to Sheppard's for a while, and, later, will drop into Metzar's. I'll make him haul in a yard or two. I don't like things I hear about his selling the youngsters rum. I'd like you to be within call."

The borderman strolled down the bluff and along the path which overhung the river. He disliked Metzar more than his brother suspected, and with more weighty reason than that of selling rum to minors. Jonathan threw himself at length on the ground and mused over the situation.

"We never had any peace in this settlement, an' never will in our day. Eb is hopeful an' looks at the bright side, always expectin' tomorrow will be different. What have the past sixteen years been? One long bloody fight, an' the next sixteen won't be any better. I make out that we'll have a mix-up soon. Metzar an' Brandt with their allies, whoever they are, will be in it, an' if Bing Legget's in the gang, we've got, as Wetzel said, a long, hard trail, which may be our last. More'n that, there'll be trouble about this chain-lightnin' girl, as Wetzel predicted. Women make trouble anyways; an' when they're winsome an' pretty they cause more; but if they're beautiful an' fiery, bent on havin' their way, as this new lass is, all hell couldn't hold a candle to them. We don't need the Shawnees an' Girtys, an' hoss thieves round this here settlement to stir up excitin' times, now we've got this dark-eyed lass. An' yet any fool could see she's sweet, an' good, an' true as gold."

Toward the middle of the afternoon Jonathan sauntered in the direction of Metzar's inn. It lay on the front of the bluff, with its main doors looking into the road. A long, one-story log structure with two doors, answered as a bar-room. The inn proper was a building more pretentious, and joined the smaller one at its western end. Several horses were hitched outside, and two great oxen yoked to a cumbersome mud-crusted wagon stood patiently by.

Jonathan bent his tall head as he entered the noisy bar-room. The dingy place reeked with tobacco smoke and the fumes of vile liquor. It was crowded with men. The lawlessness of the time and place was evident. Gaunt, red-faced frontiersmen reeled to and fro across the sawdust floor; hunters and fur-traders, raftsmen and farmers, swelled the motley crowd; young men, honest-faced, but flushed and wild with drink, hung over the bar; a group of sullen-visaged, serpent-eyed Indians held one corner. The black-bearded proprietor dealt out the rum.

From beyond the bar-room, through a door entering upon the back porch, came the rattling of dice. Jonathan crossed the bar-room apparently oblivious to the keen glance Metzar shot at him, and went out upon the porch. This also was crowded, but there was more room because of greater space. At one table sat some pioneers drinking and laughing; at another were three men playing with dice. Colonel Zane, Silas, and Sheppard were among the lookers-on at the game. Jonathan joined them, and gazed at the gamesters.

Brandt he knew well enough; he had seen that set, wolfish expression in the riverman's face before. He observed, however, that the man had flushed cheeks and trembling hands, indications of hard drinking. The player sitting next to Brandt was Williams, one of the garrison, and a good-natured fellow, but garrulous and wickedly disposed when drunk. The remaining player Jonathan at once saw was the Englishman, Mordaunt. He was a handsome man, with fair skin, and long, silken, blond mustache. Heavy lines, and purple shades under his blue eyes, were the unmistakable stamp of dissipation. Reckless, dissolute, bad as he looked, there yet clung something favorable about the man. Perhaps it was his cool, devil-may-care way as he pushed over gold piece after gold piece from the fast diminishing pile before him. His velvet frock and silken doublet had once been elegant; but were now sadly the worse for border roughing.

Behind the Englishman's chair Jonathan saw a short man with a face resembling that of a jackal. The grizzled, stubbly beard, the protruding, vicious mouth, the broad, flat nose, and deep-set, small, glittering eyes made a bad impression on the observer. This man, Jonathan concluded, was the servant, Case, who was so eager with his knife. The borderman made the reflection, that if knife-play was the little man's pastime, he was not likely to go short of sport in that vicinity.

Colonel Zane attracted Jonathan's attention at this moment. The pioneers had vacated the other table, and Silas and Sheppard now sat by it. The colonel wanted his brother to join them.

"Here, Johnny, bring drinks," he said to the serving boy. "Tell Metzar who they're for." Then turning to Sheppard he continued: "He keeps good whiskey; but few of these poor devils ever see it." At the same time Colonel Zane pressed his foot upon that of Jonathan's.

The borderman understood that the signal was intended to call attention to Brandt. The latter had leaned forward, as Jonathan passed by to take a seat with his brother, and said something in a low tone to Mordaunt and Case. Jonathan knew by the way the Englishman and his man quickly glanced up at him, that he had been the subject of the remark.

Suddenly Williams jumped to his feet with an oath.

"I'm cleaned out," he cried.

"Shall we play alone?" asked Brandt of Mordaunt.

"As you like," replied the Englishman, in a tone which showed he cared not a whit whether he played or not.

"I've got work to do. Let's have some more drinks, and play another time," said Brandt.

The liquor was served and drank. Brandt pocketed his pile of Spanish and English gold, and rose to his feet. He was a trifle unsteady; but not drunk.

"Will you gentlemen have a glass with me?" Mordaunt asked of Colonel Zane's party.

"Thank you, some other time, with pleasure. We have our drink now," Colonel Zane said courteously.

Meantime Brandt had been whispering in Case's ear. The little man laughed at something the riverman said. Then he shuffled from behind the table. He was short, his compact build gave promise of unusual strength and agility.

"What are you going to do now?" asked Mordaunt, rising also. He looked hard at Case.

"Shiver my sides, cap'n, if I don't need another drink," replied the sailor.

"You have had enough. Come upstairs with me," said Mordaunt.

"Easy with your hatch, cap'n," grinned Case. "I want to drink with that ther' Injun killer. I've had drinks with buccaneers, and bad men all over the world, and I'm not going to miss this chance."

"Come on; you will get into trouble. You must not annoy these gentlemen," said Mordaunt.

"Trouble is the name of my ship, and she's a trim, fast craft," replied the man.

His loud voice had put an end to the conversation. Men began to crowd in from the bar-room. Metzar himself came to see what had caused the excitement.

The little man threw up his cap, whooped, and addressed himself to Jonathan:

"Injun-killer, bad man of the border, will you drink with a jolly old tar from England?"

Suddenly a silence reigned, like that in the depths of the forest. To those who knew the borderman, and few did not know him, the invitation was nothing less than an insult. But it did not appear to them, as to him, like a pre-arranged plot to provoke a fight.

"Will you drink, redskin-hunter?" bawled the sailor.

"No," said Jonathan in his quiet voice.

"Maybe you mean that against old England?" demanded Case fiercely.

The borderman eyed him steadily, inscrutable as to feeling or intent, and was silent.

"Go out there and I'll see the color of your insides quicker than I'd take a drink," hissed the sailor, with his brick-red face distorted and hideous to look upon. He pointed with a long-bladed knife that no one had seen him draw, to the green sward beyond the porch.

The borderman neither spoke, nor relaxed a muscle.

"Ho! ho! my brave pirate of the plains!" cried Case, and he leered with braggart sneer into the faces of Jonathan and his companions.

It so happened that Sheppard sat nearest to him, and got the full effect of the sailor's hot, rum-soaked breath. He arose with a pale face.

"Colonel, I can't stand this," he said hastily. "Let's get away from that drunken ruffian."

"Who's a drunken ruffian?" yelled Case, more angry than ever. "I'm not drunk; but I'm going to be, and cut some of you white-livered border mates. Here, you old masthead, drink this to my health, damn you!"

The ruffian had seized a tumbler of liquor from the table, and held it toward Sheppard while he brandished his long knife.

White as snow, Sheppard backed against the wall; but did not take the drink.

The sailor had the floor; no one save him spoke a word. The action had been so rapid that there had hardly been time. Colonel Zane and Silas were as quiet and tense as the borderman.

"Drink!" hoarsely cried the sailor, advancing his knife toward Sheppard's body.

When the sharp point all but pressed against the old man, a bright object twinkled through the air. It struck Case's wrist, knocked the knife from his fingers, and, bounding against the wall, fell upon the floor. It was a tomahawk.

The borderman sprang over the table like a huge catamount, and with movement equally quick, knocked Case with a crash against the wall; closed on him before he could move a hand, and flung him like a sack of meal over the bluff.

The tension relieved, some of the crowd laughed, others looked over the embankment to see how Case had fared, and others remarked that for some reason he had gotten off better than they expected.

The borderman remained silent. He leaned against a post, with broad breast gently heaving, but his eyes sparkled as they watched Brandt, Williams, Mordaunt and Metzar. The Englishman alone spoke.

"Handily done," he said, cool and suave. "Sir, yours is an iron hand. I apologize for this unpleasant affair. My man is quarrelsome when under the influence of liquor."

"Metzar, a word with you," cried Colonel Zane curtly.

"Come inside, kunnel," said the innkeeper, plainly ill at ease.

"No; listen here. I'll speak to the point. You've got to stop running this kind of a place. No words, now, you've got to stop. Understand? You know as well as I, perhaps better, the character of your so-called inn. You'll get but one more chance."

"Wal, kunnel, this is a free country," growled Metzar. "I can't help these fellars comin' here lookin' fer blood. I runs an honest place. The men want to drink an' gamble. What's law here? What can you do?"

"You know me, Metzar," Colonel Zane said grimly. "I don't waste words. 'To hell with law!' so you say. I can say that, too. Remember, the next drunken boy I see, or shady deal, or gambling spree, out you go for good."

Metzar lowered his shaggy head and left the porch. Brandt and his friends, with serious faces, withdrew into the bar-room.

The borderman walked around the corner of the inn, and up the lane. The colonel, with Silas and Sheppard, followed in more leisurely fashion. At a shout from some one they turned to see a dusty, bloody figure, with ragged clothes, stagger up from the bluff.

"There's that blamed sailor now," said Sheppard. "He's a tough nut. My! What a knock on the head Jonathan gave him. Strikes me, too, that tomahawk came almost at the right time to save me a whole skin."

"I was furious, but not at all alarmed," rejoined Colonel Zane.

"I wondered what made you so quiet."

"I was waiting. Jonathan never acts until the right moment, and then—well, you saw him. The little villain deserved killing. I could have shot him with pleasure. Do you know, Sheppard, Jonathan's aversion to shedding blood is a singular thing. He'd never kill the worst kind of a white man until driven to it."

"That's commendable. How about Wetzel?"

"Well, Lew is different," replied Colonel Zane with a shudder. "If I told him to take an ax and clean out Metzar's place—God! what a wreck he'd make of it. Maybe I'll have to tell him, and if I do, you'll see something you can never forget."

CHAPTER IX

ON SUNDAY MORNING under the bright, warm sun, the little hamlet of Fort Henry lay peacefully quiet, as if no storms had ever rolled and thundered overhead, no roistering ever disturbed its stillness, and no Indian's yell ever horribly broke the quiet.

"'Tis a fine morning," said Colonel Zane, joining his sister on the porch. "Well, how nice you look! All in white for the first time since—well, you do look charming. You're going to church, of course."

"Yes, I invited Helen and her cousin to go. I've persuaded her to teach my Sunday-school class, and I'll take another of older children," replied Betty.

"That's well. The youngsters don't have much chance to learn out here. But we've made one great stride. A church and a preacher means very much to young people. Next shall come the village school."

"Helen and I might teach our classes an hour or two every afternoon."

"It would be a grand thing if you did! Fancy these tots growing up unable to read or write. I hate to think of it; but the Lord knows I've done my best. I've had my troubles in keeping them alive."

"Helen suggested the day school. She takes the greatest interest in everything and everybody. Her energy is remarkable. She simply must move, must do something. She overflows with kindness and sympathy. Yesterday she cried with happiness when Mabel told her Alex was eager to be married very soon. I tell you, Eb, Helen is a fine character."

"Yes, good as she is pretty, which is saying some," mused the colonel. "I wonder who'll be the lucky fellow to win her."

"It's hard to say. Not that Englishman, surely. She hates him. Jonathan might. You should see her eyes when he is mentioned."

"Say, Betts, you don't mean it?" eagerly asked her brother.

"Yes, I do," returned Betty, nodding her head positively. "I'm not easily deceived about those things. Helen's completely fascinated with Jack. She might be only a sixteen-year-old girl for the way she betrays herself to me."

"Betty, I have a beautiful plan."

"No doubt; you're full of them."

"We can do it, Betty, we can, you and I," he said, as he squeezed her arm.

"My dear old matchmaking brother," returned Betty, laughing, "it takes two to make a bargain. Jack must be considered."

"Bosh!" exclaimed the colonel, snapping his fingers. "You needn't tell me any young man—any man, could resist that glorious girl."

"Perhaps not; I couldn't if I were a man. But Jack's not like other people. He'd never realize that she cared for him. Besides, he's a borderman."

"I know, and that's the only serious obstacle. But he could scout around the fort, even if he was married. These long, lonely, terrible journeys taken by him and Wetzel are mostly unnecessary. A sweet wife could soon make him see that. The border will be civilized in a few years, and because of that he'd better give over hunting for Indians. I'd like to see him married and settled down, like all the rest of us, even Isaac. You know Jack's the last of the Zanes, that is, the old Zanes. The difficulty arising from his extreme modesty and bashfulness can easily be overcome."

"How, most wonderful brother?"

"Easy as pie. Tell Jack that Helen is dying of love for him, and tell her that Jack loves—"

"But, dear Eb, that latter part is not true," interposed Betty.

"True, of course it's true, or would be in any man who wasn't as blind as a bat. We'll tell her Jack cares for her; but he is a borderman with stern ideas of duty, and so slow and backward he'd never tell his love even if he had overcome his tricks of ranging. That would settle it with any girl worth her salt, and this one will fetch Jack in ten days, or less."

"Eb, you're a devil," said Betty gaily, and then she added in a more sober vein, "I understand, Eb. Your idea is prompted by love of Jack, and it's all right. I never see him go out of the clearing but I think it may be for the last time, even as on that day so long ago when brother Andrew waved his cap to us, and never came back. Jack is the best man in the world, and I, too, want to see him happy, with a wife, and babies, and a settled occupation in life. I think we might weave a pretty little romance. Shall we try?"

"Try? We'll do it! Now, Betts, you explain it to both. You can do it smoother than I, and telling them is really the finest point of our little plot. I'll help the good work along afterwards. He'll be out presently. Nail him at once."

Jonathan, all unconscious of the deep-laid scheme to make him happy, soon came out on the porch, and stretched his long arms as he breathed freely of the morning air.

"Hello, Jack, where are you bound?" asked Betty, clasping one of his powerful, buckskin-clad knees with her arm.

"I reckon I'll go over to the spring," he replied, patting her dark, glossy head.

"Do you know I want to tell you something, Jack, and it's quite serious," she said, blushing a little at her guilt; but resolute to carry out her part of the plot.

"Well, dear?" he asked as she hesitated.

"Do you like Helen?"

"That is a question," Jonathan replied after a moment.

"Never mind; tell me," she persisted.

He made no answer.

"Well, Jack, she's—she's wildly in love with you."

The borderman stood very still for several moments. Then, with one step he gained the lawn, and turned to confront her.

"What's that you say?"

Betty trembled a little. He spoke so sharply, his eyes were bent on her so keenly, and he looked so strong, so forceful that she was almost afraid. But remembering that she had said only what, to her mind, was absolutely true, she raised her eyes and repeated the words:

"Helen is wildly in love with you."

"Betty, you wouldn't joke about such a thing; you wouldn't lie to me, I know you wouldn't."

"No, Jack dear."

She saw his powerful frame tremble, even as she had seen more than one man tremble, during the siege, under the impact of a bullet.

Without speaking, he walked rapidly down the path toward the spring.

Colonel Zane came out of his hiding-place behind the porch and, with a face positively electrifying in its glowing pleasure, beamed upon his sister.

"Gee! Didn't he stalk off like an Indian chief!" he said, chuckling with satisfaction. "By George! Betts, you must have got in a great piece of work. I never in my life saw Jack look like that."

Colonel Zane sat down by Betty's side and laughed softly but heartily.

"We'll fix him all right, the lonely hill-climber! Why, he hasn't a ghost of a chance. Wait until she sees him after hearing your story! I tell you, Betty—why—damme! you're crying!"

He had turned to find her head lowered, while she shaded her face with her hand.

"Now, Betty, just a little innocent deceit like that—what harm?" he said, taking her hand. He was as tender as a woman.

"Oh, Eb, it wasn't that. I didn't mind telling him. Only the flash in his eyes reminded me of—of Alfred."

"Surely it did. Why not? Almost everything brings up a tender memory for some one we've loved and lost. But don't cry, Betty."

She laughed a little, and raised a face with its dark cheeks flushed and tear-stained.

"I'm silly, I suppose; but I can't help it. I cry at least once every day."

"Brace up. Here come Helen and Will. Don't let them see you grieved. My! Helen in pure white, too! This is a conspiracy to ruin the peace of the masculine portion of Fort Henry."

Betty went forward to meet her friends while Colonel Zane continued talking, but now to himself. "What a fatal beauty she has!" His eyes swept over Helen with the pleasure of an artist. The fair richness of her skin, the perfect lips, the wavy, shiny hair, the wondrous dark-blue, changing eyes, the tall figure, slender, but strong and swelling with gracious womanhood, made a picture he delighted in and loved to have near him. The girl did not possess for him any of that magnetism, so commonly felt by most of her admirers; but he did feel how subtly full she was of something, which for want of a better term he described in Wetzel's characteristic expression, as "chain-lightning."

He reflected that as he was so much older, that she, although always winsome and earnest, showed nothing of the tormenting, bewildering coquetry of her nature. Colonel Zane prided himself on his discernment, and he had already observed that Helen had different sides of character for different persons. To Betty, Mabel, Nell, and the children, she was frank, girlish, full of fun and always lovable; to her elders quiet and earnestly solicitous to please; to the young men cold; but with a penetrating, mocking promise haunting that coldness, and sometimes sweetly agreeable, often wilful, and changeable as April winds. At last the colonel concluded that she needed, as did all other spirited young women, the taming influence of a man whom she loved, a home to care for, and children to soften and temper her spirit.

"Well, young friends, I see you count on keeping the Sabbath," he said cheerily. "For my part, Will, I don't see how Jim Douns can preach this morning, before this laurel blossom and that damask rose."

"How poetical! Which is which?" asked Betty.

"Flatterer!" laughed Helen, shaking her finger.

"And a married man, too!" continued Betty.

"Well, being married has not affected my poetical sentiment, nor impaired my eyesight."

"But it has seriously inconvenienced your old propensity of making love to the girls. Not that you wouldn't if you dared," replied Betty with mischief in her eye.

"Now, Will, what do you think of that? Isn't it real sisterly regard? Come, we'll go and look at my thoroughbreds," said Colonel Zane.

"Where is Jonathan?" Helen asked presently. "Something happened at Metzar's yesterday. Papa wouldn't tell me, and I want to ask Jonathan."

"Jack is down by the spring. He spends a great deal of his time there. It's shady and cool, and the water babbles over the stones."

"How much alone he is," said Helen.

Betty took her former position on the steps, but did not raise her eyes while she continued speaking. "Yes, he's more alone than ever lately, and quieter, too. He hardly ever speaks now. There must be something on his mind more serious than horse thieves."

"What?" Helen asked quickly.

"I'd better not tell—you."

A long moment passed before Helen spoke.

"Please tell me!"

"Well, Helen, we think, Eb and I, that Jack is in love for the first time in his life, and with you, you adorable creature. But Jack's a borderman; he is stern in his principles, thinks he is wedded to his border life, and he knows that he has both red and white blood on his hands. He'd die before he'd speak of his love, because he cannot understand that would do any good, even if you loved him, which is, of course, preposterous."

"Loves me!" breathed Helen softly.

She sat down rather beside Betty, and turned her face away. She still held the young woman's hand which she squeezed so tightly as to make its owner wince. Betty stole a look at her, and saw the rich red blood mantling her cheeks, and her full bosom heave.

Helen turned presently, with no trace of emotion except a singular brilliance of the eyes. She was so slow to speak again that Colonel Zane and Will returned from the corral before she found her voice.

"Colonel Zane, please tell me about last night. When papa came home to supper he was pale and very nervous. I knew something had happened. But he would not explain, which made me all the more anxious. Won't you please tell me?"

Colonel Zane glanced again at her, and knew what had happened. Despite her self-possession those tell-tale eyes told her secret. Ever-changing and shadowing with a bounding, rapturous light, they were indeed the windows of her soul. All the emotion of a woman's heart shone there, fear, beauty, wondering appeal, trembling joy, and timid hope.

"Tell you? Indeed I will," replied Colonel Zane, softened and a little remorseful under those wonderful eyes.

No one liked to tell a story better than Colonel Zane. Briefly and graphically he related the circumstances of the affair leading to the attack on Helen's father, and, as the tale progressed, he became quite excited, speaking with animated face and forceful gestures.

"Just as the knife-point touched your father, a swiftly-flying object knocked the weapon to the floor. It was Jonathan's tomahawk. What followed was so sudden I hardly saw it. Like lightning, and flexible as steel, Jonathan jumped over the table, smashed Case against the wall, pulled him up and threw him over the bank. I tell you, Helen, it was a beautiful piece of action; but not, of course, for a woman's eyes. Now that's all. Your father was not even hurt."

"He saved papa's life," murmured Helen, standing like a statue.

She wheeled suddenly with that swift bird-like motion habitual to her, and went quickly down the path leading to the spring.

★　　★　　★　　★　　★　　★

Jonathan Zane, solitary dreamer of dreams as he was, had never been in as strange and beautiful a reverie as that which possessed him on this Sabbath morning.

Deep into his heart had sunk Betty's words. The wonder of it, the sweetness, that alone was all he felt. The glory of this girl had begun, days past, to spread its glamour round him. Swept irresistibly away now, he soared aloft in a dream-castle of fancy with its painted windows and golden walls.

For the first time in his life on the border he had entered the little glade and had no eye for the crystal water flowing over the pebbles and mossy stones, or the plot of grassy ground inclosed by tall, dark trees and shaded by a canopy of fresh green and azure blue. Nor did he hear the music of the soft rushing water, the warbling birds, or the gentle sighing breeze moving the leaves.

Gone, vanished, lost to-day was that sweet companionship of nature. That indefinable and unutterable spirit which flowed so peacefully to him from his beloved woods; that something more than merely affecting his senses, which existed for him in the stony cliffs, and breathed with life through the lonely aisles of the forest, had fled before the fateful power of a woman's love and beauty.

A long time that seemed only a moment passed while he leaned against a stone. A light step sounded on the path.

A vision in pure white entered the glade; two little hands pressed his, and two dark-blue eyes of misty beauty shed their light on him.

"Jonathan, I am come to thank you."

Sweet and tremulous, the voice sounded far away.

"Thank me? For what?"

"You saved papa's life. Oh! how can I thank you?"

No voice answered for him.

"I have nothing to give but this."

A flower-like face was held up to him; hands light as thistledown touched his shoulders; dark-blue eyes glowed upon him with all tenderness.

"May I thank you—so?"

Soft lips met his full and lingeringly.

Then came a rush as of wind, a flash of white, and the patter of flying feet. He was alone in the glade.

CHAPTER X

JUNE PASSED; JULY opened with unusually warm weather, and Fort Henry had no visits from Indians or horse-thieves, nor any inconvenience except the hot sun. It was the warmest weather for many years, and seriously dwarfed the settlers' growing corn. Nearly all the springs were dry, and a drouth menaced the farmers.

The weather gave Helen an excuse which she was not slow to adopt. Her pale face and languid air perplexed and worried her father and her friends. She explained to them that the heat affected her disagreeably.

Long days had passed since that Sunday morning when she kissed the borderman. What transports of sweet hope and fear were hers then! How shame had scorched her happiness! Yet still she gloried in the act. By that kiss had she awakened to a full consciousness of her love. With insidious stealth and ever-increasing power this flood had increased to full tide, and, bursting its bonds, surged over her with irresistible strength.

During the first days after the dawning of her passion, she lived in its sweetness, hearing only melodious sounds chiming in her soul. The hours following that Sunday were like long dreams. But as all things reach fruition, so this girlish period passed, leaving her a thoughtful woman. She began to gather up the threads of her life where love had broken them, to plan nobly, and to hope and wait.

Weeks passed, however, and her lover did not come. Betty told her that Jonathan made flying trips at break of day to hold council with Colonel Zane; that he and Wetzel were on the trail of Shawnees with stolen horses, and both bordermen were in their dark, vengeful, terrible moods. In these later days Helen passed through many stages of feeling. After the exalting mood of hot, young love, came reaction. She fell into the depths of despair.

79

Sorrow paled her face, thinned her cheeks and lent another shadow, a mournful one, to her great eyes. The constant repression of emotion, the strain of trying to seem cheerful when she was miserable, threatened even her magnificent health. She answered the solicitude of her friends by evasion, and then by that innocent falsehood in which a sensitive soul hides its secrets. Shame was only natural, because since the borderman came not, nor sent her a word, pride whispered that she had wooed him, forgetting modesty.

Pride, anger, shame, despair, however, finally fled before affection. She loved this wild borderman, and knew he loved her in return although he might not understand it himself. His simplicity, his lack of experience with women, his hazardous life and stern duty regarding it, pleaded for him and for her love. For the lack of a little understanding she would never live unhappy and alone while she was loved. Better give a thousand times more than she had sacrificed. He would return to the village some day, when the Indians and the thieves were run down, and would be his own calm, gentle self. Then she would win him, break down his allegiance to this fearful border life, and make him happy in her love.

While Helen was going through one of the fires of life to come out sweeter and purer, if a little pensive and sad, time, which waits not for love, nor life, nor death, was hastening onward, and soon the golden fields of grain were stored. September came with its fruitful promise fulfilled.

Helen entered once more into the quiet, social life of the little settlement, taught her class on Sundays, did all her own work, and even found time to bring a ray of sunshine to more than one sick child's bed. Yet she did not forget her compact with Jonathan, and bent all her intelligence to find some clew that might aid in the capture of the horse-thief. She was still groping in the darkness. She could not, however, banish the belief that the traitor was Brandt. She blamed herself for this, because of having no good reasons for suspicion; but the conviction was there, fixed by intuition. Because a man's eyes were steely gray, sharp like those of a cat's, and capable of the same contraction and enlargement, there was no reason to believe their owner was a criminal. But that, Helen acknowledged with a smile, was the only argument she had. To be sure Brandt had looked capable of anything, the night Jonathan knocked him down; she knew he had incited Case to begin the trouble at

Metzar's, and had seemed worried since that time. He had not left the settlement on short journeys, as had been his custom before the affair in the bar-room. And not a horse had disappeared from Fort Henry since that time.

Brandt had not discontinued his attentions to her; if they were less ardent it was because she had given him absolutely to understand that she could be his friend only. And she would not have allowed even so much except for Jonathan's plan. She fancied it was possible to see behind Brandt's courtesy, the real subtle, threatening man. Stripped of his kindliness, an assumed virtue, the iron man stood revealed, cold, calculating, cruel.

Mordaunt she never saw but once and then, shocking and pitiful, he lay dead drunk in the grass by the side of the road, his pale, weary, handsome face exposed to the pitiless rays of the sun. She ran home weeping over this wreck of what had once been so fine a gentleman. Ah! the curse of rum! He had learned his soft speech and courtly bearing in the refinement of a home where a proud mother adored, and gentle sisters loved him. And now, far from the kindred he had disgraced, he lay in the road like a log. How it hurt her! She almost wished she could have loved him, if love might have redeemed. She was more kind to her other admirers, more tolerant of Brandt, and could forgive the Englishman, because the pangs she had suffered through love had softened her spirit.

During this long period the growing friendship of her cousin for Betty had been a source of infinite pleasure to Helen. She hoped and believed a romance would develop between the young widow and Will, and did all in her power, slyly abetted by the matchmaking colonel, to bring the two together.

One afternoon when the sky was clear with that intense blue peculiar to bright days in early autumn, Helen started out toward Betty's, intending to remind that young lady she had promised to hunt for clematis and other fall flowers.

About half-way to Betty's home she met Brandt. He came swinging round a corner with his quick, firm step. She had not seen him for several days, and somehow he seemed different. A brightness, a flash, as of daring expectation, was in his face. The poise, too, of the man had changed.

"Well, I am fortunate. I was just going to your home," he said cheerily. "Won't you come for a walk with me?"

"You may walk with me to Betty's," Helen answered.

"No, not that. Come up the hillside. We'll get some goldenrod. I'd like to have a chat with you. I may go away—I mean I'm thinking of making a short trip," he added hurriedly.

"Please come."

"I promised to go to Betty's."

"You won't come?" His voice trembled with mingled disappointment and resentment.

"No," Helen replied in slight surprise.

"You have gone with the other fellows. Why not with me?" He was white now, and evidently laboring under powerful feelings that must have had their origin in some thought or plan which hinged on the acceptance of his invitation.

"Because I choose not to," Helen replied coldly, meeting his glance fully.

A dark red flush swelled Brandt's face and neck; his gray eyes gleamed balefully with wolfish glare; his teeth were clenched. He breathed hard and trembled with anger. Then, by a powerful effort, he conquered himself; the villainous expression left his face; the storm of rage subsided. Great incentive there must have been for him thus to repress his emotions so quickly. He looked long at her with sinister, intent regard; then, with the laugh of a desperado, a laugh which might have indicated contempt for the failure of his suit, and which was fraught with a world of meaning, of menace, he left her without so much as a salute.

Helen pondered over this sudden change, and felt relieved because she need make no further pretense of friendship. He had shown himself to be what she had instinctively believed. She hurried on toward Betty's, hoping to find Colonel Zane at home, and with Jonathan, for Brandt's hint of leaving Fort Henry, and his evident chagrin at such a slip of speech, had made her suspicious. She was informed by Mrs. Zane that the colonel had gone to a log-raising; Jonathan had not been in for several days, and Betty went away with Will.

"Where did they go?" asked Helen.

"I'm not sure; I think down to the spring."

Helen followed the familiar path through the grove of oaks into the glade. It was quite deserted. Sitting on the stone against which Jonathan had leaned the day she kissed him, she gave way to tender reflection. Suddenly she was disturbed by the sound of rapid footsteps, and looking up, saw the hulking form of Metzar, the innkeeper, coming down the path. He carried a bucket, and meant evidently to get water. Helen did not desire to be seen, and, thinking he would stay only a moment, slipped into a thicket of willows behind the stone. She could see plainly through the foliage. Metzar came into the glade, peered around in the manner of a man expecting to see some one, and then, filling his bucket at the spring, sat down on the stone.

Not a minute elapsed before soft, rapid footsteps sounded in the distance. The bushes parted, disclosing the white, set face and gray eyes of Roger Brandt. With a light spring he cleared the brook and approached Metzar.

Before speaking he glanced around the glade with the fugitive, distrustful glance of a man who suspects even the trees. Then, satisfied by the scrutiny he opened his hunting frock, taking forth a long object which he thrust toward Metzar.

It was an Indian arrow.

Metzar's dull gaze traveled from this to the ominous face of Brandt.

"See there, you! Look at this arrow! Shot by the best Indian on the border into the window of my room. I hadn't been there a minute when it came from the island. God! but it was a great shot!"

"Hell!" gasped Metzar, his dull face quickening with some awful thought.

"I guess it *is* hell," replied Brandt, his face growing whiter and wilder.

"Our game's up?" questioned Metzar with haggard cheek.

"Up? Man! We haven't a day, maybe less, to shake Fort Henry."

"What does it mean?" asked Metzar. He was the calmer of the two.

"It's a signal. The Shawnees, who were in hiding with the horses over by Blueberry swamp, have been flushed by those bordermen. Some of them have escaped; at least one, for no one but Ashbow could shoot that arrow across the river."

"Suppose he hadn't come?" whispered Metzar hoarsely.

Brandt answered him with a dark, shuddering gaze.

A twig snapped in the thicket. Like foxes at the click of a trap, these men whirled with fearsome glances.

"Ugh!" came a low, guttural voice from the bushes, and an Indian of magnificent proportions and somber, swarthy features, entered the glade.

CHAPTER XI

THE SAVAGE HAD just emerged from the river, for his graceful, copper-colored body and scanty clothing were dripping with water. He carried a long bow and a quiver of arrows.

Brandt uttered an exclamation of surprise, and Metzar a curse, as the lithe Indian leaped the brook. He was not young. His swarthy face was lined, seamed, and terrible with a dark impassiveness.

"Paleface-brother-get-arrow," he said in halting English, as his eyes flashed upon Brandt. "Chief-want-make-sure."

The white man leaned forward, grasped the Indian's arm, and addressed him in an Indian language. This questioning was evidently in regard to his signal, the whereabouts of others of the party, and why he took such fearful risks almost in the village. The Indian answered with one English word.

"Deathwind!"

Brandt drew back with drawn, white face, while a whistling breath escaped him.

"I knew it, Metz. Wetzel!" he exclaimed in a husky voice.

The blood slowly receded from Metzar's evil, murky face, leaving it haggard.

"Deathwind-on-Chief's-trail-up-Eagle Rock," continued the Indian. "Deathwind-fooled-not-for-long. Chief-wait-paleface-brothers at Two Islands."

The Indian stepped into the brook, parted the willows, and was gone as he had come, silently.

"We know what to expect," said Brandt in calmer tone as the daring cast of countenance returned to him. "There's an Indian for you! He got away, doubled like an old fox on his trail, and ran in here to give us a chance at escape. Now you know why Bing Legget can't be caught."

"Let's dig at once," replied Metzar, with no show of returning courage such as characterized his companion.

Brandt walked to and fro with bent brows, like one in deep thought. Suddenly he turned upon Metzar's eyes which were brightly hard, and reckless with resolve.

"By Heaven! I'll do it! Listen. Wetzel has gone to the top of Eagle Mountain, where he and Zane have a rendezvous. Even he won't suspect the cunning of this Indian; anyway it'll be after daylight to-morrow before he strikes the trail. I've got twenty-four hours, and more, to get this girl, and I'll do it!"

"Bad move to have weight like her on a march," said Metzar.

"Bah! The thing's easy. As for you, go on, push ahead after we're started. All I ask is that you stay by me until the time to cut loose."

"I ain't agoin' to crawfish now," growled Metzar. "Strikes me, too, I'm losin' more'n you."

"You won't be a loser if you can get back to Detroit with your scalp. I'll pay you in horses and gold. Once we reach Legget's place we're safe."

"What's yer plan about gittin' the gal?" asked Metzar.

Brandt leaned forward and spoke eagerly, but in a low tone.

"Git away on hoss-back?" questioned Metzar, visibly brightening. "Wal, that's some sense. Kin ye trust ther other party?"

"I'm sure I can," rejoined Brandt.

"It'll be a good job, a good job an' all done in daylight, too. Bing Legget couldn't plan better," Metzar said, rubbing his hands.

"We've fooled these Zanes and their fruit-raising farmers for a year, and our time is about up," Brandt muttered. "One more job and we've done. Once with Legget we're safe, and then we'll work slowly back towards Detroit. Let's get out of here now, for some one may come at any moment."

The plotters separated, Brandt going through the grove, and Metzar down the path by which he had come.

*   *   *   *   *   *

Helen, trembling with horror of what she had heard, raised herself cautiously from the willows where she had lain, and watched the innkeeper's retreating figure. When it had disappeared she gave a little gasp of relief. Free now to run home, there to plan what course must be pursued, she conquered her fear and weakness, and hurried from the glade. Luckily, so far as she was able to tell, no one saw her return. She resolved that she would be cool, deliberate, clever, worthy of the borderman's confidence.

First she tried to determine the purport of this interview between Brandt and Metzar. She recalled to mind all that was said, and supplied what she thought had been suggested. Brandt and Metzar were horse-thieves, aids of Bing Legget. They had repaired to the glade to plan. The Indian had been a surprise. Wetzel had routed the Shawnees, and was now on the trail of this chieftain. The Indian warned them to leave Fort Henry and to meet him at a place called Two Islands. Brandt's plan, presumably somewhat changed by the advent of the red-man, was to steal horses, abduct a girl in broad daylight, and before to-morrow's sunset escape to join the ruffian Legget.

"I am the girl," murmured Helen shudderingly, as she relapsed momentarily into girlish fears. But at once she rose above selfish feelings.

Secondly, while it was easy to determine what the outlaws meant, the wisest course was difficult to conceive. She had promised the borderman to help him, and not speak of anything she learned to any but himself. She could not be true to him if she asked advice. The point was clear; either she must remain in the settlement hoping for Jonathan's return in time to frustrate Brandt's villainous scheme, or find the borderman. Suddenly she remembered Metzar's allusion to a second person whom Brandt felt certain he could trust. This meant another traitor in Fort Henry, another horse-thief, another desperado willing to make off with helpless women.

Helen's spirit rose in arms. She had their secret, and could ruin them. She would find the borderman.

Wetzel was on the trail at Eagle Rock. What for? Trailing an Indian who was then five miles east of that rock? Not Wetzel! He was on that track to meet Jonathan. Otherwise, with the redskins near the river, he would have been closer to them. He would meet Jonathan there at sunset to-day, Helen decided.

She paced the room, trying to still her throbbing heart and trembling hands.

"I must be calm," she said sternly. "Time is precious. I have not a moment to lose. I will find him. I've watched that mountain many a time, and can find the trail and the rock. I am in more danger here, than out there in the forest. With Wetzel and Jonathan on the mountain side, the Indians have fled it. But what about the savage who warned Brandt? Let me think. Yes, he'll avoid the river; he'll go round south of the settlement, and, therefore, can't see me cross. How fortunate that I have paddled a canoe many times across the river. How glad that I made Colonel Zane describe the course up the mountains!"

Her resolution fixed, Helen changed her skirt for one of buck-skin, putting on leggings and moccasins of the same serviceable material. She filled the pockets of a short, rain-proof jacket with biscuits, and, thus equipped, sallied forth with a spirit and exulta-tion she could not subdue. Only one thing she feared, which was that Brandt or Metzar might see her cross the river. She launched her canoe and paddled down stream, under cover of the bluff, to a point opposite the end of the island, then straight across, keeping the island between her and the settlement. Gaining the other shore, Helen pulled the canoe into the willows, and mounted the bank. A thicket of willow and alder made progress up the steep incline dif-ficult, but once out of it she faced a long stretch of grassy meadow-land. A mile beyond began the green, billowy rise of that mountain which she intended to climb.

Helen's whole soul was thrown into the adventure. She felt her strong young limbs in accord with her heart.

"Now, Mr. Brandt, horse-thief and girl-snatcher, we'll see," she said with scornful lips. "If I can't beat you now I'm not fit to be Betty Zane's friend; and am unworthy of a borderman's trust."

She traversed the whole length of meadowland close under the shadow of the fringed bank, and gained the forest. Here she hesi-tated. All was so wild and still. No definite course through the woods seemed to invite, and yet all was open. Trees, trees, dark, immovable trees everywhere. The violent trembling of poplar and aspen leaves, when all others were so calm, struck her strangely, and the fearful stillness awed her. Drawing a deep breath she started forward up the gently rising ground.

As she advanced the open forest became darker, and of wilder aspect. The trees were larger and closer together. Still she made fair progress without deviating from the course she had determined upon. Before her rose a ridge, with a ravine on either side, reaching nearly to the summit of the mountain. Here the underbrush was scanty, the fallen trees had slipped down the side, and the rocks were not so numerous, all of which gave her reason to be proud, so far, of her judgment.

Helen, pressing onward and upward, forgot time and danger, while she reveled in the wonder of the forestland. Birds and squirrels fled before her; whistling and wheezing of alarm, or heavy crashings in the bushes, told of frightened wild beasts. A dull, faint roar, like a distant wind, suggested tumbling waters. A single birch tree, gleaming white among the black trees, enlivened the gloomy forest. Patches of sunlight brightened the shade. Giant ferns, just tinging with autumn colors, waved tips of sculptured perfection. Most wonderful of all were the colored leaves, as they floated downward with a sad, gentle rustle.

Helen was brought to a realization of her hazardous undertaking by a sudden roar of water, and the abrupt termination of the ridge in a deep gorge. Grasping a tree she leaned over to look down. It was fully a hundred feet deep, with impassable walls, green-stained and damp, at the bottom of which a brawling, brown brook rushed on its way. Fully twenty feet wide, it presented an insurmountable barrier to further progress in that direction.

But Helen looked upon it merely as a difficulty to be overcome. She studied the situation, and decided to go to the left because higher ground was to be seen that way. Abandoning the ridge, she pressed on, keeping as close to the gorge as she dared, and came presently to a fallen tree lying across the dark cleft. Without a second's hesitation, for she knew such would be fatal, she stepped upon the tree and started across, looking at nothing but the log under her feet, while she tried to imagine herself walking across the water-gate, at home in Virginia.

She accomplished the venture without a misstep. When safely on the ground once more she felt her knees tremble and a queer, light feeling came into her head. She laughed, however, as she rested a moment. It would take more than a gorge to discourage her, she resolved with set lips, as once again she made her way along the rising ground.

Perilous, if not desperate, work was ahead of her. Broken, rocky ground, matted thicket, and seemingly impenetrable forest, rose darkly in advance. But she was not even tired, and climbed, crawled, twisted and turned on her way upward. She surmounted a rocky ledge, to face a higher ridge covered with splintered, uneven stones, and the fallen trees of many storms. Once she slipped and fell, spraining her wrist. At length this uphill labor began to weary her. To breathe caused a pain in her side and she was compelled to rest.

Already the gray light of coming night shrouded the forest. She was surprised at seeing the trees become indistinct; because the shadows hovered over the thickets, and noted that the dark, dim outline of the ridges was fading into obscurity.

She struggled on up the uneven slope with a tightening at her heart which was not all exhaustion. For the first time she doubted herself, but it was too late. She could not turn back. Suddenly she felt that she was on a smoother, easier course. Not to strike a stone or break a twig seemed unusual. It might be a path worn by deer going to a spring. Then into her troubled mind flashed the joyful thought, she had found a trail.

Soft, wiry grass, springing from a wet soil, rose under her feet. A little rill trickled alongside the trail. Mossy, soft-cushioned stones lay imbedded here and there. Young maples and hickories grew breast-high on either side, and the way wound in and out under the lowering shade of forest monarchs.

Swiftly ascending this path she came at length to a point where it was possible to see some distance ahead. The ascent became hardly noticeable. Then, as she turned a bend of the trail, the light grew brighter and brighter, until presently all was open and clear. An oval space, covered with stones, lay before her. A big, blasted chestnut stood near by. Beyond was the dim, purple haze of distance. Above, the pale, blue sky just faintly rose-tinted by the setting sun. Far to her left the scraggly trees of a low hill were tipped with orange and russet shades. She had reached the summit.

Desolate and lonely was this little plateau. Helen felt immeasurably far away from home. Yet she could see in the blue distance the glancing river, the dark fort, and that cluster of cabins which marked the location of Fort Henry. Sitting upon the roots of the big chestnut tree she gazed around. There were the remains of a small camp-fire. Beyond, a hollow under a shelving rock. A bed of dry leaves lay packed in this shelter. Some one had been here, and she doubted not that it was the borderman.

She was so tired and her wrist pained so severely that she lay back against the tree-trunk, closed her eyes and rested. A weariness, the apathy of utter exhaustion, came over her. She wished the bordermen would hurry and come before she went to sleep.

Drowsily she was sinking into slumber when a long, low rumble aroused her. How dark it had suddenly become! A sheet of pale light flared across the overcast heavens.

"A storm!" exclaimed Helen. "Alone on this mountain-top with a storm coming. Am I frightened? I don't believe it. At least I'm safe from that ruffian Brandt. Oh! if my borderman would only come!"

Helen changed her position from beside the tree, to the hollow under the stone. It was high enough to permit of her sitting upright, and offered a safe retreat from the storm. The bed of leaves was soft and comfortable. She sat there peering out at the darkening heavens.

All beneath her, southward and westward was gray twilight. The settlement faded from sight; the river grew wan and shadowy. The ruddy light in the west was fast succumbing to the rolling clouds. Darker and darker it became, until only one break in the overspreading vapors admitted the last crimson gleam of sunshine over hills and valley, brightening the river until it resembled a stream of fire. Then the light failed, the glow faded. The intense blackness of night prevailed.

Out of the ebon west came presently another flare of light, a quick, spreading flush, like a flicker from a monster candle; it was followed by a long, low, rumbling roll.

Helen felt in those intervals of unutterably vast silence, that she must shriek aloud. The thunder was a friend. She prayed for the storm to break. She had withstood danger and toilsome effort with fortitude; but could not brave this awful, boding, wilderness stillness.

Flashes of lightning now revealed the rolling, pushing, turbulent clouds, and peals of thunder sounded nearer and louder.

A long swelling moan, sad, low, like the uneasy sigh of the sea, breathed far in the west. It was the wind, the ominous warning of the storm. Sheets of light were now mingled with long, straggling ropes of fire, and the rumblings were often broken by louder, quicker detonations.

Then a period, longer than usual, of inky blackness succeeded the sharp flaring of light. A faint breeze ruffled the leaves of the thicket, and fanned Helen's hot cheek. The moan of the wind became more distinct, then louder, and in another instant like the far-off roar of a rushing river. The storm was upon her. Helen shrank closer against the stone, and pulled her jacket tighter around her trembling form.

A sudden, intense, dazzling, blinding, white light enveloped her. The rocky promontory, the weird, giant chestnut tree, the open plateau, and beyond, the stormy heavens, were all luridly clear in the flash of lightning. She fancied it was possible to see a tall, dark figure emerging from the thicket. As the thunderclap rolled and pealed overhead, she strained her eyes into the blackness waiting for the next lightning flash.

It came with brilliant, dazing splendor. The whole plateau and thicket were as light as in the day. Close by the stone where she lay crept the tall, dark figure of an Indian. With starting eyes she saw the fringed clothing, the long, flying hair, and supple body peculiar to the savage. He was creeping upon her.

Helen's blood ran cold; terror held her voiceless. She felt herself sinking slowly down upon the leaves.

CHAPTER XII

THE SUN HAD begun to cast long shadows the afternoon of Helen's hunt for Jonathan, when the borderman, accompanied by Wetzel, led a string of horses along the base of the very mountain she had ascended.

"Last night's job was a good one, I ain't gainsayin'; but the red-skin I wanted got away," Wetzel said gloomily.

"He's safe now as a squirrel in a hole. I saw him dartin' among the trees with his white eagle feathers stickin' up like a buck's flag," replied Jonathan. "He can run. If I'd only had my rifle loaded! But I'm not sure he was that arrow-shootin' Shawnee."

"It was him. I saw his bow. We ought'er taken more time an' picked him out," Wetzel replied, shaking his head gravely. "Though mebbe that'd been useless. I think he was hidin'. He's precious shy of his red skin. I've been after him these ten year, an' never ketched him nappin' yet. We'd have done much toward snuffin' out Legget an' his gang if we'd winged the Shawnee."

"He left a plain trail."

"One of his tricks. He's slicker on a trail than any other Injun on the border, unless mebbe it's old Wingenund, the Huron. This Shawnee'd lead us many a mile for nuthin', if we'd stick to his trail. I'm long ago used to him. He's doubled like an old fox, run harder'n a skeered fawn, an', if needs be, he'll lay low as a cunnin' buck. I calkilate once over the mountain, he's made a bee-line east. We'll go on with the hosses, an' then strike across country to find his trail."

"It 'pears to me, Lew, that we've taken a long time in makin' a show against these hoss-thieves," said Jonathan.

"I ain't sayin' much; but I've felt it," replied Wetzel.

"All summer, an' nothin' done. It was more luck than sense that we run into those Injuns with the hosses. We only got three out of four, an' let the best redskin give us the slip. Here fall is nigh on us, with winter comin' soon, an' still we don't know who's the white traitor in the settlement."

"I said it's be a long, an' mebbe, our last trail."

"Why?"

"Because these fellars, red or white, are in with a picked gang of the best woodsmen as ever outlawed the border. We'll get the Fort Henry hoss-thief. I'll back the bright-eyed lass for that."

"I haven't seen her lately, an' allow she'd left me word if she learned anythin'."

"Wal, mebbe it's as well you hain't seen so much of her."

In silence they traveled and, arriving at the edge of the meadow, were about to mount two of the horses, when Wetzel said in a sharp tone:

"Look!"

He pointed to a small, well-defined moccasin track in the black earth on the margin of a rill.

"Lew, it's a woman's, sure's you're born," declared Jonathan.

Wetzel knelt and closely examined the footprint; "Yes, a woman's, an' no Injun."

"What?" Jonathan exclaimed, as he knelt to scrutinize the imprint.

"This ain't half a day old," added Wetzel. "An' not a redskin's moccasin near. What d'you reckon?"

"A white girl, alone," replied Jonathan as he followed the trail a short distance along the brook. "See, she's makin' upland. Wetzel, these tracks could hardly be my sister's, an' there's only one other girl on the border whose feet will match 'em! Helen Sheppard has passed here, on her way up the mountain to find you or me."

"I like your reckonin'."

"She's suddenly discovered somethin', Injuns, hoss-thieves, the Fort Henry traitor, or mebbe, an' most likely, some plottin'. Bein' bound to secrecy by me, she's not told my brother. An' it must be call for hurry. She knows we frequent this mountain-top; said Eb told her about the way we get here."

"I'd calkilate about the same."

"What'll you do? Go with me after her?" asked Jonathan.

"I'll take the hosses, an' be at the fort inside of an hour. If Helen's gone, I'll tell her father you're close on her trail. Now listen! It'll be dark soon, an' a storm's comin'. Don't waste time on her trail. Hurry up to the rock. She'll be there, if any lass could climb there. If not, come back in the mornin', hunt her trail out, an' find her. I'm thinkin', Jack, we'll find the Shawnee had somethin' to do with this. Whatever happens after I get back to the fort, I'll expect you hard on my trail."

Jonathan bounded across the brook and with an easy lope began the gradual ascent. Soon he came upon a winding path. He ran along this for perhaps a quarter of an hour, until it became too steep for rapid traveling, when he settled down to a rapid walk. The forest was already dark. A slight rustling of the leaves beneath his feet was the only sound, except at long intervals the distant rumbling of thunder.

The mere possibility of Helen's being alone on that mountain seeking him, made Jonathan's heart beat as it never had before. For weeks he had avoided her, almost forgot her. He had conquered the strange, yearning weakness which assailed him after that memorable Sunday, and once more the silent shaded glens, the mystery of the woods, the breath of his wild, free life had claimed him. But now as this evidence of her spirit, her recklessness, was before him, and he remembered Betty's avowal, a pain which was almost physical, tore at his heart. How terrible it would be if she came to her death through him! He pictured the big, alluring eyes, the perfect lips, the haunting face, cold in death. And he shuddered.

The dim gloom of the woods soon darkened into blackness. The flashes of lightning, momentarily streaking the foliage, or sweeping overhead in pale yellow sheets, aided Jonathan in keeping the trail.

He gained the plateau just as a great flash illumined it, and distinctly saw the dark hollow where he had taken refuge in many a storm, and where he now hoped to find the girl. Picking his way carefully over the sharp, loose stones, he at last put his hand on the huge rock. Another blue-white, dazzling flash enveloped the scene.

Under the rock he saw a dark form huddled, and a face as white as snow, with wide, horrified eyes.

"Lass," he said, when the thunder had rumbled away. He received no answer, and called again. Kneeling, he groped about until touching Helen's dress. He spoke again; but she did not reply.

Jonathan crawled under the ledge beside the quiet figure. He touched her hands; they were very cold. Bending over, he was relieved to hear her heart beating. He called her name, but still she made no reply. Dipping his hand into a little rill that ran beside the stone, he bathed her face. Soon she stirred uneasily, moaned, and suddenly sat up.

"'Tis Jonathan," he said quickly; "don't be scared."

Another illuminating flare of lightning brightened the plateau.

"Oh! thank Heaven!" cried Helen. "I thought you were an Indian!"

Helen sank trembling against the borderman, who enfolded her in his long arms. Her relief and thankfulness were so great that she could not speak. Her hands clasped and unclasped round his strong fingers. Her tears flowed freely.

The storm broke with terrific fury. A seething torrent of rain and hail came with the rushing wind. Great heaven-broad sheets of lightning played across the black dome overhead. Zigzag ropes, steel-blue in color, shot downward. Crash, and crack, and boom the thunder split and rolled the clouds above. The lightning flashes showed the fall of rain in columns like white waterfalls, borne on the irresistible wind.

The grandeur of the storm awed, and stilled Helen's emotion. She sat there watching the lightning, listening to the peals of thunder, and thrilling with the wonder of the situation.

Gradually the roar abated, the flashes became less frequent, the thunder decreased, as the storm wore out its strength in passing. The wind and rain ceased on the mountain-top almost as quickly as they had begun, and the roar died slowly away in the distance. Far to the eastward flashes of light illumined scowling clouds, and brightened many a dark, wooded hill and valley.

"Lass, how is't I find you here?" asked Jonathan gravely.

With many a pause and broken phrase, Helen told the story of what she had seen and heard at the spring.

"Child, why didn't you go to my brother?" asked Jonathan. "You don't know what you undertook!"

"I thought of everything; but I wanted to find you myself. Besides, I was just as safe alone on this mountain as in the village."

"I don't know but you're right," replied Jonathan thoughtfully. "So Brandt planned to make off with you to-morrow?"

"Yes, and when I heard it I wanted to run away from the village."

"You've done a wondrous clever thing, lass. This Brandt is a bad man, an' hard to match. But if he hasn't shaken Fort Henry by now, his career'll end mighty sudden, an' his bad trails stop short on the hillside among the graves, for Eb will always give outlaws or Injuns decent burial."

"What will the colonel, or anyone, think has become of me?"

"Wetzel knows, lass, for he found your trail below."

"Then he'll tell papa you came after me? Oh! poor papa! I forgot him. Shall we stay here until daylight?"

"We'd gain nothin' by startin' now. The brooks are full, an' in the dark we'd make little distance. You're dry here, an' comfortable. What's more, lass, you're safe."

"I feel perfectly safe, with you," Helen said softly.

"Aren't you tired, lass?"

"Tired? I'm nearly dead. My feet are cut and bruised, my wrist is sprained, and I ache all over. But, Jonathan, I don't care. I am so happy to have my wild venture turn out successfully."

"You can lie here an' sleep while I keep watch."

Jonathan made a move to withdraw his arm, which was still between Helen and the rock but had dropped from her waist.

"I am very comfortable. I'll sit here with you, watching for daybreak. My! how dark it is! I cannot see my hand before my eyes."

Helen settled herself back upon the stone, leaned a very little against his shoulder, and tried to think over her adventure. But her mind refused to entertain any ideas, except those of the present. Mingled with the dreamy lassitude that grew stronger every moment, was a sense of delight in her situation. She was alone on a wild mountain, in the night, with this borderman, the one she loved. By chance and her own foolhardiness this had come about, yet she was fortunate to have it tend to some good beyond her own happiness. All she would suffer from her perilous climb would be aching bones, and, perhaps, a scolding from her father. What she might gain was more than she had dared hope. The breaking up of the horse-thief gang would be a boon to the harassed settlement. How proudly Colonel Zane would smile! Her name would go on that long roll of border honor and heroism. That was not, however, one thousandth part so pleasing, as to be alone with her borderman.

With a sigh of mingled weariness and content, Helen leaned her head on Jonathan's shoulder and fell asleep.

The borderman trembled. The sudden nestling of her head against him, the light caress of her fragrant hair across his cheek, revived a sweet, almost-conquered, almost-forgotten emotion. He felt an inexplicable thrill vibrate through him. No untrodden, ambushed wild, no perilous trail, no dark and bloody encounter had ever made him feel fear as had the kiss of this maiden. He had sternly silenced faint, unfamiliar, yet tender, voices whispering in his heart; and now his rigorous discipline was as if it were not, for at her touch he trembled. Still he did not move away. He knew she had succumbed to weariness, and was fast asleep. He could, gently, without awakening her, have laid her head upon the pillow of leaves; indeed, he thought of doing it, but made no effort. A woman's head softly lying against him was a thing novel, strange, wonderful. For all the power he had then, each tumbling lock of her hair might as well have been a chain linking him fast to the mountain.

With the memory of his former yearning, unsatisfied moods, and the unrest and pain his awakening tenderness had caused him, came a determination to look things fairly in the face, to be just in thought toward this innocent, impulsive girl, and be honest with himself.

Duty commanded that he resist all charm other than that pertaining to his life in the woods. Years ago he had accepted a borderman's destiny, well content to be recompensed by its untamed freedom from restraint; to be always under the trees he loved so well; to lend his cunning and woodcraft in the pioneer's cause; to haunt the savage trails; to live from day to day a menace to the foes of civilization. That was the life he had chosen; it was all he could ever have.

In view of this, justice demanded that he allow no friendship to spring up between himself and this girl. If his sister's belief was really true, if Helen really was interested in him, it must be a romantic infatuation which, not encouraged, would wear itself out. What was he, to win the love of any girl? An unlettered borderman, who knew only the woods, whose life was hard and cruel, whose hands were red with Indian blood, whose vengeance had not spared men even of his own race. He could not believe she really loved him. Wildly impulsive as girls were at times, she had kissed him. She had been grateful, carried away by a generous feeling for him as the protector of her father. When she did not see him for a long time, as he vowed should be the case after he had carried her safely home, she would forget.

Then honesty demanded that he probe his own feelings. Sternly, as if judging a renegade, he searched out in his simple way the truth. This big-eyed lass with her nameless charm would bewitch even a borderman, unless he avoided her. So much he had not admitted until now. Love he had never believed could be possible for him. When she fell asleep her hand had slipped from his arm to his fingers, and now rested there lightly as a leaf. The contact was delight. The gentle night breeze blew a tress of hair across his lips. He trembled. Her rounded shoulder pressed against him until he could feel her slow, deep breathing. He almost held his own breath lest he disturb her rest.

No, he was no longer indifferent. As surely as those pale stars blinked far above, he knew the delight of a woman's presence. It moved him to study the emotion, as he studied all things, which was the habit of his borderman's life. Did it come from knowledge of her beauty, matchless as that of the mountain-laurel? He recalled the dark glance of her challenging eyes, her tall, supple figure, and the bewildering excitement and magnetism of her presence. Beauty was wonderful, but not everything. Beauty belonged to her, but she would have been irresistible without it. Was it not because she was a woman? That was the secret. She was a woman with all a woman's charm to bewitch, to twine round the strength of men as the ivy encircles the oak; with all a woman's weakness to pity and to guard; with all a woman's wilful burning love, and with all a woman's mystery.

At last so much of life was intelligible to him. The renegade committed his worst crimes because even in his outlawed, homeless state, he could not exist without the companionship, if not the love, of a woman. The pioneer's toil and privation were for a woman, and the joy of loving her and living for her. The Indian brave, when not on the war-path, walked hand in hand with a dusky, soft-eyed maiden, and sang to her of moonlit lakes and western winds. Even the birds and beasts mated. The robins returned to their old nest; the eagles paired once and were constant in life and death. The buck followed the doe through the forest. All nature sang that love made life worth living. Love, then, was everything.

The borderman sat out the long vigil of the night watching the stars, and trying to decide that love was not for him. If Wetzel had locked a secret within his breast, and never in all these years spoke of it to his companion, then surely that companion could as well live without love. Stern, dark, deadly work must stain and blot all tenderness from his life, else it would be unutterably barren. The joy of living, of unharassed freedom he had always known. If a fair face and dark, mournful eyes were to haunt him on every lonely trail, then it were better an Indian should end his existence.

The darkest hour before dawn, as well as the darkest of doubt and longing in Jonathan's life, passed away. A gray gloom obscured the pale, winking stars; the east slowly whitened, then brightened, and at length day broke misty and fresh.

The borderman rose to stretch his cramped limbs. When he turned to the little cavern the girl's eyes were wide open. All the darkness, the shadow, the beauty, and the thought of the past night, lay in their blue depths. He looked away across the valley where the sky was reddening and a pale rim of gold appeared above the hill-tops.

"Well, if I haven't been asleep!" exclaimed Helen, with a low, soft laugh.

"You're rested, I hope," said Jonathan, with averted eyes. He dared not look at her.

"Oh, yes, indeed. I am ready to start at once. How gray, how beautiful the morning is! Shall we be long? I hope papa knows."

In silence the borderman led the way across the rocky plateau, and into the winding, narrow trail. His pale, slightly drawn and stern, face did not invite conversation, therefore Helen followed silently in his footsteps. The way was steep, and at times he was forced to lend her aid. She put her hand in his and jumped lightly as a fawn. Presently a brawling brook, over-crowding its banks, impeded further progress.

"I'll have to carry you across," said Jonathan.

"I'm very heavy," replied Helen, with a smile in her eyes.

She flushed as the borderman put his right arm around her waist. Then a clasp as of steel enclosed her; she felt herself swinging easily into the air, and over the muddy brook.

Farther down the mountain this troublesome brook again crossed the trail, this time much wider and more formidable. Helen looked with some vexation and embarrassment into the border-man's face. It was always the same, stern, almost cold.

"Perhaps I'd better wade," she said hesitatingly.

"Why? The water's deep an' cold. You'd better not get wet."

Helen flushed, but did not answer. With downcast eyes she let herself be carried on his powerful arm.

The wading was difficult this time. The water foamed furiously around his knees. Once he slipped on a stone, and nearly lost his balance. Uttering a little scream Helen grasped at him wildly, and her arm encircled his neck. What was still more trying, when he put her on her feet again, it was found that her hair had become entangled in the porcupine quills on his hunting-coat.

She stood before him while with clumsy fingers he endeavored to untangle the shimmering strands; but in vain. Helen unwound the snarl of wavy hair. Most alluring she was then, with a certain softness on her face, and light and laughter, and something warm in her eyes.

The borderman felt that he breathed a subtle exhilaration which emanated from her glowing, gracious beauty. She radiated with the gladness of life, with an uncontainable sweetness and joy. But, giving no token of his feeling, he turned to march on down through the woods.

From this point the trail broadened, descending at an easier angle. Jonathan's stride lengthened until Helen was forced to walk rapidly, and sometimes run, in order to keep close behind him. A quick journey home was expedient, and in order to accomplish this she would gladly have exerted herself to a greater extent. When they reached the end of the trail where the forest opened clear of brush, finally to merge into the broad, verdant plain, the sun had chased the mist-clouds from the eastern hill-tops, and was gloriously brightening the valley.

With the touch of sentiment natural to her, Helen gazed backward for one more view of the mountain-top. The wall of rugged rock she had so often admired from her window at home, which henceforth would ever hold a tender place of remembrance in her heart, rose out of a gray-blue bank of mist. The long, swelling slope lay clear to the sunshine. With the rays of the sun gleaming and glistening upon the variegated foliage, and upon the shiny rolling haze above, a beautiful picture of autumn splendor was before her. Tall pines, here and there towered high and lonely over the surrounding trees. Their dark, green, graceful heads stood in bold relief above the gold and yellow crests beneath. Maples, tinged from faintest pink to deepest rose, added warm color to the scene, and chestnuts with their brown-white burrs lent fresher beauty to the undulating slope.

The remaining distance to the settlement was short. Jonathan spoke only once to Helen, then questioning her as to where she had left her canoe. They traversed the meadow, found the boat in the thicket of willows, and were soon under the frowning bluff of Fort Henry. Ascending the steep path, they followed the road leading to Colonel Zane's cabin.

A crowd of boys, men and women loitering near the bluff arrested Helen's attention. Struck by this unusual occurrence, she wondered what was the cause of such idleness among the busy pioneer people. They were standing in little groups. Some made vehement gestures, others conversed earnestly, and yet more were silent. On seeing Jonathan, a number shouted and pointed toward the inn. The borderman hurried Helen along the path, giving no heed to the throng.

But Helen had seen the cause of all this excitement. At first glance she thought Metzar's inn had been burned; but a second later it could be seen that the smoke came from a smoldering heap of rubbish in the road. The inn, nevertheless, had been wrecked. Windows stared with that vacantness peculiar to deserted houses. The doors were broken from their hinges. A pile of furniture, rude tables, chairs, beds, and other articles, were heaped beside the smoking rubbish. Scattered around lay barrels and kegs all with gaping sides and broken heads. Liquor had stained the road, where it had been soaked up by the thirsty dust.

Upon a shattered cellar-door lay a figure covered with a piece of rag carpet. When Helen's quick eyes took in this last, she turned away in horror. That motionless form might be Brandt's. Remorse and womanly sympathy surged over her, for bad as the man had shown himself, he had loved her.

She followed the borderman, trying to compose herself. As they neared Colonel Zane's cabin she saw her father, Will, the colonel, Betty, Nell, Mrs. Zane, Silas Zane, and others whom she did not recognize. They were all looking at her. Helen's throat swelled, and her eyes filled when she got near enough to see her father's haggard, eager face. The others were grave. She wondered guiltily if she had done much wrong.

In another moment she was among them. Tears fell as her father extended his trembling hands to clasp her, and as she hid her burning face on his breast, he cried: "My dear, dear child!" Then Betty gave her a great hug, and Nell flew about them like a happy bird. Colonel Zane's face was pale, and wore a clouded, stern expression.

She smiled timidly at him through her tears. "Well! well! well!" he mused, while his gaze softened. That was all he said; but he took her hand and held it while he turned to Jonathan.

The borderman leaned on his long rifle, regarding him with expectant eyes.

"Well, Jack, you missed a little scrimmage this morning. Wetzel got in at daybreak. The storm and horses held him up on the other side of the river until daylight. He told me of your suspicions, with the additional news that he'd found a fresh Indian trail on the island just across from the inn. We went down not expecting to find any one awake; but Metzar was hurriedly packing some of his traps. Half a dozen men were there, having probably stayed all night. That little English cuss was one of them, and another, an ugly fellow, a stranger to us, but evidently a woodsman. Things looked bad. Metzar told a decidedly conflicting story. Wetzel and I went outside to talk over the situation, with the result that I ordered him to clean out the place."

Here Colonel Zane paused to indulge in a grim, meaning laugh.

"Well, he cleaned out the place all right. The ugly stranger got rattlesnake-mad, and yanked out a big knife. Sam is hitching up the team now to haul what's left of him up on the hillside. Metzar resisted arrest, and got badly hurt. He's in the guardhouse. Case, who has been drunk for a week, got in Wetzel's way and was kicked into the middle of next week. He's been spitting blood for the last hour, but I guess he's not much hurt. Brandt flew the coop last night. Wetzel found this hid in his room."

Colonel Zane took a long, feathered arrow from where it lay on a bench, and held it out to Jonathan.

"The Shawnee signal! Wetzel had it right," muttered the borderman.

"Exactly. Lew found where the arrow struck in the wall of Brandt's room. It was shot from the island at the exact spot where Lew came to an end of the Indian's trail in the water."

"That Shawnee got away from us."

"So Lew said. Well, he's gone now. So is Brandt. We're well rid of the gang, if only we never hear of them again."

The borderman shook his head. During the colonel's recital his face changed. The dark eyes had become deadly; the square jaw was shut, the lines of the cheek had grown tense, and over his usually expressive countenance had settled a chill, lowering shade.

"Lew thinks Brandt's in with Bing Legget. Well, d—his black traitor heart! He's a good man for the worst and strongest gang that ever tracked the border."

The borderman was silent; but the furtive, restless shifting of his eyes over the river and island, hill and valley, spoke more plainly than words.

"You're to take his trail at once," added Colonel Zane. "I had Bess put you up some bread, meat and parched corn. No doubt you'll have a long, hard tramp. Good luck."

The borderman went into the cabin, presently emerging with a buckskin knapsack strapped to his shoulder. He set off eastward with a long, swinging stride.

The women had taken Helen within the house where, no doubt, they could discuss with greater freedom the events of the previous day.

"Sheppard," said Colonel Zane, turning with a sparkle in his eyes. "Brandt was after Helen sure as a bad weed grows fast. And certain as death Jonathan and Wetzel will see him cold and quiet back in the woods. That's a border saying, and it means a good deal. I never saw Wetzel so implacable, nor Jonathan so fatally cold but once, and that was when Miller, another traitor, much like Brandt, tried to make away with Betty. It would have chilled your blood to see Wetzel go at that fool this morning. Why did he want to pull a knife on the borderman? It was a sad sight. Well, these things are justifiable. We must protect ourselves, and above all our women. We've had bad men, and a bad man out here is something you cannot yet appreciate, come here and slip into the life of the settlement, because on the border you can never tell what a man is until he proves himself. There have been scores of criminals spread over the frontier, and some better men, like Simon Girty, who were driven to outlaw life. Simon must not be confounded with Jim Girty, absolutely the most fiendish desperado who ever lived. Why, even the Indians feared Jim so much that after his death his skeleton remained unmolested in the glade where he was killed. The place is believed to be haunted now, by all Indians and many white hunters, and I believe the bones stand there yet."

"Stand?" asked Sheppard, deeply interested.

"Yes, it stands where Girty stood and died, upright against a tree, pinned, pinned there by a big knife."

"Heavens, man! Who did it?" Sheppard cried in horror.

Again Colonel Zane's laugh, almost metallic, broke grimly from his lips.

"Who? Why, Wetzel, of course. Lew hunted Jim Girty five long years. When he caught him—God! I'll tell you some other time. Jonathan saw Wetzel handle Jim and his pal, Deering, as if they were mere boys. Well, as I said, the border has had, and still has, its bad men. Simon Girty took McKee and Elliott, the Tories, from Fort Pitt, when he deserted, and ten men besides. They're all, except those who are dead, outlaws of the worst type. The other bad men drifted out here from Lord only knows where. They're scattered all over. Simon Girty, since his crowning black deed, the massacre of the Christian Indians, is in hiding. Bing Legget now has the field. He's a hard nut, a cunning woodsman, and capable leader who surrounds himself with only the most desperate Indians and renegades. Brandt is an agent of Legget's and I'll bet we'll hear from him again."

CHAPTER XIII

JONATHAN TRAVELED TOWARD the east straight as a crow flies. Wetzel's trail as he pursued Brandt had been left designedly plain. Branches of young maples had been broken by the borderman; they were glaring evidences of his passage. On open ground, or through swampy meadows he had contrived to leave other means to facilitate his comrade's progress. Bits of sumach lay strewn along the way, every red, leafy branch a bright marker of the course; crimson maple leaves served their turn, and even long-bladed ferns were scattered at intervals.

Ten miles east of Fort Henry, at a point where two islands lay opposite each other, Wetzel had crossed the Ohio. Jonathan removed his clothing, and tying these, together with his knapsack, to the rifle, held them above the water while he swam the three narrow channels. He took up the trail again, finding here, as he expected, where Brandt had joined the waiting Shawnee chief. The borderman pressed on harder to the eastward.

About the middle of the afternoon signs betokened that Wetzel and his quarry were not far in advance. Fresh imprints in the grass; crushed asters and moss, broken branches with un-withered leaves, and plots of grassy ground where Jonathan saw that the blades of grass were yet springing back to their original position, proved to the borderman's practiced eye that he was close upon Wetzel.

In time he came to a grove of yellow birch trees. The ground was nearly free from brush, beautifully carpeted with flowers and ferns, and, except where bushy windfalls obstructed the way, was singularly open to the gaze for several hundred yards ahead.

Upon entering this wood Wetzel's plain, intentional markings became manifest, then wavered, and finally disappeared. Jonathan pondered a moment. He concluded that the way was so open and

clear, with nothing but grass and moss to mark a trail, that Wetzel
had simply considered it waste of time for, perhaps, the short length
of this grove.

Jonathan knew he was wrong after taking a dozen steps more.
Wetzel's trail, known so well to him, as never to be mistaken,
sheered abruptly off to the left, and, after a few yards, the distance
between the footsteps widened perceptibly. Then came a point
where they were so far apart that they could only have been made
by long leaps.

On the instant the borderman knew that some unforeseen peril
or urgent cause had put Wetzel to flight, and he now bent piercing
eyes around the grove. Retracing his steps to where he had found
the break in the trail, he followed up Brandt's tracks for several
rods. Not one hundred paces beyond where Wetzel had quit the
pursuit, were the remains of a camp fire, the embers still smoldering, and moccasin tracks of a small band of Indians. The trail of
Brandt and his Shawnee guide met the others at almost right angles.

The Indian, either by accident or design, had guided Brandt to a
band of his fellows, and thus led Wetzel almost into an ambush.

Evidence was not clear, however, that the Indians had discovered the keen tracker who had run almost into their midst.

While studying the forest ahead Jonathan's mind was running
over the possibilities. How close was Wetzel? Was he still in flight?
Had the savages an inkling of his pursuit? Or was he now working
out one of his cunning tricks of woodcraft? The borderman had no
other idea than that of following the trail to learn all this. Taking
the desperate chances warranted under the circumstances, he
walked boldly forward in his comrade's footsteps.

Deep and gloomy was the forest adjoining the birch grove. It was
a heavy growth of hardwood trees, interspersed with slender ash
and maples, which with their scanty foliage resembled a labyrinth
of green and yellow network, like filmy dotted lace, hung on the
taller, darker oaks. Jonathan felt safer in this deep wood. He could
still see several rods in advance. Following the trail, he was relieved
to see that Wetzel's leaps had become shorter and shorter, until
they once again were about the length of a long stride. The borderman was, moreover, swinging in a curve to the northeast. This was
proof that the borderman had not been pursued, but was making a
wide detour to get ahead of the enemy. Five hundred yards farther
on the trail turned sharply toward the birch grove in the rear.

The trail was fresh. Wetzel was possibly within signal call; surely within sound of a rifle shot. But even more stirring was the certainty that Brandt and his Indians were inside the circle Wetzel had made.

Once again in sight of the more open woodland, Jonathan crawled on his hands and knees, keeping close to the cluster of ferns, until well within the eastern end of the grove. He lay for some minutes listening. A threatening silence, like the hush before a storm, permeated the wilderness. He peered out from his covert; but, owing to its location in a little hollow, he could not see far. Crawling to the nearest tree he rose to his feet slowly, cautiously.

No unnatural sight or sound arrested his attention. Repeatedly, with the acute, unsatisfied gaze of the borderman who knew that every tree, every patch of ferns, every tangled brush-heap might harbor a foe, he searched the grove with his eyes; but the curly-barked birches, the clumps of colored ferns, the bushy windfalls kept their secrets.

For the borderman, however, the whole aspect of the birch-grove had changed. Over the forest was a deep calm. A gentle, barely perceptible wind sighed among the leaves, like rustling silk. The far-off drowsy drum of a grouse intruded on the vast stillness. The silence of the birds betokened a message. That mysterious breathing, that beautiful life of the woods lay hushed, locked in a waiting, brooding silence. Far away among the somber trees, where the shade deepened into impenetrable gloom, lay a menace, invisible and indefinable.

A wind, a breath, a chill, terribly potent, seemed to pass over the borderman. Long experience had given him intuition of danger.

As he moved slightly, with lynx-eyes fixed on the grove before him, a sharp, clear, perfect bird-note broke the ominous quiet. It was like the melancholy cry of an oriole, short, deep, suggestive of lonely forest dells. By a slight variation in the short call, Jonathan recognized it as a signal from Wetzel. The borderman smiled as he realized that with all his stealth. Wetzel had heard or seen him re-enter the grove. The signal was a warning to stand still or retreat.

Jonathan's gaze narrowed down to the particular point whence had come the signal. Some two hundred yards ahead in this direction were several large trees standing in a group. With one exception, they all had straight trunks. This deviated from the others in that it possessed an irregular, bulging trunk, or else half-shielded the form of Wetzel. So indistinct and immovable was this irregularity, that the watcher could not be certain. Out of line, somewhat, with this tree which he suspected screened his comrade, lay a huge windfall large enough to conceal in ambush a whole band of savages.

Even as he gazed a sheet of flame flashed from this covert.

Crack!

A loud report followed; then the whistle and zip of a bullet as it whizzed close by his head.

"Shawnee lead!" muttered Jonathan.

Unfortunately the tree he had selected did not hide him sufficiently. His shoulders were so wide that either one or the other was exposed, affording a fine target for a marksman.

A quick glance showed him a change in the knotty tree-trunk; the seeming bulge was now the well-known figure of Wetzel.

Jonathan dodged as some object glanced slantingly before his eyes.

Twang. Whizz. Thud. Three familiar and distinct sounds caused him to press hard against the tree.

A tufted arrow quivered in the bark not a foot from his head.

"Glose shave! Damn that arrow-shootin' Shawnee!" muttered Jonathan. "An' he ain't in that windfall either." His eyes searched to the left for the source of this new peril.

Another sheet of flame, another report from the windfall. A bullet sang, close overhead, and, glancing on a branch, went harmlessly into the forest.

"Injuns all around; I guess I'd better be makin' tracks," Jonathan said to himself, peering out to learn if Wetzel was still under cover.

He saw the tall figure straighten up; a long, black rifle rise to a level and become rigid; a red fire belch forth, followed by a puff of white smoke.

Spang!

An Indian's horrible, strangely-breaking death yell rent the silence.

Then a chorus of plaintive howls, followed by angry shouts, rang through the forest. Naked, painted savages darted out of the windfall toward the tree that had sheltered Wetzel.

Quick as thought Jonathan covered the foremost Indian, and with the crack of his rifle saw the redskin drop his gun, stop in his mad run, stagger sideways, and fall. Then the borderman looked to see what had become of his ally. The cracking of the Indian's rifle told him that Wetzel had been seen by his foes.

With almost incredible fleetness a brown figure with long black hair streaming behind, darted in and out among the trees, flashed through the sunlit glade, and vanished in the dark depths of the forest.

Jonathan turned to flee also, when he heard again the twanging of an Indian's bow. A wind smote his cheek, a shock blinded him, an excruciating pain seized upon his breast. A feathered arrow had pinned his shoulder to the tree. He raised his hand to pull it out; but, slippery with blood, it afforded a poor hold for his fingers. Violently exerting himself, with both hands he wrenched away the weapon. The flint-head lacerating his flesh and scraping his shoulder bones caused sharpest agony. The pain gave away to a sudden sense of giddiness; he tried to run; a dark mist veiled his sight; he stumbled and fell. Then he seemed to sink into a great darkness, and knew no more.

When consciousness returned to Jonathan it was night. He lay on his back, and knew because of his cramped limbs that he had been securely bound. He saw the glimmer of a fire, but could not raise his head. A rustling of leaves in the wind told that he was yet in the woods, and the distant rumble of a waterfall sounded familiar. He felt drowsy; his wound smarted slightly, still he did not suffer any pain. Presently he fell asleep.

Broad daylight had come when again he opened his eyes. The blue sky was directly above, and before him he saw a ledge covered with dwarfed pine trees. He turned his head, and saw that he was in a sort of amphitheater of about two acres in extent enclosed by low cliffs. A cleft in the stony wall let out a brawling brook, and served, no doubt, as entrance to the place. Several rude log cabins stood on that side of the enclosure. Jonathan knew he had been brought to Bing Legget's retreat.

Voices attracted his attention, and, turning his head to the other side, he saw a big Indian pacing near him, and beyond, seven savages and three white men reclining in the shade.

The powerful, dark-visaged savage near him he at once recognized as Ashbow, the Shawnee chief, and noted emissary of Bing Legget. Of the other Indians, three were Delawares, and four Shawnees, all veterans, with swarthy, somber faces and glistening heads on which the scalp-locks were trimmed and tufted. Their naked, muscular bodies were painted for the war-path with their strange emblems of death. A trio of white men, nearly as bronzed as their savage comrades, completed the group. One, a desperate-looking outlaw, Jonathan did not know. The blond-bearded giant in the center was Legget. Steel-blue, inhuman eyes, with the expression of a free but hunted animal; a set, mastiff-like jaw, brutal and coarse, individualized him. The last man was the haggard-faced Brandt.

"I tell ye, Brandt, I ain't agoin' against this Injun," Legget was saying positively. "He's the best reddy on the border, an' has saved me scores of times. This fellar Zane belongs to him, an' while I'd much rather see the scout knifed right here an' now, I won't do nothin' to interfere with the Shawnee's plans."

"Why does the redskin want to take him away to his village?" Brandt growled. "All Injun vanity and pride."

"It's Injun ways, an' we can't do nothin' to change 'em."

"But you're boss here. You could make him put this borderman out of the way."

"Wal, I ain't agoin' ter interfere. Anyways, Brandt, the Shawnee'll make short work of the scout when he gits him among the tribe. Injuns is Injuns. It's a great honor fer him to git Zane, an' he wants his own people to figger in the finish. Quite nat'r'l, I reckon."

"I understand all that; but it's not safe for us, and it's courting death for Ashbow. Why don't he keep Zane here until you can spare more than three Indians to go with him? These bordermen can't be stopped. You don't know them, because you're new in this part of the country."

"I've been here as long as you, an' agoin' some, too, I reckon," replied Legget complacently.

"But you've not been hunted until lately by these bordermen, and you've had little opportunity to hear of them except from Indians. What can you learn from these silent redskins? I tell you, letting this fellow get out of here alive, even for an hour is a fatal mistake. It's two full days' tramp to the Shawnee village. You don't suppose Wetzel will be afraid of four savages? Why, he sneaked right into eight of us, when we were ambushed, waiting for him. He killed one and then was gone like a streak. It was only a piece of pure luck we got Zane."

"I've reason to know this Wetzel, this Deathwind, as the Delawares call him. I never seen him though, an' anyways, I reckon I can handle him if ever I get the chance."

"Man, you're crazy!" cried Brandt. "He'd cut you to pieces before you'd have time to draw. He could give you a tomahawk, then take it away and split your head. I tell you I know! You remember Jake Deering? He came from up your way. Wetzel fought Deering and Jim Girty together, and killed them. You know how he left Girty."

"I'll allow he must be a fighter; but I ain't afraid of him."

"That's not the question. I am talking sense. You've got a chance now to put one of these bordermen out of the way. Do it quick! That's my advice."

Brandt spoke so vehemently that Legget seemed impressed. He stroked his yellow beard, and puffed thoughtfully on his pipe. Presently he addressed the Shawnee chief in the native tongue.

"Will Ashbow take five horses for his prisoner?"

The Indian shook his head.

"How many will he take?"

The chief strode with dignity to and fro before his captive. His dark, impassive face gave no clew to his thoughts; but his lofty bearing, his measured, stately walk were indicative of great pride. Then he spoke in his deep bass:

"The Shawnee knows the woods from the Great Lakes where the sun sets, to the Blue Hills where it rises. He has met the great paleface hunters. Only for Deathwind will Ashbow trade his captive."

"See? It ain't no use," said Legget, spreading out his hands. "Let him go. He'll outwit the bordermen if any redskin's able to. The sooner he goes the quicker he'll git back, an' we can go to work. You ought'er be satisfied to git the girl——"

"Shut up!" interrupted Brandt sharply.

"'Pears to me, Brandt, bein' in love hes kinder worked on your nerves. You used to be game. Now you're afeerd of a bound an' tied man who ain't got long to live."

"I fear no man," answered Brandt, scowling darkly. "But I know what you don't seem to have sense enough to see. If this Zane gets away, which is probable, he and Wetzel will clean up your gang."

"Haw! haw! haw!" roared Legget, slapping his knees. "Then you'd hev little chanst of gittin' the lass, eh?"

"All right. I've no more to say," snapped Brandt, rising and turning on his heel. As he passed Jonathan he paused. "Zane, if I could, I'd get even with you for that punch you once gave me. As it is, I'll stop at the Shawnee village on my way west——"

"With the pretty lass," interposed Legget.

"Where I hope to see your scalp drying in the chief's lodge."

The borderman eyed him steadily; but in silence. Words could not so well have conveyed his thought as did the cold glance of dark scorn and merciless meaning.

Brandt shuffled on with a curse. No coward was he. No man ever saw him flinch. But his intelligence was against him as a desperado. While such as these bordermen lived, an outlaw should never sleep, for he was a marked and doomed man. The deadly, cold-pointed flame which scintillated in the prisoner's eyes was only a gleam of what the border felt towards outlaws.

While Jonathan was considering all he had heard, three more Shawnees entered the retreat, and were at once called aside in consultation by Ashbow. At the conclusion of this brief conference the chief advanced to Jonathan, cut the bonds round his feet, and motioned for him to rise. The prisoner complied to find himself weak and sore, but able to walk. He concluded that his wound, while very painful, was not of a serious nature, and that he would be taken at once on the march toward the Shawnee village.

He was correct, for the chief led him, with the three Shawnees following, toward the outlet of the enclosure. Jonathan's sharp eye took in every detail of Legget's rendezvous. In a corral near the entrance, he saw a number of fine horses, and among them his sister's pony. A more inaccessible, natural refuge than Legget's, could hardly have been found in that country. The entrance was a narrow opening in the wall, and could be held by half a dozen against an army of besiegers. It opened, moreover, on the side of a barren hill, from which could be had a good survey of the surrounding forests and plains.

As Jonathan went with his captors down the hill his hopes, which while ever alive, had been flagging, now rose. The long journey to the Shawnee town led through an untracked wilderness. The Delaware villages lay far to the north; the Wyandot to the west. No likelihood was there of falling in with a band of Indians hunting, because this region, stony, barren, and poorly watered, afforded sparse pasture for deer or bison. From the prisoner's point of view this enterprise of Ashbow's was reckless and vainglorious. Cunning as the chief was, he erred in one point, a great warrior's only weakness, love of show, of pride, of his achievement. In Indian nature this desire for fame was as strong as love of life. The brave risked everything to win his eagle feathers, and the matured warrior found death while keeping bright the glory of the plumes he had won.

Wetzel was in the woods, fleet as a deer, fierce and fearless as a lion. Somewhere among those glades he trod, stealthily, with the ears of a doe and eyes of a hawk strained for sound or sight of his comrade's captors. When he found their trail he would stick to it as the wolf to that of a bleeding buck's. The rescue would not be attempted until the right moment, even though that came within rifle-shot of the Shawnee encampment. Wonderful as his other gifts, was the borderman's patience.

CHAPTER XIV

"GOOD MORNING, COLONEL Zane," said Helen cheerily, coming into the yard where the colonel was at work. "Did Will come over this way?"

"I reckon you'll find him if you find Betty," replied Colonel Zane dryly.

"Come to think of it, that's true," Helen said, laughing. "I've a suspicion Will ran off from me this morning."

"He and Betty have gone nutting."

"I declare it's mean of Will," Helen said petulantly. "I have been wanting to go so much, and both he and Betty promised to take me."

"Say, Helen, let me tell you something," said the colonel, resting on his spade and looking at her quizzically. "I told them we hadn't had enough frost yet to ripen hickory-nuts and chestnuts. But they went anyhow. Will did remember to say if you came along, to tell you he'd bring the colored leaves you wanted."

"How extremely kind of him. I've a mind to follow them."

"Now see here, Helen, it might be a right good idea for you not to," returned the colonel, with a twinkle and a meaning in his eye.

"Oh, I understand. How singularly dull I've been."

"It's this way. We're mighty glad to have a fine young fellow like Will come along and interest Betty. Lord knows we had a time with her after Alfred died. She's just beginning to brighten up now, and, Helen, the point is that young people on the border must get married. No, my dear, you needn't laugh, you'll have to find a husband same as the other girls. It's not here as it was back east, where a lass might have her fling, so to speak, and take her time choosing. An unmarried girl on the border is a positive menace. I saw, not many years ago, two first-rate youngsters, wild with border

114

fire and spirit, fight and kill each other over a lass who wouldn't choose. Like as not, if she had done so, the three would have been good friends, for out here we're like one big family. Remember this, Helen, and as far as Betty and Will are concerned you will be wise to follow our example: Leave them to themselves. Nothing else will so quickly strike fire between a boy and a girl."

"Betty and Will! I'm sure I'd love to see them care for each other." Then with big, bright eyes bent gravely on him she continued, "May I ask, Colonel Zane, who you have picked out for me?"

"There, now you've said it, and that's the problem. I've looked over every marriageable young man in the settlement, except Jack. Of course you couldn't care for him, a borderman, a fighter and all that; but I can't find a fellow I think quite up to you."

"Colonel Zane, is not a borderman such as Jonathan worthy a woman's regard?" Helen asked a little wistfully.

"Bless your heart, lass, yes!" replied Colonel Zane heartily. "People out here are not as they are back east. An educated man, polished and all that, but incapable of hard labor, or shrinking from dirt and sweat on his hands, or even blood, would not help us in the winning of the West. Plain as Jonathan is, and with his lack of schooling, he is greatly superior to the majority of young men on the frontier. But, unlettered or not, he is as fine a man as ever stepped in moccasins, or any other kind of foot gear."

"Then why did you say—that—what you did?"

"Well, it's this way," replied Colonel Zane, stealing a glance at her pensive, downcast face. "Girls all like to be wooed. Almost every one I ever knew wanted the young man of her choice to outstrip all her other admirers, and then, for a spell, nearly die of love for her, after which she'd give in. Now, Jack, being a borderman, a man with no occupation except scouting, will never look at a girl, let alone make up to her. I imagine, my dear, it'd take some mighty tall courting to fetch home Helen Sheppard a bride. On the other hand, if some pretty and spirited lass, like, say for instance, Helen Sheppard, would come along and just make Jack forget Indians and fighting, she'd get the finest husband in the world. True, he's wild; but only in the woods. A simpler, kinder, cleaner man cannot be found."

"I believe that, Colonel Zane; but where is the girl who would interest him?" Helen asked with spirit. "These bordermen are unapproachable. Imagine a girl interesting that great, cold, stern

Wetzel! All her flatteries, her wiles, the little coquetries that might attract ordinary men, would not be noticed by him, or Jonathan either."

"I grant it'd not be easy, but woman was made to subjugate man, and always, everlastingly, until the end of life here on this beautiful earth, she will do it."

"Do you think Jonathan and Wetzel will catch Brandt?" asked Helen, changing the subject abruptly.

"I'd stake my all that this year's autumn leaves will fall on Brandt's grave."

Colonel Zane's calm, matter-of-fact coldness made Helen shiver.

"Why, the leaves have already begun to fall. Papa told me Brandt had gone to join the most powerful outlaw band on the border. How can these two men, alone, cope with savages, as I've heard they do, and break up such an outlaw band as Legget's?"

"That's a question I've heard Daniel Boone ask about Wetzel, and Boone, though not a borderman in all the name implies, was a great Indian fighter. I've heard old frontiersmen, grown grizzled on the frontier, use the same words. I've been twenty years with that man, yet I can't answer it. Jonathan, of course, is only a shadow of him; Wetzel is the type of these men who have held the frontier for us. He was the first borderman, and no doubt he'll be the last."

"What have Jonathan and Wetzel that other men do not possess?"

"In them is united a marvelously developed woodcraft, with wonderful physical powers. Imagine a man having a sense, almost an animal instinct, for what is going on in the woods. Take for instance the fleetness of foot. That is one of the greatest factors. It is absolutely necessary to run, to get away when to hold ground would be death. Whether at home or in the woods, the bordermen retreat every day. You wouldn't think they practiced anything of the kind, would you? Well, a man can't be great in anything without keeping at it. Jonathan says he exercises to keep his feet light. Wetzel would just as soon run as walk. Think of the magnificent condition of these men. When a dash of speed is called for, when to be fleet of foot is to elude vengeance-seeking Indians, they must travel as swiftly as the deer. The Zanes were all sprinters. I could do something of the kind; Betty was fast on her feet, as that old fort will testify until the logs rot; Isaac was fleet, too, and Jonathan can get over the ground like a scared buck. But, even so, Wetzel can beat him."

"Goodness me, Helen!" exclaimed the colonel's buxom wife, from the window, "don't you ever get tired hearing Eb talk of Wetzel, and Jack, and Indians? Come in with me. I venture to say my gossip will do you more good than his stories."

Therefore Helen went in to chat with Mrs. Zane, for she was always glad to listen to the colonel's wife, who was so bright and pleasant, so helpful and kindly in her womanly way. In the course of their conversation, which drifted from weaving linsey, Mrs. Zane's occupation at the time, to the costly silks and satins of remembered days, and then to matters of more present interest, Helen spoke of Colonel Zane's hint about Will and Betty.

"Isn't Eb a terror? He's the worst matchmatcher you ever saw," declared the colonel's good spouse.

"There's no harm in that."

"No, indeed; it's a good thing, but he makes me laugh, and Betty, he sets her furious."

"The colonel said he had designs on me."

"Of course he has, dear old Eb! How he'd love to see you happily married. His heart is as big as that mountain yonder. He has given this settlement his whole life."

"I believe you. He has such interest, such zeal for everybody. Only the other day he was speaking to me of Mr. Mordaunt, telling how sorry he was for the Englishman, and how much he'd like to help him. It does seem a pity a man of Mordaunt's blood and attainments should sink to utter worthlessness."

"Yes, 'tis a pity for any man, blood or no, and the world's full of such wrecks. I always liked that man's looks. I never had a word with him, of course; but I've seen him often, and something about him appealed to me. I don't believe it was just his handsome face; still I know women are susceptible that way."

"I, too, liked him once as a friend," said Helen feelingly. "Well, I'm glad he's gone."

"Gone?"

"Yes, he left Fort Henry yesterday. He came to say good-bye to me, and, except for his pale face and trembling hands, was much as he used to be in Virginia. Said he was going home to England, and wanted to tell me he was sorry—for—for all he'd done to make papa and me suffer. Drink had broken him, he said, and surely he looked a broken man. I shook hands with him, and then slipped upstairs and cried."

"Poor fellow!" sighed Mrs. Zane.

"Papa said he left Fort Pitt with one of Metzar's men as a guide."

"Then he didn't take the 'little cuss,' as Eb calls his man Case?"

"No, if I remember rightly papa said Case wouldn't go."

"I wish he had. He's no addition to our village."

Voices outside attracted their attention. Mrs. Zane glanced from the window and said: "There come Betty and Will."

Helen went on the porch to see her cousin and Betty entering the yard, and Colonel Zane once again leaning on his spade.

"Gather any hickory-nuts from birch or any other kind of trees?" asked the colonel grimly.

"No," replied Will cheerily, "the shells haven't opened yet."

"Too bad the frost is so backward," said Colonel Zane with a laugh. "But I can't see that it makes any difference."

"Where are my leaves?" asked Helen, with a smile and a nod to Betty.

"What leaves?" inquired that young woman, plainly mystified.

"Why, the autumn leaves Will promised to gather with me, then changed his mind, and said he'd bring them."

"I forgot," Will replied a little awkwardly.

Colonel Zane coughed, and then, catching Betty's glance, which had begun to flash, he plied his spade vigorously.

Betty's face had colored warmly at her brother's first question; it toned down slightly when she understood that he was not going to tease her as usual, and suddenly, as she looked over his head, it paled white as snow.

"Eb, look down the lane!" she cried.

Two tall men were approaching with labored tread, one half-supporting his companion.

"Wetzel! Jack! and Jack's hurt!" cried Betty.

"My dear, be calm," said Colonel Zane, in that quiet tone he always used during moments of excitement. He turned toward the bordermen, and helped Wetzel lead Jonathan up the walk into the yard.

From Wetzel's clothing water ran, his long hair was disheveled, his aspect frightful. Jonathan's face was white and drawn. His buckskin hunting coat was covered with blood, and the hand which he held tightly against his left breast showed dark red stains.

Helen shuddered. Almost fainting, she leaned against the porch, too horrified to cry out, with contracting heart and a chill stealing through her veins.

"Jack! Jack!" cried Betty, in agonized appeal.

"Betty, it's nothin'," said Wetzel.

"Now, Betts, don't be scared of a little blood," Jonathan said with a faint smile flitting across his haggard face.

"Bring water, shears an' some linsey cloth," added Wetzel, as Mrs. Zane came running out.

"Come inside," cried the colonel's wife, as she disappeared again immediately.

"No," replied the borderman, removing his coat, and, with the assistance of his brother, he unlaced his hunting shirt, pulling it down from a wounded shoulder. A great gory hole gaped just beneath his left collar-bone.

Although stricken with fear, when Helen saw the bronzed, massive shoulder, the long, powerful arm with its cords of muscles playing under the brown skin, she felt a thrill of admiration.

"Just missed the lung," said Mrs. Zane. "Eb, no bullet ever made that hole."

Wetzel washed the bloody wound, and, placing on it a wad of leaves he took from his pocket, bound up the shoulder tightly.

"What made that hole?" asked Colonel Zane.

Wetzel lifted the quiver of arrows Jonathan had laid on the porch, and, selecting one, handed it to the colonel. The flint-head and a portion of the shaft were stained with blood.

"The Shawnee!" exclaimed Colonel Zane. Then he led Wetzel aside, and began conversing in low tones while Jonathan, with Betty holding his arm, ascended the steps and went within the dwelling.

Helen ran home, and, once in her room, gave vent to her emotions. She cried because of fright, nervousness, relief, and joy. Then she bathed her face, tried to rub some color into her pale cheeks, and set about getting dinner as one in a trance. She could not forget that broad shoulder with its frightful wound. What a man Jonathan must be to receive a blow like that and live! Exhausted, almost spent, had been his strength when he reached home, yet how calm and cool he was! What would she not have given for the faint smile that shone in his eyes for Betty?

The afternoon was long for Helen. When at last supper was over she changed her gown, and, asking Will to accompany her, went down the lane toward Colonel Zane's cabin. At this hour the colonel almost invariably could be found sitting on his doorstep puffing a long Indian pipe, and gazing with dreamy eyes over the valley.

"Well, well, how sweet you look!" he said to Helen; then with a wink of his eyelid, "Hello, Willie, you'll find Elizabeth inside with Jack."

"How is he?" asked Helen eagerly, as Will with a laugh and a retort mounted the steps.

"Jack's doing splendidly. He slept all day. I don't think his injury amounts to much, at least not for such as him or Wetzel. It would have finished ordinary men. Bess says if complications don't set in, blood-poison or something to start a fever, he'll be up shortly. Wetzel believes the two of 'em will be on the trail inside of a week."

"Did they find Brandt?" asked Helen in a low voice.

"Yes, they ran him to his hole, and, as might have been expected, it was Bing Legget's camp. The Indians took Jonathan there."

"Then Jack was captured?"

Colonel Zane related the events, as told briefly by Wetzel, that had taken place during the preceding three days.

"The Indian I saw at the spring carried that bow Jonathan brought back. He must have shot the arrow. He was a magnificent savage."

"He was indeed a great, and a bad Indian, one of the craftiest spies who ever stepped in moccasins; but he lies quiet now on the moss and the leaves. Bing Legget will never find another runner like that Shawnee. Let us go indoors."

He led Helen into the large sitting-room where Jonathan lay on a couch, with Betty and Will sitting beside him. The colonel's wife and children, Silas Zane, and several neighbors, were present.

"Here, Jack, is a lady inquiring after your health. Betts, this reminds me of the time Isaac came home wounded, after his escape from the Hurons. Strikes me he and his Indian bride should be about due here on a visit."

Helen forgot every one except the wounded man lying so quiet and pale upon the couch. She looked down upon him with eyes strangely dilated, and darkly bright.

"How are you?" she asked softly.

"I'm all right, thank you, lass," answered Jonathan.

Colonel Zane contrived, with inimitable skill, to get Betty, Will, Silas, Bessie and the others interested in some remarkable news he had just heard, or made up, and this left Jonathan and Helen comparatively alone for the moment.

The wise old colonel thought perhaps this might be the right time. He saw Helen's face as she leaned over Jonathan, and that was enough for him. He would have taxed his ingenuity to the utmost to keep the others away from the young couple.

"I was so frightened," murmured Helen.

"Why?" asked Jonathan.

"Oh! You looked so deathly—the blood, and that awful wound!"

"It's nothin', lass."

Helen smiled down upon him. Whether or not the hurt amounted to anything in the borderman's opinion, she knew from his weakness, and his white, drawn face, that the strain of the march home had been fearful. His dark eyes held now nothing of the coldness and glitter so natural to them. They were weary, almost sad. She did not feel afraid of him now. He lay there so helpless, his long, powerful frame as quiet as a sleeping child's! Hitherto an almost indefinable antagonism in him had made itself felt; now there was only gentleness, as of a man too weary to fight longer. Helen's heart swelled with pity, and tenderness, and love. His weakness affected her as had never his strength. With an involuntary gesture of sympathy she placed her hand softly on his.

Jonathan looked up at her with eyes no longer blind. Pain had softened him. For the moment he felt carried out of himself, as it were, and saw things differently. The melting tenderness of her gaze, the glowing softness of her face, the beauty, bewitched him; and beyond that, a sweet, impelling gladness stirred within him and would not be denied. He thrilled as her fingers lightly, timidly touched his, and opened his broad hand to press hers closely and warmly.

"Lass," he whispered, with a huskiness and unsteadiness unnatural to his deep voice.

Helen bent her head closer to him; she saw his lips tremble, and his nostrils dilate; but an unutterable sadness shaded the brightness in his eyes.

"I love you."

The low whisper reached Helen's ears. She seemed to float dreamily away to some beautiful world, with the music of those words ringing in her ears. She looked at him again. Had she been dreaming? No; his dark eyes met hers with a love that he could no longer deny. An exquisite emotion, keen, strangely sweet and strong, yet terrible with sharp pain, pulsated through her being. The revelation had been too abrupt. It was so wonderfully different from what she had ever dared hope. She lowered her head, trembling.

The next moment she felt Colonel Zane's hand on her chair, and heard him say in a cheery voice:

"Well, well, see here, lass, you mustn't make Jack talk too much. See how white and tired he looks."

CHAPTER XV

IN FORTY-EIGHT hours Jonathan Zane was up and about the cabin as though he had never been wounded; the third day he walked to the spring; in a week he was waiting for Wetzel, ready to go on the trail.

On the eighth day of his enforced idleness, as he sat with Betty and the colonel in the yard, Wetzel appeared on a ridge east of the fort. Soon he rounded the stockade fence, and came straight toward them. To Colonel Zane and Betty, Wetzel's expression was terrible. The stern kindliness, the calm, though cold, gravity of his countenance, as they usually saw it, had disappeared. Yet it showed no trace of his unnatural passion to pursue and slay. No doubt that terrible instinct, or lust, was at white heat; but it wore a mask of impenetrable stone-gray gloom.

Wetzel spoke briefly. After telling Jonathan to meet him at sunset on the following day at a point five miles up the river, he reported to the colonel that Legget with his band had left their retreat, moving southward, apparently on a marauding expedition. Then he shook hands with Colonel Zane and turned to Betty.

"Good-bye, Betty," he said, in his deep, sonorous voice.

"Good-bye, Lew," answered Betty slowly, as if surprised. "God save you," she added.

He shouldered his rifle, and hurried down the lane, halting before entering the thicket that bounded the clearing, to look back at the settlement. In another moment his dark figure had disappeared among the bushes.

"Betts, I've seen Wetzel go like that hundreds of times, though he never shook hands before; but I feel sort of queer about it now. Wasn't he strange?"

Betty did not answer until Jonathan, who had started to go within, was out of hearing.

"Lew looked and acted the same the morning he struck Miller's trail," Betty replied in a low voice. "I believe, despite his indifference to danger, he realizes that the chances are greatly against him, as they were when he began the trailing of Miller, certain it would lead him into Girty's camp. Then I know Lew has an affection for us, though it is never shown in ordinary ways. I pray he and Jack will come home safe."

"This is a bad trail they're taking up; the worst, perhaps, in border warfare," said Colonel Zane gloomily. "Did you notice how Jack's face darkened when his comrade came? Much of this borderman-life of his is due to Wetzel's influence."

"Eb, I'll tell you one thing," returned Betty, with a flash of her old spirit. "This is Jack's last trail."

"Why do you think so?"

"If he doesn't return he'll be gone the way of all bordermen; but if he comes back once more he'll never get away from Helen."

"Ugh!" exclaimed Zane, venting his pleasure in characteristic Indian way.

"That night after Jack came home wounded," continued Betty, "I saw him, as he lay on the couch, gaze at Helen. Such a look! Eb, she has won."

"I hope so, but I fear, I fear," replied her brother gloomily. "If only he returns, that's the thing! Betts, be sure he sees Helen before he goes away."

"I shall try. Here he comes now," said Betty.

"Hello, Jack!" cried the colonel, as his brother came out in somewhat of a hurry. "What have you got? By George! It's that blamed arrow the Shawnee shot into you. Where are you going with it? What the deuce—Say—Betts, eh?"

Betty had given him a sharp little kick.

The borderman looked embarrassed. He hesitated and flushed. Evidently he would have liked to avoid his brother's question; but the inquiry came direct. Dissimulation with him was impossible.

"Helen wanted this, an' I reckon that's where I'm goin' with it," he said finally, and walked away.

"Eb, you're stupid!" exclaimed Betty.

"Hang it! Who'd have thought he was going to give her that blamed, bloody arrow?"

$$\star \quad \star \quad \star \quad \star \quad \star \quad \star$$

As Helen ushered Jonathan, for the first time, into her cosy little sitting-room, her heart began to thump so hard she could hear it.

She had not seen him since the night he whispered the words which gave such happiness. She had stayed at home, thankful beyond expression to learn every day of his rapid improvement, living in the sweetness of her joy, and waiting for him. And now as he had come, so dark, so grave, so unlike a lover to woo, that she felt a chill steal over her.

"I'm so glad you've brought the arrow," she faltered, "for, of course, coming so far means that you're well once more."

"You asked me for it, an' I've fetched it over. To-morrow I'm off on a trail I may never return from," he answered simply, and his voice seemed cold.

An immeasurable distance stretched once more between them. Helen's happiness slowly died.

"I thank you," she said with a voice that was tremulous despite all her efforts.

"It's not much of a keepsake."

"I did not ask for it as a keepsake, but because—because I wanted it. I need nothing tangible to keep alive my memory. A few words whispered to me not many days ago will suffice for remembrance—or—or did I dream them?"

Bitter disappointment almost choked Helen. This was not the gentle, soft-voiced man who had said he loved her. It was the indifferent borderman. Again he was the embodiment of his strange, quiet woods. Once more he seemed the comrade of the cold, inscrutable Wetzel.

"No, lass, I reckon you didn't dream," he replied.

Helen swayed from sick bitterness and a suffocating sense of pain, back to her old, sweet, joyous, tumultuous heart-throbbing.

"Tell me, if I didn't dream," she said softly, her face flashing warm again. She came close to him and looked up with all her heart in her great dark eyes, and love trembling on her red lips.

Calmness deserted the borderman after one glance at her. He paced the floor; twisted and clasped his hands while his eyes gleamed.

"Lass, I'm only human," he cried hoarsely, facing her again.

But only for a moment did he stand before her; but it was long enough for him to see her shrink a little, the gladness in her eyes giving way to uncertainty and a fugitive hope. Suddenly he began to pace the room again, and to talk incoherently. With the flow of words he gradually grew calmer, and, with something of his natural dignity, spoke more rationally.

"I said I loved you, an' it's true, but I didn't mean to speak. I oughtn't have done it. Somethin' made it so easy, so natural like. I'd have died before letting you know, if any idea had come to me of what I was sayin'. I've fought this feelin' for months. I allowed myself to think of you at first, an' there's the wrong. I went on the trail with your big eyes pictured in my mind, an' before I'd dreamed of it you'd crept into my heart. Life has never been the same since—that kiss. Betty said as how you cared for me, an' that made me worse, only I never really believed. Today I came over here to say good-bye, expectin' to hold myself well in hand; but the first glance of your eyes unmans me. Nothin' can come of it, lass, nothin' but trouble. Even if you cared, an' I don't dare believe you do, nothin' can come of it! I've my own life to live, an' there's no sweetheart in it. Mebbe, as Lew says, there's one in Heaven. Oh! girl, this has been hard on me. I see you always on my lonely tramps; I see your glorious eyes in the sunny fields an' in the woods, at gray twilight, an' when the stars shine brightest. They haunt me. Ah! you're the sweetest lass as ever tormented a man, an' I love you, I love you!"

He turned to the window only to hear a soft, broken cry, and a flurry of skirts. A rush of wind seemed to envelop him. Then two soft, rounded arms encircled his neck, and a golden head lay on his breast.

"My borderman! My hero! My love!"

Jonathan clasped the beautiful, quivering girl to his heart.

"Lass, for God's sake don't say you love me," he implored, thrilling with contact of her warm arms.

"Ah!" she breathed, and raised her head. Her radiant eyes darkly wonderful with unutterable love, burned into his.

He had almost pressed his lips to the sweet red ones so near his, when he drew back with a start, and his frame straightened.

"Am I a man, or only a coward?" he muttered. "Lass, let me think. Don't believe I'm harsh, nor cold, nor nothin' except that I want to do what's right."

He leaned out of the window while Helen stood near him with a hand on his quivering shoulder. When at last he turned, his face was colorless, white as marble, and sad, and set, and stern.

"Lass, it mustn't be; I'll not ruin your life."

"But you will if you give me up."

"No, no, lass."

"I cannot live without you."

"You must. My life is not mine to give."

"But you love me."

"I am a borderman."

"I will not live without you."

"Hush! lass, hush!"

"I love you."

Jonathan breathed hard; once more the tremor, which seemed pitiful in such a strong man, came upon him. His face was gray.

"I love you," she repeated, her rich voice indescribably deep and full. She opened wide her arms and stood before him with heaving bosom, with great eyes dark with woman's sadness, passionate with woman's promise, perfect in her beauty, glorious in her abandonment.

The borderman bowed and bent like a broken reed.

"Listen," she whispered, coming closer to him, "go if you must leave me; but let this be your last trail. Come back to me, Jack, come back to me! You have had enough of this terrible life; you have won a name that will never be forgotten; you have done your duty to the border. The Indians and outlaws will be gone soon. Take the farm your brother wants you to have, and live for me. We will be happy. I shall learn to keep your home. Oh! my dear, I will recompense you for the loss of all this wild hunting and fighting. Let me persuade you, as much for your sake as for mine, for you are my heart, and soul, and life. Go out upon your last trail, Jack, and come back to me."

"An' let Wetzel go always alone?"

"He is different; he lives only for revenge. What are those poor savages to you? You have a better, nobler life opening."

"Lass, I can't give him up."

"You need not; but give up this useless seeking of adventure. That, you know, is half a borderman's life. Give it up, Jack, if not for your own, then for my sake."

"No—no—never—I can't—I won't be a coward! After all these years I won't desert him. No—no—"

"Do not say more," she pleaded, stealing closer to him until she was against his breast. She slipped her arms around his neck. For love and more than life she was fighting now. "Good-bye, my love." She kissed him, a long, lingering pressure of her soft full lips on his. "Dearest, do not shame me further. Dearest Jack, come back to me, for I love you."

She released him, and ran sobbing from the room.

Unsteady as a blind man, he groped for the door, found it, and went out.

CHAPTER XVI

THE LONGEST DAY in Jonathan Zane's life, the oddest, the most terrible and complex with unintelligible emotions, was that one in which he learned that the wilderness no longer sufficed for him.

He wandered through the forest like a man lost, searching for, he knew not what. Rambling along the shady trails he looked for that contentment which had always been his, but found it not. He plunged into the depths of deep, gloomy ravines; into the fastnesses of heavy-timbered hollows where the trees hid the light of day; he sought the open, grassy hillsides, and roamed far over meadow and plain. Yet something always eluded him. The invisible and beautiful life of all inanimate things sang no more in his heart. The springy moss, the quivering leaf, the tell-tale bark of the trees, the limpid, misty, eddying pools under green banks, the myriads of natural objects from which he had learned so much, and the manifold joyous life around him, no longer spoke with soul-satisfying faithfulness. The environment of his boyish days, of his youth, and manhood, rendered not a sweetness as of old.

His intelligence, sharpened by the pain of new experience, told him he had been vain to imagine that he, because he was a borderman, could escape the universal destiny of human life. Dimly he could feel the broadening, the awakening into a fuller existence, but he did not welcome this new light. He realized that men had always turned, at some time in their lives, to women even as the cypress leans toward the sun. This weakening of the sterner stuff in him; this softening of his heart, and especially the inquietude, and lack of joy and harmony in his old pursuits of the forest trails bewildered him, and troubled him some. Thousands of times his borderman's trail had been crossed, yet never to his sorrow until now when it had been crossed by a woman.

Sick at heart, hurt in his pride, darkly savage, sad, remorseful, and thrilling with awakened passion, all in turn, he roamed the woodland unconsciously visiting the scenes where he had formerly found contentment.

He paused by many a shady glen, and beautiful quiet glade; by gray cliffs and mossy banks, searching with moody eyes for the spirit which evaded him.

Here in the green and golden woods rose before him a rugged, giant rock, moss-stained, and gleaming with trickling water. Tangled ferns dressed in autumn's russet hue lay at the base of the green-gray cliff, and circled a dark, deep pool dotted with yellow leaves. Half-way up, the perpendicular ascent was broken by a protruding ledge upon which waved broad-leaved plants and rusty ferns. Above, the cliff sheered out with many cracks and seams in its weather-beaten front.

The forest grew to the verge of the precipice. A full foliaged oak and a luxuriant maple, the former still fresh with its dark green leaves, the latter making a vivid contrast with its pale yellow, purple-red, and orange hues, leaned far out over the bluff. A mighty chestnut grasped with gnarled roots deep into the broken cliff. Dainty plumes of goldenrod swayed on the brink; red berries, amber moss, and green trailing vines peeped over the edge, and every little niche and cranny sported fragile ferns and pale-faced asters. A second cliff, higher than the first, and more heavily wooded, loomed above, and over it sprayed a transparent film of water, thin as smoke, and iridescent in the sunshine. Far above where the glancing rill caressed the mossy cliff and shone like gleaming gold against the dark branches with their green and red and purple leaves, lay the faint blue of the sky.

Jonathan pulled on down the stream with humbler heart. His favorite waterfall had denied him. The gold that had gleamed there was his sweetheart's hair; the red was of her lips; the dark pool with its lights and shades, its unfathomable mystery, was like her eyes.

He came at length to another scene of milder aspect. An open glade where the dancing, dimpling brook raced under dark hemlocks, and where blood-red sumach leaves, and beech leaves like flashes of sunshine, lay against the green. Under a leaning birch he found a patch of purple asters, and a little apart from them, by a mossy stone, a lonely fringed gentian. Its deep color brought to him the dark blue eyes that haunted him, and once again, like one possessed of an evil spirit, he wandered along the merry water-course.

But finally pain and unrest left him. When he surrendered to his love, peace returned. Though he said in his heart that Helen was not for him, he felt he did not need to torture himself by fighting against resistless power. He could love her without being a coward. He would take up his life where it had been changed, and live it, carrying this bitter-sweet burden always.

Memory, now that he admitted himself conquered, made a toy of him, bringing the sweetness of fragrant hair, and eloquent eyes, and clinging arms, and dewy lips. A thousand-fold harder to fight than pain was the seductive thought that he had but to go back to Helen to feel again the charm of her presence, to see the grace of her person, to hear the music of her voice, to have again her lips on his.

Jonathan knew then that his trial had but begun; that the pain and suffering of a borderman's broken pride and conquered spirit was nothing; that to steel his heart against the joy, the sweetness, the longing of love was everything.

So a tumult raged within his heart. No bitterness, nor wretchedness stabbed him as before, but a passionate yearning, born of memory, and unquenchable as the fires of the sun, burned there.

Helen's reply to his pale excuses, to his duty, to his life, was that she loved him. The wonder of it made him weak. Was not her answer enough? "I love you!" Three words only; but they changed the world. A beautiful girl loved him, she had kissed him, and his life could never again be the same. She had held out her arms to him—and he, cold, churlish, unfeeling brute, had let her shame herself, fighting for her happiness, for the joy that is a woman's divine right. He had been blind; he had not understood the significance of her gracious action; he had never realized until too late, what it must have cost her, what heart-burning shame and scorn his refusal brought upon her. If she ever looked tenderly at him again with her great eyes; or leaned toward him with her beautiful arms outstretched, he would fall at her feet and throw his duty to the winds, swearing his love was hers always and his life forever.

So love stormed in the borderman's heart.

Slowly the melancholy Indian-summer day waned as Jonathan strode out of the woods into a plain beyond, where he was to meet Wetzel at sunset. A smoky haze like a purple cloud lay upon the gently waving grass. He could not see across the stretch of prairie-land, though at this point he knew it was hardly a mile wide. With the trilling of the grasshoppers alone disturbing the serene quiet of this autumn afternoon, all nature seemed in harmony with the declining season. He stood a while, his thoughts becoming the calmer for the silence and loneliness of this breathing meadow.

When the shadows of the trees began to lengthen, and to steal far out over the yellow grass, he knew the time had come, and glided out upon the plain. He crossed it, and sat down upon a huge stone which lay with one shelving end overhanging the river.

Far in the west the gold-red sun, too fiery for his direct gaze, lost the brilliance of its under circle behind the fringe of the wooded hill. Slowly the red ball sank. When the last bright gleam had vanished in the dark horizon Jonathan turned to search wood and plain. Wetzel was to meet him at sunset. Even as his first glance swept around a light step sounded behind him. He did not move, for that step was familiar. In another moment the tall form of Wetzel stood beside him.

"I'm about as much behind as you was ahead of time," said Wetzel. "We'll stay here fer the night, an' be off early in the mornin'."

Under the shelving side of the rock, and in the shade of the thicket, the bordermen built a little fire and roasted strips of deer-meat. Then, puffing at their long pipes they sat for a long time in silence, while twilight let fall a dark, gray cloak over river and plain.

"Legget's move up the river was a blind, as I suspected," said Wetzel, presently. "He's not far back in the woods from here, an' seems to be waitin' fer somethin' or somebody. Brandt an' seven redskins are with him. We'd hev a good chance at them in the mornin'; now we've got 'em a long ways from their camp, so we'll wait, an' see what deviltry they're up to."

"Mebbe he's waitin' for some Injun band," suggested Jonathan.

"Thar's redskins in the valley an' close to him; but I reckon he's barkin' up another tree."

"Suppose we run into some of these Injuns?"

"We'll hev to take what comes," replied Wetzel, lying down on a bed of leaves.

When darkness enveloped the spot Wetzel lay wrapped in deep slumber, while Jonathan sat against the rock, watching the last flickerings of the camp-fire.

CHAPTER XVII

WILL AND HELEN hurried back along the river road. Beguiled by the soft beauty of the autumn morning they ventured farther from the fort than ever before, and had been suddenly brought to a realization of the fact by a crackling in the underbrush. Instantly their minds reverted to bears and panthers, such as they had heard invested the thickets round the settlement.

"Oh! Will! I saw a dark form stealing along in the woods from tree to tree!" exclaimed Helen in a startled whisper.

"So did I. It was an Indian, or I never saw one. Walk faster. Once round the bend in the road we'll be within sight of the fort; then we'll run," replied Will. He had turned pale, but maintained his composure.

They increased their speed, and had almost come up to the curve in the road, marked by dense undergrowth on both sides, when the branches in the thicket swayed violently, a sturdy little man armed with a musket appeared from among them.

"Avast! Heave to!" he commanded in a low, fierce voice, leveling his weapon. "One breeze from ye, an' I let sail this broadside."

"What do you want? We have no valuables," said Will, speaking low.

Helen stared at the little man. She was speechless with terror. It flashed into her mind as soon as she recognized the red, evil face of the sailor, that he was the accomplice upon whom Brandt had told Metzar he could rely.

"Shut up! It's not ye I want, nor valuables, but this wench," growled Case. He pushed Will around with the muzzle of the musket, which action caused the young man to turn a sickly white and shrink involuntarily with fear. The hammer of the musket was raised, and might fall at the slightest jar.

133

"For God's sake! Will, do as he says," cried Helen, who saw murder in Case's eyes. Capture or anything was better than sacrifice of life.

"March!" ordered Case, with the musket against Will's back.

Will hurriedly started forward, jostling Helen, who had preceded him. He was forced to hurry, because every few moments Case pressed the gun to his back or side.

Without another word the sailor marched them swiftly along the road, which now narrowed down to a trail. His intention, no doubt, was to put as much distance between him and the fort as was possible. No more than a mile had been thus traversed when two Indians stepped into view.

"My God! My God!" cried Will as the savages proceeded first to bind Helen's arms behind her, and then his in the same manner. After this the journey was continued in silence, the Indians walking beside the prisoners, and Case in the rear.

Helen was so terrified that for a long time she could not think coherently. It seemed as if she had walked miles, yet did not feel tired. Always in front wound the narrow, leaf-girt trail, and to the left the broad river gleamed at intervals through open spaces in the thickets. Flocks of birds rose in the line of march. They seemed tame, and uttered plaintive notes as if in sympathy.

About noon the trail led to the river bank. One of the savages disappeared in a copse of willows, and presently reappeared carrying a birch-bark canoe. Case ordered Helen and Will into the boat, got in himself, and the savages, taking stations at bow and stern, paddled out into the stream. They shot over under the lee of an island, around a rocky point, and across a strait to another island. Beyond this they gained the Ohio shore, and beached the canoe.

"Ahoy! there, cap'n," cried Case, pushing Helen up the bank before him, and she, gazing upward, was more than amazed to see Mordaunt leaning against a tree.

"Mordaunt, had you anything to do with this?" cried Helen breathlessly.

"I had all to do with it," answered the Englishman.

"What do you mean?"

He did not meet her gaze, nor make reply; but turned to address a few words in a low tone to a white man sitting on a log.

Helen knew she had seen this person before, and doubted not he was one of Metzar's men. She saw a rude, bark lean to, the remains of a camp-fire, and a pack tied in blankets. Evidently Mordaunt and his men had tarried here awaiting such developments as had come to pass.

"You white-faced hound!" hissed Will, beside himself with rage when he realized the situation. Bound though he was, he leaped up and tried to get at Mordaunt. Case knocked him on the head with the handle of his knife. Will fell with blood streaming from a cut over the temple.

The dastardly act aroused all Helen's fiery courage. She turned to the Englishman with eyes ablaze.

"So you've at last found your level. Border-outlaw! Kill me at once. I'd rather be dead than breathe the same air with such a coward!"

"I swore I'd have you, if not by fair means then by foul," he answered, with dark and haggard face.

"What do you intend to do with me now that I am tied?" she demanded scornfully.

"Keep you a prisoner in the woods till you consent to marry me."

Helen laughed in scorn. Desperate as was the plight, her natural courage had arisen at the cruel blow dealt her cousin, and she faced the Englishman with flashing eyes and undaunted mien. She saw he was again unsteady, and had the cough and catching breath habitual to certain men under the influence of liquor. She turned her attention to Will. He lay as he had fallen, with blood streaming over his pale face and fair hair. While she gazed at him Case whipped out his long knife, and looked up at Mordaunt.

"Cap'n, I'd better loosen a hatch fer him," he said brutally. "He's dead cargo fer us, an' in the way."

He lowered the gleaming point upon Will's chest.

"Oh-h-h!" breathed Helen in horror. She tried to close her eyes but was so fascinated she could not.

"Get up. I'll have no murder," ordered Mordaunt. "Leave him here."

"He's not got a bad cut," said the man sitting on the log. "He'll come to after a spell, go back to ther fort, an' give an alarm."

"What's that to me?" asked Mordaunt sharply. "We shall be safe. I won't have him with us because some Indian or another will kill him. It's not my purpose to murder any one."

"Ugh!" grunted one of the savages, and pointed eastward with his hand. "Hurry-long-way-go," he said in English. With the Indians in the lead the party turned from the river into the forest.

Helen looked back into the sandy glade and saw Will lying as they had left him, unconscious, with his hands still bound tightly behind him, and blood running over his face. Painful as was the thought of leaving him thus, it afforded her relief. She assured herself he had not been badly hurt, would recover consciousness before long, and, even bound as he was, could make his way back to the settlement.

Her own situation, now that she knew Mordaunt had instigated the abduction, did not seem hopeless. Although dreading Brandt with unspeakable horror, she did not in the least fear the Englishman. He was mad to carry her off like this into the wilderness, but would force her to do nothing. He could not keep her a prisoner long while Jonathan Zane and Wetzel were free to take his trail. What were his intentions? Where was he taking her? Such questions as these, however, troubled Helen ·more than a little. They brought her thoughts back to the Indians leading the way with lithe and stealthy step. How had Mordaunt associated himself with these savages? Then, suddenly, it dawned upon her that Brandt also might be in this scheme to carry her off. She scouted the idea; but it returned. Perhaps Mordaunt was only a tool; perhaps he himself was being deceived. Helen turned pale at the very thought. She had never forgotten the strange, unreadable, yet threatening, expression which Brandt had worn the day she had refused to walk with him.

Meanwhile the party made rapid progress through the forest. Not a word was spoken, nor did any noise of rustling leaves or crackling twigs follow their footsteps. The savage in the lead chose the open and less difficult ground; he took advantage of glades, mossy places, and rocky ridges. This careful choosing was, evidently, to avoid noise, and make the trail as difficult to follow as possible. Once he stopped suddenly, and listened.

Helen had a good look at the savage while he was in this position. His lean, athletic figure resembled, in its half-clothed condition, a bronzed statue; his powerful visage was set, changeless like iron. His dark eyes seemed to take in all points of the forest before him.

Whatever had caused the halt was an enigma to all save his red-skinned companion.

The silence of the wood was the silence of the desert. No bird chirped; no breath of wind sighed in the treetops; even the aspens remained unagitated. Pale yellow leaves sailed slowly, reluctantly down from above.

But some faint sound, something unusual had jarred upon the exquisitely sensitive ears of the leader, for with a meaning shake of the head to his followers, he resumed the march in a direction at right angles with the original course.

This caution, and evident distrust of the forest ahead, made Helen think again of Jonathan and Wetzel. Those great bordermen might already be on the trail of her captors. The thought thrilled her. Presently she realized, from another long, silent march through forest thickets, glades, aisles, and groves, over rock-strewn ridges, and down mossy-stoned ravines, that her strength was beginning to fail.

"I can go no further with my arms tied in this way," she declared, stopping suddenly.

"Ugh!" uttered the savage before her, turning sharply. He brandished a tomahawk before her eyes.

Mordaunt hurriedly set free her wrists. His pale face flushed a dark, flaming red when she shrank from his touch as if he were a viper.

After they had traveled what seemed to Helen many miles, the vigilance of the leaders relaxed.

On the banks of the willow-skirted stream the Indian guide halted them, and proceeded on alone to disappear in a green thicket. Presently he reappeared, and motioned for them to come on. He led the way over smooth, sandy paths between clumps of willows, into a heavy growth of alder bushes and prickly thorns, at length to emerge upon a beautiful grassy plot enclosed by green and yellow shrubbery. Above the stream, which cut the edge of the glade, rose a sloping, wooded ridge, with huge rocks projecting here and there out of the brown forest.

Several birch-bark huts could be seen; then two rough bearded men lolling upon the grass, and beyond them a group of painted Indians.

A whoop so shrill, so savage, so exultant, that it seemingly froze her blood, rent the silence. A man, unseen before, came crashing through the willows on the side of the ridge. He leaped the stream with the spring of a wild horse. He was big and broad, with disheveled hair, keen, hard face, and wild, gray eyes.

Helen's sight almost failed her; her head whirled dizzily; it was as if her heart had stopped beating and was become a cold, dead weight. She recognized in this man the one whom she feared most of all—Brandt.

He cast one glance full at her, the same threatening, cool, and evil-meaning look she remembered so well, and then engaged the Indian guide in low conversation.

Helen sank at the foot of a tree, leaning against it. Despite her weariness she had retained some spirit until this direful revelation broke her courage. What worse could have happened? Mordaunt had led her, for some reason that she could not divine, into the clutches of Brandt, into the power of Legget and his outlaws.

But Helen was not one to remain long dispirited or hopeless. As this plot thickened, as every added misfortune weighed upon her, when just ready to give up to despair she remembered the bordermen. Then Colonel Zane's tales of their fearless, implacable pursuit when bent on rescue or revenge, recurred to her, and fortitude returned. While she had life she would hope.

The advent of the party with their prisoner enlivened Legget's gang. A great giant of a man, blond-bearded, and handsome in a wild, rugged, uncouth way, a man Helen instinctively knew to be Legget, slapped Brandt on the shoulder.

"Damme, Roge, if she ain't a regular little daisy! Never seed such a purty lass in my life."

Brandt spoke hurriedly, and Legget laughed.

All this time Case had been sitting on the grass, saying nothing, but with his little eyes watchful. Mordaunt stood near him, his head bowed, his face gloomy.

"Say, cap'n, I don't like this mess," whispered Case to his master. "They ain't no crew fer us. I know men, fer I've sailed the seas, an' you're goin' to get what Metz calls the double-cross."

Mordaunt seemed to arouse from his gloomy reverie. He looked at Brandt and Legget who were now in earnest council. Then his eyes wandered toward Helen. She beckoned him to come to her.

"Why did you bring me here?" she asked.

"Brandt understood my case. He planned this thing, and seemed to be a good friend of mine. He said if I once got you out of the settlement, he would give me protection until I crossed the border into Canada. There we could be married," replied Mordaunt unsteadily.

"Then you meant marriage by me, if I could be made to consent?"

"Of course. I'm not utterly vile," he replied, with face lowered in shame.

"Have you any idea what you've done?"

"Done? I don't understand."

"You have ruined yourself, lost your manhood, become an out-law, a fugitive, made yourself the worst thing on the border—a girl-thief, and all for nothing."

"No, I have you. You are more to me than all."

"But can't you see? You've brought me out here for Brandt!"

"My God!" exclaimed Mordaunt. He rose slowly to his feet and gazed around like a man suddenly wakened from a dream. "I see it all now! Miserable, drunken wretch that I am!"

Helen saw his face change and lighten as if a cloud of darkness had passed away from it. She understood that love of liquor had made him a party to this plot. Brandt had cunningly worked upon his weakness, proposed a daring scheme; and filled his befogged mind with hopes that, in a moment of clear-sightedness, he would have seen to be vain and impossible. And Helen understood also that the sudden shock of surprise, pain, possible fury, had sobered Mordaunt, probably for the first time in weeks.

The Englishman's face became exceedingly pale. Seating himself on a stone near Case, he bowed his head, remaining silent and motionless.

The conference between Legget and Brandt lasted for some time. When it ended the latter strode toward the motionless figure on the rock.

"Mordaunt, you and Case will do well to follow this Indian at once to the river, where you can strike the Fort Pitt trail," said Brandt.

He spoke arrogantly and authoritatively. His keen, hard face, his steely eyes, bespoke the iron will and purpose of the man.

Mordaunt rose with cold dignity. If he had been a dupe, he was one no longer, as could be plainly read on his calm, pale face. The old listlessness, the unsteadiness had vanished. He wore a manner of extreme quietude; but his eyes were like balls of blazing blue steel.

"Mr. Brandt, I seem to have done you a service, and am no longer required," he said in a courteous tone.

Brandt eyed his man; but judged him wrongly. An English gentleman was new to the border-outlaw.

"I swore the girl should be mine," he hissed.

"Doomed men cannot be choosers!" cried Helen, who had heard him. Her dark eyes burned with scorn and hatred.

All the party heard her passionate outburst. Case arose as if unconcernedly, and stood by the side of his master. Legget and the other two outlaws came up. The Indians turned their swarthy faces.

"Hah! ain't she sassy?" cried Legget.

Brandt looked at Helen, understood the meaning of her words, and laughed. But his face paled, and involuntarily his shifty glance sought the rocks and trees upon the ridge.

"You played me from the first?" asked Mordaunt quietly.

"I did," replied Brandt.

"You meant nothing of your promise to help me across the border?"

"No."

"You intended to let me shift for myself out here in this wilderness?"

"Yes, after this Indian guides you to the river-trail," said Brandt, indicating with his finger the nearest savage.

"I get what you frontier men call 'the double-cross'?"

"That's it," replied Brandt with a hard laugh, in which Legget joined.

A short pause ensued.

"What will you do with the girl?"

"That's my affair."

"Marry her?" Mordaunt's voice was low and quiet.

"No!" cried Brandt. "She flaunted my love in my face, scorned me! She saw that borderman strike me, and by God! I'll get even. I'll keep her here in the woods until I'm tired of her, and when her beauty fades I'll turn her over to Legget."

Scarcely had the words dropped from his vile lips when Mordaunt moved with tigerish agility. He seized a knife from the belt of one of the Indians.

"Die!" he screamed.

Brandt grasped his tomahawk. At the same instant the man who had acted as Mordaunt's guide grasped the Englishman from behind.

Brandt struck ineffectually at the struggling man.

"Fair play!" roared Case, leaping at Mordaunt's second assailant. His long knife sheathed its glittering length in the man's breast. Without even a groan he dropped. "Clear the decks!" Case yelled, sweeping round in a circle. All fell back before that whirling knife.

Several of the Indians started as if to raise their rifles; but Legget's stern command caused them to desist.

The Englishman and the outlaw now engaged in a fearful encounter. The practiced, rugged, frontier desperado apparently had found his match in this pale-faced, slender man. His border skill with the hatchet seemed offset by Mordaunt's terrible rage. Brandt whirled and swung the weapon as he leaped around his antagonist. With his left arm the Englishman sought only to protect his head, while with his right he brandished the knife. Whirling here and there they struggled across the cleared space, plunging out of sight among the willows. During a moment there was a sound as of breaking branches; then a dull blow, horrible to hear, followed by a low moan, and then deep silence.

CHAPTER XVIII

A BLACK WEIGHT was seemingly lifted from Helen's weary eyelids. The sun shone; the golden forest surrounded her; the brook babbled merrily; but where were the struggling, panting men? She noticed presently, when her vision had grown more clear, that the scene differed entirely from the willow-glade where she had closed her eyes upon the fight. Then came the knowledge that she had fainted, and, during the time of unconsciousness, been moved.

She lay upon a mossy mound a few feet higher than a swiftly running brook. A magnificent chestnut tree spread its leafy branches above her. Directly opposite, about a hundred feet away, loomed a gray, ragged, moss-stained cliff. She noted this particularly because the dense forest encroaching to its very edge excited her admiration. Such wonderful coloring seemed unreal. Dead gold and bright red foliage flamed everywhere.

Two Indians stood near by silent, immovable. No other of Legget's band was visible. Helen watched the red men.

Sinewy, muscular warriors they were, with bodies partially painted, and long, straight hair, black as burnt wood, interwoven with bits of white bone, and plaited around waving eagle plumes. At first glance their dark faces and dark eyes were expressive of craft, cunning, cruelty, courage, all attributes of the savage.

Yet wild as these savages appeared, Helen did not fear them as she did the outlaws. Brandt's eyes, and Legget's, too, when turned on her, emitted a flame that seemed to scorch and shrivel her soul. When the savages met her gaze, which was but seldom, she imagined she saw intelligence, even pity, in their dusky eyes. Certain it was she did not shrink from them as from Brandt.

Suddenly, with a sensation of relief and joy, she remembered Mordaunt's terrible onslaught upon Brandt. Although she could

142

not recollect the termination of that furious struggle, she did recall Brandt's scream of mortal agony, and the death of the other at Case's hands. This meant, whether Brandt was dead or not, that the fighting strength of her captors had been diminished. Surely as the sun had risen that morning, Helen believed Jonathan and Wetzel lurked on the trail of these renegades. She prayed that her courage, hope, strength, might be continued.

"Ugh!" exclaimed one of the savages, pointing across the open space. A slight swaying of the bushes told that some living thing was moving among them, and an instant later the huge frame of the leader came into view. The other outlaw, and Case, followed closely. Farther down the margin of the thicket the Indians appeared; but without the slightest noise or disturbance of the shrubbery.

It required but a glance to show Helen that Case was in high spirits. His repulsive face glowed with satisfaction. He carried a bundle, which Helen saw, with a sickening sense of horror, was made up of Mordaunt's clothing. Brandt had killed the Englishman. Legget also had a package under his arm, which he threw down when he reached the chestnut tree, to draw from his pocket a long, leather belt, such as travelers use for the carrying of valuables. It was evidently heavy, and the musical clink which accompanied his motion proclaimed the contents to be gold.

Brandt appeared next; he was white and held his hand to his breast. There were dark stains on his hunting coat, which he removed to expose a shirt blotched with red.

"You ain't much hurt, I reckon?" inquired Legget solicitously.

"No; but I'm bleeding bad," replied Brandt coolly. He then called an Indian and went among the willows skirting the stream.

"So I'm to be in this border crew?" asked Case, looking up at Legget.

"Sure," replied the big outlaw. "You're a handy fellar, Case, an' after I break you into border ways you will fit in here tip-top. Now you'd better stick by me. When Eb Zane, his brother Jack, an' Wetzel find out this here day's work, hell will be a cool place compared with their whereabouts. You'll be safe with me, an' this is the only place on the border, I reckon, where you can say your life is your own."

"I'm yer mate, cap'n. I've sailed with soldiers, pirates, sailors, an' I guess I can navigate this borderland. Do we mess here? You didn't come far."

"Wal, I ain't pertikuler, but I don't like eatin' with buzzards," said Legget, with a grin. "Thet's why we moved a bit."

"What's buzzards?"

"Ho! ho! Mebbe you'll hev 'em closer'n you'd like, some day, if you'd only know it. Buzzards are fine birds, most particular birds, as won't eat nothin' but flesh, an' white man or Injun is pie fer 'em."

"Cap'n, I've seed birds as wouldn't wait till a man was dead," said Case.

"Haw! haw! you can't come no sailor yarns on this fellar. Wal, now, we've got ther Englishman's gold. One or t'other of us might jest as well hev it all."

"Right yer are, cap'n. Dice, cards, anyways, so long as I knows the game."

"Here, Jenks, hand over yer clickers, an' bring us a flat stone," said Legget, sitting on the moss and emptying the belt in front of him. Case took a small bag from the dark blue jacket that had so lately covered Mordaunt's shoulders, and poured out its bright contents.

"This coat ain't worth keepin'," he said, holding it up. The garment was rent and slashed, and under the left sleeve was a small, blood-stained hole where one of Brandt's blows had fallen. "Hullo, what's this?" muttered the sailor, feeling in the pocket of the jacket. "Blast my timbers, hooray!"

He held up a small, silver-mounted whiskey flask, unscrewed the lid, and lifted the vessel to his mouth.

"I'm kinder thirsty myself," suggested Legget.

"Cap'n, a nip an' no more," Case replied, holding the flask to Legget's lips.

The outlaw called Jenks now returned with a flat stone which he placed between the two men. The Indians gathered around. With greedy eyes they bent their heads over the gamblers, and watched every movement with breathless interest. At each click of the dice, or clink of gold, they uttered deep exclamations.

"Luck's again' ye, cap'n," said Case, skilfully shaking the ivory cubes.

"Hain't I got eyes?" growled the outlaw.

Steadily his pile of gold diminished, and darker grew his face.

"Cap'n, I'm a bad wind to draw," Case rejoined, drinking again from the flask. His naturally red face had become livid, his skin moist, and his eyes wild with excitement.

"Hullo! If them dice wasn't Jenks's, an' I hadn't played afore with him, I'd swear they's loaded."

"You ain't insinuatin' nothin', cap'n?" inquired Case softly, hesitating with the dice in his hands, his evil eyes glinting at Legget.

"No, you're fair enough," growled the leader. "It's my tough luck."

The game progressed with infrequent runs of fortune for the outlaw, and presently every piece of gold lay in a shining heap before the sailor.

"Clean busted!" exclaimed Legget in disgust.

"Can't you find nothin' more?" asked Case.

The outlaw's bold eyes wandered here and there until they rested upon the prisoner.

"I'll play ther lass against yer pile of gold," he growled. "Best two throws out 'en three. See here, she's as much mine as Brandt's."

"Make it half my pile an' I'll go you."

"Nary time. Bet, or give me back what yer win," replied Legget gruffly.

"She's a trim little craft, no mistake," said Case, critically surveying Helen. "All right, cap'n, I've sportin' blood, an' I'll bet. Yer throw first."

Legget won the first cast, and Case the second. With deliberation the outlaw shook the dice in his huge fist, and rattled them out upon the stone. "Hah!" he cried in delight. He had come within one of the highest score possible. Case nonchalantly flipped the little white blocks. The Indians crowded forward, their dusky eyes shining.

Legget swore in a terrible voice which re-echoed from the stony cliff. The sailor was victorious. The outlaw got up, kicked the stone and dice in the brook, and walked away from the group. He strode to and fro under one of the trees. Gruffly he gave an order to the Indians. Several of them began at once to kindle a fire. Presently he called Jenks, who was fishing the dice out of the brook, and began to converse earnestly with him, making fierce gestures and casting lowering glances at the sailor.

Case was too drunk now to see that he had incurred the enmity of the outlaw leader. He drank the last of the rum, and tossed the silver flask to an Indian, who received the present with every show of delight.

Case then, with the slow, uncertain movements of a man whose mind is befogged, began to count his gold; but only to gather up a few pieces when they slipped out of his trembling hands to roll on the moss. Laboriously, seriously, he kept at it with the doggedness of a drunken man. Apparently he had forgotten the others. Failing to learn the value of the coins by taking up each in turn, he arranged them in several piles, and began to estimate his wealth in sections.

In the meanwhile Helen, who had not failed to take in the slightest detail of what was going on, saw that a plot was hatching which boded ill to the sailor. Moreover, she heard Legget and Jenks whispering.

"I kin take him from right here 'atwixt his eyes," said Jenks softly, and tapped his rifle significantly.

"Wal, go ahead, only I ruther hev it done quieter," answered Legget. "We're yet a long ways, near thirty miles, from my camp, an' there's no tellin' who's in ther woods. But we've got ter git rid of ther fresh sailor, an' there's no surer way."

Cautiously cocking his rifle, Jenks deliberately raised it to his shoulder. One of the Indian sentinels who stood near at hand, sprang forward and struck up the weapon. He spoke a single word to Legget, pointed to the woods above the cliff, and then resumed his statue-like attitude.

"I told yer, Jenks, that it wouldn't do. The redskin scents somethin' in the woods, an' ther's an Injun I never seed fooled. We mustn't make a noise. Take yer knife an' tomahawk, crawl down below the edge o' the bank an' slip up on him. I'll give half ther gold fer ther job."

Jenks buckled his belt more tightly, gave one threatening glance at the sailor, and slipped over the bank. The bed of the brook lay about six feet below the level of the ground. This afforded an opportunity for the outlaw to get behind Case without being observed. A moment passed. Jenks disappeared round a bend of the stream. Presently his grizzled head appeared above the bank. He was immediately behind the sailor; but still some thirty feet away. This ground must be covered quickly and noiselessly. The outlaw began to crawl. In his right hand he grasped a tomahawk, and between his teeth was a long knife. He looked like a huge, yellow bear.

The savages, with the exception of the sentinel who seemed absorbed in the dense thicket on the cliff, sat with their knees between their hands, watching the impending tragedy.

Nothing but the merest chance, or some extraordinary intervention, could avert Case's doom. He was gloating over his gold. The creeping outlaw made no more noise than a snake. Nearer and nearer he came; his sweaty face shining in the sun; his eyes tigerish; his long body slipping silently over the grass. At length he was within five feet of the sailor. His knotty hands were dug into the sward as he gathered energy for a sudden spring.

At that very moment Case, with his hand on his knife, rose quickly and turned round.

The outlaw, discovered in the act of leaping, had no alternative, and spring he did, like a panther.

The little sailor stepped out of line with remarkable quickness, and as the yellow body whirled past him, his knife flashed blue-bright in the sunshine.

Jenks fell forward, his knife buried in the grass beneath him, and his outstretched hand still holding the tomahawk.

"Tryin' ter double-cross me fer my gold," muttered the sailor, sheathing his weapon. He never looked to see whether or not his blow had been fatal. "These border fellars might think a man as sails the seas can't handle a knife." He calmly began gathering up his gold, evidently indifferent to further attack.

Helen saw Legget raise his own rifle, but only to have it struck aside as had Jenks's. This time the savage whispered earnestly to Legget, who called the other Indians around him. The sentinel's low throaty tones mingled with the soft babbling of the stream. No sooner had he ceased speaking than the effect of his words showed how serious had been the information, warning or advice. The Indians cast furtive glances toward the woods. Two of them melted like shadows into the red and gold thicket. Another stealthily slipped from tree to tree until he reached the open ground, then dropped into the grass, and was seen no more until his dark body rose under the cliff. He stole along the green-stained wall, climbed a rugged corner, and vanished amid the dense foliage.

Helen felt that she was almost past discernment or thought. The events of the day succeeding one another so swiftly, and fraught with panic, had, despite her hope and fortitude, reduced her to a helpless condition of piteous fear. She understood that the savages scented danger, or had, in their mysterious way, received intelligence such as rendered them wary and watchful.

"Come on, now, an' make no noise," said Legget to Case. "Bring the girl, an' see that she steps light."

"Ay, ay, cap'n," replied the sailor. "Where's Brandt?"

"He'll be comin' soon's his cut stops bleedin'. I reckon he's weak yet."

Case gathered up his goods, and, tucking it under his arm, grasped Helen's arm. She was leaning against the tree, and when he pulled her, she wrenched herself free, rising with difficulty. His disgusting touch and revolting face had revived her sensibilities.

"Yer kin begin duty by carryin' thet," said Case, thrusting the package into Helen's arms. She let it drop without moving a hand.

"I'm runnin' this ship. Yer belong to me," hissed Case, and then he struck her on the head. Helen uttered a low cry of distress, and half staggered against the tree. The sailor picked up the package. This time she took it, trembling with horror.

"Thet's right. Now, give ther cap'n a kiss," he leered, and jostled against her.

Helen pushed him violently. With agonized eyes she appealed to the Indians. They were engaged tying up their packs. Legget looked on with a lazy grin.

"Oh! oh!" breathed Helen as Case seized her again. She tried to scream, but could not make a sound. The evil eyes, the beastly face, transfixed her with terror.

Case struck her twice, then roughly pulled her toward him.

Half-fainting, unable to move, Helen gazed at the heated, bloated face approaching hers.

When his coarse lips were within a few inches of her lips something hot hissed across her brow. Following so closely as to be an accompaniment, rang out with singular clearness the sharp crack of a rifle.

Case's face changed. The hot, surging flush faded; the expression became shaded, dulled into vacant emptiness; his eyes rolled wildly, then remained fixed, with a look of dark surprise. He stood upright an instant, swayed with the regular poise of a falling oak, and then plunged backward to the ground. His face, ghastly and livid, took on the awful calm of death.

A very small hole, reddish-blue round the edges, dotted the center of his temple.

Legget stared aghast at the dead sailor; then he possessed himself of the bag of gold.

"Saved me ther trouble," he muttered, giving Case a kick.

The Indians glanced at the little figure, then out into the flaming thickets. Each savage sprang behind a tree with incredible quickness. Legget saw this, and grasping Helen, he quickly led her within cover of the chestnut.

Brandt appeared with his Indian companion, and both leaped to shelter behind a clump of birches near where Legget stood. Brandt's hawk eyes flashed upon the dead Jenks and Case. Without asking a question he seemed to take in the situation. He stepped over and grasped Helen by the arm.

"Who killed Case?" he asked in a whisper, staring at the little blue hole in the sailor's temple.

No one answered.

The two Indians who had gone into the woods to the right of the stream, now returned. Hardly were they under the trees with their party, when the savage who had gone off alone arose out of the grass in the left of the brook, took it with a flying leap, and darted into their midst. He was the sentinel who had knocked up the weapons, thereby saving Case's life twice. He was lithe and supple, but not young. His grave, shadowy-lined, iron visage showed the traces of time and experience. All gazed at him as at one whose wisdom was greater than theirs.

"Old Horse," said Brandt in English. "Haven't I seen bullet holes like this?"

The Chippewa bent over Case, and then slowly straightened his tall form.

"Deathwind!" he replied, answering in the white man's language.

His Indian companions uttered low, plaintive murmurs, not signifying fear so much as respect.

Brandt turned as pale as the clean birch-bark on the tree near him. The gray flare of his eyes gave out a terrible light of certainty and terror.

"Legget, you needn't try to hide your trail," he hissed, and is seemed as if there was a bitter, reckless pleasure in these words.

Then the Chippewa glided into the low bushes bordering the creek. Legget followed him, with Brandt leading Helen, and the other Indians brought up the rear, each one sending wild, savage glances into the dark, surrounding forest.

CHAPTER XIX

A DENSE WHITE fog rose from the river, obscuring all objects, when the bordermen rolled out of their snug bed of leaves. The air was cool and bracing, faintly fragrant with dying foliage and the damp, dewy luxuriance of the ripened season. Wetzel pulled from under the protecting ledge a bundle of bark and sticks he had put there to keep dry, and built a fire, while Jonathan fashioned a cup from a green fruit resembling a gourd, filling it at a spring near by.

"Lew, there's a frosty nip in the water this mornin'," said Jonathan.

"I reckon. It's gettin' along into fall now. Any clear, still night'll fetch all the leaves, an' strip the trees bare as burned timber," answered Wetzel, brushing the ashes off the strip of meat he had roasted. "Get a stick, an' help me cook the rest of this chunk of bison. The sun'll be an hour breakin' up thet mist, an' we can't clear out till then. Mebbe we won't have no chance to light another fire soon."

With these bordermen everything pertaining to their lonely lives, from the lighting of a fire to the trailing of a redskin, was singularly serious. No gladsome song ever came from their lips; there was no jollity around their camp-fire. Hunters had their moments of rapturous delight; bordermen knew the peace, the content of the wilderness, but their pursuits racked nerve and heart. Wetzel had his moments of frenzied joy, but they passed with the echo of his vengeful yell. Jonathan's happiness, such as it was, had been to roam the forests. That, before a woman's eyes had dispelled it, had been enough, and compensated him for the gloomy, bloody phantoms which haunted him.

The bordermen, having partaken of the frugal breakfast, stowed in their spacious pockets all the meat that was left, and were ready for the day's march. They sat silent for a time waiting for the mist to lift. It broke in places, rolled in huge billows, sailed aloft like great white clouds, and again hung tenaciously to the river and the plain. Away in the west blue patches of sky shone through the rifts, and eastward banks of misty vapor reddened beneath the rising sun. Suddenly from beneath the silver edge of the rising pall the sun burst gleaming gold, disclosing the winding valley with its steaming river.

"We'll make up stream fer Two Islands, an' cross there if so be we've reason," Wetzel had said.

Through the dewy dells, avoiding the wet grass and bushes, along the dark, damp glades with their yellow carpets, under the thinning arches of the trees, down the gentle slopes of the ridges, rich with green moss, the bordermen glided like gray shadows. The forest was yet asleep. A squirrel frisked up an oak and barked quarrelsomely at these strange, noiseless visitors. A crow cawed from somewhere overhead. These were the only sounds disturbing the quiet early hour.

As the bordermen advanced the woods lightened and awoke to life and joy. Birds sang, trilled, warbled, or whistled their plaintive songs, peculiar to the dying season, and in harmony with the glory of the earth. Birds that in earlier seasons would have screeched and fought, now sang and fluttered side by side, in fraternal parade on their slow pilgrimage to the far south.

"Bad time fer us, when the birds are so tame, an' chipper. We can't put faith in them these days," said Wetzel. "Seems like they never was wild. I can tell, 'cept at this season, by the way they whistle an' act in the woods, if there's been any Injuns along the trails."

The greater part of the morning passed thus with the bordermen steadily traversing the forest; here, through a spare and gloomy wood, blasted by fire, worn by age, with many a dethroned monarch of bygone times rotting to punk and duff under the ferns, with many a dark, seamed and ragged king still standing, but gray and bald of head and almost ready to take his place in the forest of the past; there, through a maze of young saplings where each ash, maple, hickory and oak added some new and beautiful hue to the riot of color.

"I just had a glimpse of the lower island, as we passed an opening in the thicket," said Jonathan.

"We ain't far away," replied Wetzel.

The bordermen walked less rapidly in order to proceed with more watchfulness. Every rod or two they stopped to listen.

"You think Legget's across the river?" asked Jonathan.

"He was two days back, an' had his gang with him. He's up to some bad work, but I can't make out what. One thing, I never seen his trail so near Fort Henry."

They emerged at length into a more open forest which skirted the river. At a point still some distance ahead, but plainly in sight, two small islands rose out of the water.

"Hist! What's that?" whispered Wetzel, slipping his hand in Jonathan's arm.

A hundred yards beyond lay a long, dark figure stretched at full length under one of the trees close to the bank.

"Looks like a man," said Jonathan.

"You've hit the mark. Take a good peep roun' now, Jack, fer we're comin' somewhere near the trail we want."

Minutes passed while the patient bordermen searched the forest with their eyes, seeking out every tree within rifle range, or surveyed the level glades, scrutinized the hollows, and bent piercing eyes upon the patches of ferns.

"If there's a redskin around he ain't big enough to hold a gun," said Wetzel, moving forward again, yet still with that same stealthy step and keen caution.

Finally they were gazing down upon the object which had attracted Wetzel's attention.

"Will Sheppard!" cried Jonathan. "Is he dead? What's this mean?"

Wetzel leaned over the prostrate lad, and then quickly turned to his companion.

"Get some water. Take his cap. No, he ain't even hurt bad, unless he's got some wound as don't show."

Jonathan returned with the water, and Wetzel bathed the bloody face. When the gash on Will's forehead was clean, it told the bordermen much.

"Not an hour old, that blow," muttered Wetzel.

"He's comin' to," said Jonathan as Will stirred uneasily and moaned. Presently the lad opened his eyes and sat bolt upright. He looked bewildered for a moment, and felt of his head while gazing vaguely at the bordermen. Suddenly he cried:

"I remember! We were captured, brought here, and I was struck down by that villain Case."

"We? Who was with you?" asked Jonathan slowly.

"Helen. We came after flowers and leaves. While in full sight of the fort I saw an Indian. We hurried back," he cried, and proceeded with broken, panting voice to tell his story.

Jonathan Zane leaped to his feet with face deathly white and eyes blue-black, like burning stars.

"Jack, study the trail while I get the lad acrost the river, an' steered fer home," said Wetzel, and then he asked Will if he could swim.

"Yes; but you will find a canoe there in those willows."

"Come, lad, we've no time to spare," added Wetzel, sliding down the bank and entering the willows. He came out almost immediately with the canoe which he launched.

Will turned that he might make a parting appeal to Jonathan to save Helen; but could not speak. The expression on the borderman's face frightened him.

Motionless and erect Jonathan stood, his arms folded and his white, stern face distorted with the agony of remorse, fear, and anguish, which, even as Will gazed, froze into an awful, deadly look of fateful purpose.

Wetzel pushed the canoe off, and paddled with powerful strokes; he left Will on the opposite bank, and returned as swiftly as he could propel the light craft.

The bordermen met each other's glance, and had little need of words. Wetzel's great shoulders began to sag slightly, and his head lowered as his eyes sought the grass; a dark and gloomy shade overcast his features. Thus he passed from borderman to Deathwind. The sough of the wind overhead among the almost naked branches might well have warned Indians and renegades that Deathwind was on the trail!

"Brandt's had a hand in this, an' the Englishman's a fool!" said Wetzel.

"An hour ahead; can we come up with them before they join Brandt an' Legget?"

"We can try, but like as not we'll fail. Legget's gang is thirteen strong by now. I said it! Somethin' told me—a hard trail, a long trail, an' our last trail."

"It's over thirty miles to Legget's camp. We know the woods, an' every stream, an' every cover," hissed Jonathan Zane.

With no further words Wetzel took the trail on the run, and so plain was it to his keen eyes that he did not relax his steady lope except to stop and listen at regular intervals. Jonathan followed with easy swing. Through forest and meadow, over hill and valley, they ran, fleet and tireless. Once, with unerring instinct, they abruptly left the broad trail and cut far across a wide and rugged ridge to come again upon the tracks of the marching band. Then, in open country they reduced their speed to a walk. Ahead, in a narrow valley, rose a thicket of willows, yellow in the sunlight, and impenetrable to human vision. Like huge snakes the bordermen crept into this copse, over the sand, under the low branches, hard on the trail. Finally, in a light, open space, where the sun shone through a network of yellow branches and foliage, Wetzel's hand was laid upon Jonathan's shoulder.

"Listen! Hear that!" he whispered.

Jonathan heard the flapping of wings, and a low, hissing sound, not unlike that made by a goose.

"Buzzards!" he said, with a dark, grim smile. "Mebbe Brandt has begun our work. Come."

Out into the open they crawled to put to flight a flock of huge black birds with grisly, naked necks, hooked beaks, and long, yellow claws. Upon the green grass lay three half-naked men, ghastly, bloody, in terribly limp and lifeless positions.

"Metzar's man Smith, Jenks, the outlaw, and Mordaunt!"

Jonathan Zane gazed darkly into the steely, sightless eyes of the traitor. Death's awful calm had set the expression; but the man's whole life was there, its better part sadly shining forth among the cruel shadows.

His body was mutilated in a frightful manner. Cuts, stabs, and slashes told the tale of a long encounter, brought to an end by one clean stroke.

"Come here, Lew. You've seen men chopped up; but look at this dead Englishman," called Zane.

Mordaunt lay weltering in a crimson tide. Strangely though, his face was uninjured. A black bruise showed under his fair hair. The ghost of a smile seemed to hover around his set lips, yet almost intangible though it was, it showed that at last he had died a man. His left shoulder, side and arm showed where the brunt of Brandt's attack had fallen.

"How'd he ever fight so?" mused Jonathan.

"You never can tell," replied Wetzel. "Mebbe he killed this other fellar, too; but I reckon not. Come, we must go slow now, fer Legget is near at hand."

Jonathan brought huge, flat stones from the brook, and laid them over Mordaunt; then, cautiously he left the glade on Wetzel's trail.

Five hundred yards farther on Wetzel had ceased following the outlaw's tracks to cross the creek and climb a ridge. He was beginning his favorite trick of making a wide detour. Jonathan hurried forward, feeling he was safe from observation. Soon he distinguished the tall, brown figure of his comrade gliding ahead from tree to tree, from bush to bush.

"See them maples an' chestnuts down thar," said Wetzel when Jonathan had come up, pointing through an opening in the foliage. "They've stopped fer some reason."

On through the forest the bordermen glided. They kept near the summit of the ridge, under the best cover they could find, and passed swiftly over this half-circle. When beginning once more to draw toward the open grove in the valley, they saw a long, irregular cliff, densely wooded. They swerved a little, and made for this excellent covert.

They crawled the last hundred yards and never shook a fern, moved a leaf, or broke a twig. Having reached the brink of the low precipice, they saw the grassy meadow below, the straggling trees, the brook, the group of Indians crowding round the white men.

"See that point of rock thar? It's better cover," whispered Wetzel.

Patiently, with no hurry or excitement, they slowly made their difficult way among the rocks and ferns to the vantage point desired. Taking a position like this was one the bordermen strongly favored. They could see everywhere in front, and had the thick woods at their backs.

"What are they up to?" whispered Jonathan, as he and Wetzel lay close together under a mass of grapevine still tenacious of its broad leaves.

"Dicin'," answered Wetzel. "I can see 'em throw; anyways, nothin' but bettin' ever makes redskins act like that."

"Who's playin'? Where's Brandt?"

"I can make out Legget; see his shaggy head. The other must be Case. Brandt ain't in sight. Nursin' a hurt perhaps. Ah! See thar!

Over under the big tree as stands dark-like agin the thicket. Thet's an Injun, an' he looks too quiet an' keen to suit me. We'll have a care of him."

"Must be playin' fer Mordaunt's gold."

"Like as not, for where'd them ruffians get any 'cept they stole it."

"Aha! They're gettin' up! See Legget walk away shakin' his big head. He's mad. Mebbe he'll be madder presently," growled Jonathan.

"Case's left alone. He's countin' his winnin's. Jack, look out fer more work took off our hands."

"By gum! See that Injun knock up a leveled rifle."

"I told you, an' thet redskin has his suspicions. He's seen us down along ther ridge. There's Helen, sittin' behind the biggest tree. Thet Injun guard, 'afore he moved, kept us from seein' her."

Jonathan made no answer to this; but his breath literally hissed through his clenched teeth.

"Thar goes the other outlaw," whispered Wetzel, as if his comrade could not see. "It's all up with Case. See the sneak bendin' down the bank. Now, thet's a poor way. It'd better be done from the front, walkin' up natural-like, instead of tryin' to cover thet wide stretch. Case'll see him or hear him sure. Thar, he's up now, an' crawlin'. He's too slow, too slow. Aha! I knew it—Case turns. Look at the outlaw spring! Well, did you see thet little cuss whip his knife? One more less fer us to quiet. Thet makes four, Jack, an' mebbe, soon, it'll be five."

"They're holdin' a council," said Jonathan.

"I see two Injuns sneakin' off into the woods, an' here comes thet guard. He's a keen redskin, Jack, fer we did come light through the brush. Mebbe it'd be well to stop his scoutin'.''

"Lew, that villain Case is bullyin' Helen!" cried Jonathan.

"Sh-sh-h," whispered Wetzel.

"See! He's pulled her to her feet. Oh! He struck her! Oh!"

Jonathan leveled his rifle and would have fired, but for the iron grasp on his wrist.

"Hev you lost yer senses? It's full two hundred paces, an' too far fer your piece," said Wetzel in a whisper. "An' it ain't sense to try from here."

"Lend me your gun! Lend me your gun!"

Silently Wetzel handed him the long, black rifle.

Jonathan raised it, but trembled so violently that the barrel wavered like a leaf in the breeze.

"Take it, I can't cover him," groaned Jonathan. "This is new to me. I ain't myself. God! Lew, he struck her again! *Again!* He's tryin' to kiss her! Wetzel, if you're my friend, kill him!"

"Jack, it'd be better to wait, an'—"

"I love her," breathed Jonathan.

The long, black barrel swept up to a level and stopped. White smoke belched from among the green leaves; the report rang throughout the forest.

"Ah! I saw him stop an' pause," hissed Jonathan. "He stands, he sways, he falls! Death for yours, you sailor-beast!"

CHAPTER XX

THE BORDERMEN WATCHED Legget and his band disappear into the thicket adjoining the grove. When the last dark, lithe form glided out of sight among the yellowing copse, Jonathan leaped from the low cliff, and had hardly reached the ground before Wetzel dashed down to the grassy turf.

Again they followed the outlaw's trail, darker-faced, fiercer-visaged than ever, with cocked, tightly-gripped rifles thrust well before them, and light feet that scarcely brushed the leaves.

Wetzel halted after a long tramp up and down the ridges, and surveyed with keen intent the lay of the land ahead.

"Sooner or later we'll hear from that redskin as discovered us a ways back," whispered he. "I wish we might get a crack at him afore he hinders us bad. I ain't seen many keener Injuns. It's lucky we fixed ther arrow-shootin' Shawnee. We'd never hev beat thet combination. An' fer all of thet I'm worrin' some about the goin' ahead."

"Ambush?" Jonathan asked.

"Like as not. Legget'll send thet Injun back, an' mebbe more'n him. Jack, see them little footprints? They're Helen's. Look how she's draggin' along. Almost tuckered out. Legget can't travel many more miles to-day. He'll make a stand somewheres, an' lose all his redskins afore he gives up the lass."

"I'll never live through to-night with her in that gang. She'll be saved, or dead, before the stars pale in the light of the moon."

"I reckon we're nigh the end for some of us. It'll be moonlight an hour after dusk, an' now it's only the middle of the afternoon; we've time enough fer anythin'. Now, Jack, let's not tackle the trail straight. We'll split, an' go round to head 'em off. See thet dead white oak standin' high over thar?"

Jonathan looked out between the spreading branches of a beech, and saw, far over a low meadow, luxuriant with grasses and rushes and bright with sparkling ponds and streams, a dense wood out of which towered a bare, bleached tree-top.

"You slip around along the right side of this meader, an' I'll take the left side. Go slow, an' hev yer eyes open. We'll meet under thet big dead tree. I allow we can see it from anywhere around. We'll leave the trail here, an' take it up farther on. Legget's goin' straight for his camp; he ain't losin' an inch. He wants to get in that rocky hole of his'n."

Wetzel stepped off the trail, glided into the woods, and vanished.

Jonathan turned to the right, traversed the summit of the ridge, softly traveled down its slope, and, after crossing a slow, eddying, quiet stream, gained the edge of the forest on that side of the swamp. A fringe of briars and prickly thorns bordered this wood affording an excellent cover. On the right the land rose rather abruptly. He saw that by walking up a few paces he could command a view of the entire swamp, as well as the ridge beyond, which contained Wetzel, and, probably, the outlaw and his band.

Remembering his comrade's admonition, Jonathan curbed his unusual impatience and moved slowly. The wind swayed the tree-tops, and rustled the fallen leaves. Birds sang as if thinking the warm, soft weather was summer come again. Squirrels dropped heavy nuts that cracked on the limbs, or fell with a thud to the ground, and they scampered over the dry earth, scratching up the leaves as they barked and scolded. Crows cawed clamorously after a hawk that had darted under the tree-tops to escape them; deer loped swiftly up the hill, and a lordly elk rose from a wallow in the grassy swamp, crashing into the thicket.

When two-thirds around this oval plain, which was a mile long and perhaps one-fourth as wide, Jonathan ascended the hill to make a survey. The grass waved bright brown and golden in the sunshine, swished in the wind, and swept like a choppy sea to the opposite ridge. The hill was not densely wooded. In many places the red-brown foliage opened upon irregular patches, some black, as if having been burned over, others showing the yellow and purple colors of the low thickets and the gray, barren stones.

Suddenly Jonathan saw something darken one of these sunlit plots. It might have been a deer. He studied the rolling, rounded tree-tops, the narrow strips between the black trunks, and the open places that were clear in the sunshine. He had nearly come to believe he had seen a small animal or bird flit across the white of the sky far in the background, when he distinctly saw dark figures stealing along past a green-gray rock, only to disappear under colored banks of foliage. Presently, lower down, they reappeared and crossed an open patch of yellow fern. Jonathan counted them. Two were rather yellow in color, the hue of buckskin; another, slight of stature as compared with the first, and light gray by contrast. Then six black, slender, gliding forms crossed the space. Jonathan then lost sight of them, and did not get another glimpse. He knew them to be Legget and his band. The slight figure was Helen.

Jonathan broke into a run, completed the circle around the swamp, and slowed into a walk when approaching the big dead tree where he was to wait for Wetzel.

Several rods beyond the lowland he came to a wood of white oaks, all giants rugged and old, with scarcely a sapling intermingled with them. Although he could not see the objective point, he knew from his accurate sense of distance that he was near it. As he entered the wood he swept its whole length and width with his eyes, he darted forward twenty paces to halt suddenly behind a tree. He knew full well that a sharply moving object was more difficult to see in the woods, than one stationary. Again he ran, fleet and light, a few paces ahead to take up a position as before behind a tree. Thus he traversed the forest. On the other side he found the dead oak of which Wetzel had spoken.

Its trunk was hollow. Jonathan squeezed himself into the blackened space, with his head in a favorable position behind a projecting knot, where he could see what might occur near at hand.

He waited for what seemed to him a long while, during which he neither saw nor heard anything, and then, suddenly, the report of a rifle rang out. A single, piercing scream followed. Hardly had the echo ceased when three hollow reports, distinctly different in tone from the first, could be heard from the same direction. In quick succession short, fierce yells attended rather than succeeded, the reports.

Jonathan stepped out of the hiding-place, cocked his rifle, and fixed a sharp eye on the ridge before him whence those startling cries had come. The first rifle-shot, unlike any other in its short, spiteful, stinging quality, was unmistakably Wetzel's. Zane had heard it, followed many times, as now, by the wild death-cry of a savage. The other reports were of Indian guns, and the yells were the clamoring, exultant cries of Indians in pursuit.

Far down where the open forest met the gloom of the thickets, a brown figure flashed across the yellow ground. Darting among the trees, across the glades, it moved so swiftly that Jonathan knew it was Wetzel. In another instant a chorus of yelps resounded from the foliage, and three savages burst through the thicket almost at right angles with the fleeing borderman, running to intercept him. The borderman did not swerve from his course; but came on straight toward the dead tree, with the wonderful fleetness that so often had served him well.

Even in that moment Jonathan thought of what desperate chances his comrade had taken. The trick was plain. Wetzel had, most likely, shot the dangerous scout, and, taking to his heels, raced past the others, trusting to his speed and their poor marksmanship to escape with a whole skin.

When within a hundred yards of the oak Wetzel's strength apparently gave out. His speed deserted him; he ran awkwardly, and limped. The savages burst out into full cry like a pack of hungry wolves. They had already emptied their rifles at him, and now, supposing one of the shots had taken effect, redoubled their efforts, making the forest ring with their short, savage yells. One gaunt, dark-bodied Indian with a long, powerful, springy stride easily distanced his companions, and, evidently sure of gaining the coveted scalp of the borderman, rapidly closed the gap between them as he swung aloft his tomahawk, yelling the war-cry.

The sight on Jonathan's rifle had several times covered this savage's dark face; but when he was about to press the trigger Wetzel's fleeting form, also in line with the savage, made it extremely hazardous to take a shot.

Jonathan stepped from his place of concealment, and let out a yell that pealed high over the cries of the savages.

Wetzel suddenly dropped flat on the ground.

With a whipping crack of Jonathan's rifle, the big Indian plunged forward on his face.

The other Indians, not fifty yards away, stopped aghast at the fate of their comrade, and were about to seek the shelter of trees when, with his terrible yell, Wetzel sprang up and charged upon them. He had left his rifle where he fell; but his tomahawk glittered as he ran.

The lameness had been a trick, for now he covered ground with a swiftness which caused his former progress to seem slow.

The Indians, matured and seasoned warriors though they were, gave but one glance at this huge, brown figure bearing down upon them like a fiend, and, uttering the Indian name of *Deathwind,* wavered, broke and ran.

One, not so fleet as his companion, Wetzel overtook and cut down with a single stroke. The other gained a hundred-yard start in the slight interval of Wetzel's attack, and, spurred on by a pealing, awful cry in the rear, sped swiftly in and out among the trees until he was lost to view.

Wetzel scalped the two dead savages, and, after returning to regain his rifle, joined Jonathan at the dead oak.

"Jack, you can never tell how things is comin' out. Thet redskin I allowed might worry us a bit, fooled me as slick as you ever saw, an' I hed to shoot him. Knowin' it was a case of runnin', I just cut fer this oak, drew the redskins' fire, an' hed 'em after me quicker 'n you'd say Jack Robinson. I was hopin' you'd be here; but wasn't sure till I'd seen your rifle. Then I kinder got a kink in my leg jest to coax the brutes on."

"Three more quiet," said Jonathan Zane. "What now?"

"We've headed Legget, an' we'll keep nosin' him off his course. Already he's lookin' fer a safe campin' place for the night."

"There is none in these woods, fer him."

"We didn't plan this gettin' between him an' his camp; but couldn't be better fixed. A mile farther along the ridge, is a campin' place, with a spring in a little dell close under a big stone, an' well wooded. Legget's headin' straight fer it. With a couple of Injuns guardin' thet spot, he'll think he's safe. But I know the place, an' can crawl to thet rock the darkest night thet ever was an' never crack a stick."

★　★　★　★　★　★

In the gray of the deepening twilight Jonathan Zane sat alone. An owl hooted dismally in the dark woods beyond the thicket where the borderman crouched waiting for Wetzel. His listening ear detected a soft, rustling sound like the play of a mole under the leaves. A branch trembled and swung back; a soft footstep followed and Wetzel came into the retreat.

"Well?" asked Jonathan impatiently, as Wetzel deliberately sat down and laid his rifle across his knees.

"Easy, Jack, easy. We've an hour to wait."

"The time I've already waited has been long for me."

"They're thar," said Wetzel grimly.

"How far from here?"

"A half-hour's slow crawl."

"Close by?" hissed Jonathan.

"Too near fer you to get excited."

"Let us go; it's as light now as in the gray of mornin'."

"Mornin' would be best. Injuns get sleepy along towards day. I've ever found thet time the best. But we'll be lucky if we ketch these redskins asleep."

"Lew, I can't wait here all night. I won't leave her longer with that renegade. I've got to free or kill her."

"Most likely it'll be the last," said Wetzel simply.

"Well, so be it then," and the borderman hung his head.

"You needn't worry none, 'bout Helen. I jest had a good look at her, not half an hour back. She's fagged out; but full of spunk yet. I seen thet when Brandt went near her. Legget's got his hands full jest now with the redskins. He's hevin' trouble keepin' them on this slow trail. I ain't sayin' they're skeered; but they're mighty restless."

"Will you take the chance now?"

"I reckon you needn't hev asked thet."

"Tell me the lay of the land."

"Wal, if we get to this rock I spoke 'bout, we'll be right over 'em. It's ten feet high, an' we can jump straight amongst 'em. Most likely two or three'll be guardin' the openin' which is a little ways to the right. Ther's a big tree, the only one, low down by the spring. Helen's under it, half-sittin', half-leanin' against the roots. When I first looked, her hands were free; but I saw Brandt bind her feet. An' he had to get an Injun to help him, fer she kicked like a spirited little filly. There's moss under the tree an' there's where the redskins'll lay down to rest."

"I've got that; now out with your plan."

"Wal, I calkilate it's this. The moon'll be up in about an hour. We'll crawl as we've never crawled afore, because Helen's life depends as much on our not makin' a noise, as it does on fightin' when the time comes. If they hear us afore we're ready to shoot, the lass'll be tomahawked quicker'n lightnin'. If they don't suspicion us, when the right moment comes you shoot Brandt, yell louder'n you ever did afore, leap amongst 'em, an' cut down the first Injun thet's near you on your way to Helen. Swing her over your arm, an' dig into the woods."

"Well?" asked Jonathan when Wetzel finished.

"That's all," the borderman replied grimly.

"An' leave you all alone to fight Legget an' the rest of 'em?"

"I reckon."

"Not to be thought of."

"Ther's no other way."

"There must be! Let me think; I can't, I'm not myself."

"No other way," repeated Wetzel curtly.

Jonathan's broad hand fastened on Wetzel's shoulder and wheeled him around.

"Have I ever left you alone?"

"This's different," and Wetzel turned away again. His voice was cold and hard.

"How is it different? We've had the same thing to do, almost, more than once."

"We've never had as bad a bunch to handle as Legget's. They're lookin' fer us, an' will be hard to beat."

"That's no reason."

"We never had to save a girl one of us loved."

Jonathan was silent.

"I said this'd be my last trail," continued Wetzel. "I felt it, an' I know it'll be yours."

"Why?"

"If you get away with the girl she'll keep you at home, an' it'll be well. If you don't succeed, you'll die tryin', so it's sure your last trail."

Wetzel's deep, cold voice rang with truth.

"Lew, I can't run away an' leave you to fight those devils alone, after all these years we've been together, I can't."

"No other chance to save the lass."

Jonathan quivered with the force of his emotion. His black eyes glittered; his hands grasped at nothing. Once more he was between love and duty. Again he fought over the old battle, but this time it left him weak.

"You love the big-eyed lass, don't you?" asked Wetzel, turning with softened face and voice.

"I have gone mad!" cried Jonathan, tortured by the simple question of his friend. Those big, dear, wonderful eyes he loved so well, looked at him now from the gloom of the thicket. The old, beautiful, soft glow, the tender light, was there, and more, a beseeching prayer to save her.

Jonathan bowed his head, ashamed to let his friend see the tears that dimmed his eyes.

"Jack, we've follered the trail fer years together. Always you've been true an' staunch. This is our last, but whatever bides we'll break up Legget's band to-night, an' the border'll be cleared, mebbe, for always. At least his race is run. Let thet content you. Our time'd have to come, sooner or later, so why not now? I know how it is, that you want to stick by me; but the lass draws you to her. I understand, an' want you to save her. Mebbe you never dreamed it; but I can tell jest how you feel. All the tremblin', an' softness, an' sweetness, an' delight you've got for thet girl, is no mystery to Lew Wetzel."

"You loved a lass?"

Wetzel bowed his head, as perhaps he had never before in all his life.

"Betty—always," he answered softly.

"My sister!" exclaimed Jonathan, and then his hand closed hard on his comrade's, his mind going back to many things, strange in the past, but now explained. Wetzel had revealed his secret.

"An' it's been all my life, since she wasn't higher 'n my knee. There was a time when I might hev been closer to you than I am now. But I was a mad an' bloody Injun hater, so I never let her know till I seen it was too late. Wal, wal, no more of me. I only told it fer you."

Jonathan was silent.

"An' now to come back where we left off," continued Wetzel. "Let's take a more hopeful look at this comin' fight. Sure I said it was my last trail, but mebbe it's not. You can never tell. Feelin' as we do, I imagine they've no odds on us. Never in my life did I say to you, least of all to any one else, what I was goin' to do; but I'll tell it now. If I land uninjured amongst thet bunch, I'll kill them all."

The giant borderman's low voice hissed, and stung. His eyes glittered with unearthly fire. His face was cold and gray. He spread out his brawny arms and clenched his huge fists, making the muscles of his broad shoulders roll and bulge.

"I hate the thought, Lew, I hate the thought. Ain't there no other way?"

"No other way."

"I'll do it, Lew, because I'd do the same for you; because I have to, because I love her; but God! it hurts."

"Thet's right," answered Wetzel, his deep voice softening until it was singularly low and rich. "I'm glad you've come to it. An' sure it hurts. I want you to feel so at leavin' me to go it alone. If we both get out alive, I'll come many times to see you an' Helen. If you live an' I don't, think of me sometimes, think of the trails we've crossed together. When the fall comes with its soft, cool air, an' smoky mornin's an' starry nights, when the wind's sad among the bare branches, an' the leaves drop down, remember they're fallin' on my grave."

Twilight darkened into gloom; the red tinge in the west changed to opal light; through the trees over a dark ridge a rim of silver glinted and moved.

The moon had risen; the hour was come.

The bordermen tightened their belts, replaced their leggings, tied their hunting coats, loosened their hatchets, looked to the priming of their rifles, and were ready.

Wetzel walked twenty paces and turned. His face was white in the moonlight; his dark eyes softened into a look of love as he gripped his comrade's outstretched hand.

Then he dropped flat on the ground, carefully saw to the position of his rifle, and began to creep. Jonathan kept close at his heels.

Slowly but steadily they crawled, minute after minute. The hazel-nut bushes above them had not yet shed their leaves; the ground was clean and hard, and the course fatefully perfect for their deadly purpose.

A slight rustling of their buckskin garments sounded like the rustling of leaves in a faint breeze.

The moon came out above the trees and still Wetzel advanced softly, steadily, surely.

The owl, lonely sentinel of that wood, hooted dismally. Even his night eyes, which made the darkness seem clear as day, missed those gliding figures. Even he, sure guardian of the wilderness, failed the savages.

Jonathan felt soft moss beneath him; he was now in the woods under the trees. The thicket had been passed.

Wetzel's moccasin pressed softly against Jonathan's head. The first signal!

Jonathan crawled forward, and slightly raised himself.

He was on a rock. The trees were thick and gloomy. Below, the little hollow was almost in the wan moonbeams. Dark figures lay close together. Two savages paced noiselessly to and fro. A slight form rolled in a blanket lay against a tree.

Jonathan felt his arm gently squeezed.

The second signal!

Slowly he thrust forward his rifle, and raised it in unison with Wetzel's. Slowly he rose to his feet as if the same muscles guided them both.

Over his head a twig snapped. In the darkness he had not seen a low branch.

The Indian guards stopped suddenly, and became motionless as stone.

They had heard; but too late.

With the blended roar of the rifles both dropped, lifeless.

Almost under the spouting flame and white cloud of smoke, Jonathan leaped behind Wetzel, over the bank. His yells were mingled with Wetzel's vengeful cry. Like leaping shadows the bordermen were upon their foes.

An Indian sprang up, raised a weapon, and fell beneath Jonathan's savage blow, to rise no more. Over his prostrate body the borderman bounded. A dark, nimble form darted upon the captive. He swung high a blade that shone like silver in the moonlight. His shrill war-cry of death rang out with Helen's scream of despair. Even as he swung back her head with one hand in her long hair, his arm descended; but it fell upon the borderman's body. Jonathan and the Indian rolled upon the moss. There was a terrific struggle, a whirling blade, a dull blow which silenced the yell, and the borderman rose alone.

He lifted Helen as if she were a child, leaped the brook, and plunged into the thicket.

The noise of the fearful conflict he left behind, swelled high and hideously on the night air. Above the shrill cries of the Indians, and the furious yells of Legget, rose the mad, booming roar of Wetzel. No rifle cracked; but sodden blows, the clash of steel, the threshing of struggling men, told of the dreadful strife.

Jonathan gained the woods, sped through the moonlit glades, and far on under light and shadow.

The shrill cries ceased; only the hoarse yells and the mad roar could be heard. Gradually these also died away, and the forest was still.

CHAPTER XXI

NEXT MORNING, WHEN the mist was breaking and rolling away under the warm rays of the Indian-summer sun, Jonathan Zane beached his canoe on the steep bank before Fort Henry. A pioneer, attracted by the borderman's halloo, ran to the bluff and sounded the alarm with shrill whoops. Among the hurrying, brown-clad figures that answered this summons, was Colonel Zane.

"It's Jack, kurnel, an' he's got her!" cried one.

The doughty colonel gained the bluff to see his brother climbing the bank with a white-faced girl in his arms.

"Well?" he asked, looking darkly at Jonathan. Nothing kindly or genial was visible in his manner now; rather grim and forbidding he seemed, thus showing he had the same blood in his veins as the borderman.

"Lend a hand," said Jonathan. "As far as I know she's not hurt."

They carried Helen toward Colonel Zane's cabin. Many women of the settlement saw them as they passed, and looked gravely at one another, but none spoke. This return of an abducted girl was by no means a strange event.

"Somebody run for Sheppard," ordered Colonel Zane, as they entered his cabin.

Betty, who was in the sitting-room, sprang up and cried: "Oh! Eb! Eb! Don't say she's—"

"No, no, Betts, she's all right. Where's my wife? Ah! Bess here, get to work."

The colonel left Helen in the tender, skilful hands of his wife and sister, and followed Jonathan into the kitchen.

"I was just ready for breakfast when I heard some one yell," said he. "Come, Jack, eat something."

They ate in silence. From the sitting-room came excited whispers, a joyous cry from Betty, and a faint voice. Then heavy, hurrying footsteps, followed by Sheppard's words of thanksgiving.

"Where's Wetzel?" began Colonel Zane.

The borderman shook his head gloomily.

"Where did you leave him?"

"We jumped Legget's bunch last night, when the moon was about an hour high. I reckon about fifteen miles northeast. I got away with the lass."

"Ah! Left Lew fighting?"

The borderman answered the question with bowed head.

"You got off well. Not a hurt that I can see, and more than lucky to save Helen. Well, Jack, what do you think about Lew?"

"I'm goin' back," replied Jonathan.

"No! no!"

The door opened to admit Mrs. Zane. She looked bright and cheerful. "Hello, Jack; glad you're home. Helen's all right, only faint from hunger and over-exertion. I want something for her to eat—well! you men didn't leave much."

Colonel Zane went into the sitting-room. Sheppard sat beside the couch where Helen lay, white and wan. Betty and Nell were looking on with their hearts in their eyes. Silas Zane was there, and his wife, with several women neighbors.

"Betty, go fetch Jack in here," whispered the colonel in his sister's ear. "Drag him, if you have to," he added fiercely.

The young woman left the room, to reappear directly with her brother. He came in reluctantly.

As the stern-faced borderman crossed the threshold a smile, beautiful to see, dawned in Helen's eyes.

"I'm glad to see you're comin' round," said Jonathan, but he spoke dully as if his mind was on other things.

"She's a little flighty; but a night's sleep will cure that," cried Mrs. Zane from the kitchen.

"What do you think?" interrupted the colonel. "Jack's not satisfied to get back with Helen unharmed, and a whole skin himself; but he's going on the trail again."

"No, Jack, no, no!" cried Betty.

"What's that I hear?" asked Mrs. Zane as she came in. "Jack's going out again? Well, all I want to say is that he's as mad as a March hare."

"Jonathan, look here," said Silas seriously. "Can't you stay home now?"

"Jack, listen," whispered Betty, going close to him. "Not one of us ever expected to see either you or Helen again, and oh! we are so happy. Do not go away again. You are a man; you do not know, you cannot understand all a woman feels. She must sit and wait, and hope, and pray for the safe return of husband or brother or sweetheart. The long days! Oh, the long sleepless nights, with the wail of the wind in the pines, and the rain on the roof! It is maddening. Do not leave us! Do not leave me! Do not leave Helen! Say you will not, Jack."

To these entreaties the borderman remained silent. He stood leaning on his rifle, a tall, dark, strangely sad and stern man.

"Helen, beg him to stay!" implored Betty.

Colonel Zane took Helen's hand, and stroked it. "Yes," he said, "you ask him, lass. I'm sure you can persuade him to stay."

Helen raised her head. "Is Brandt dead?" she whispered faintly.

Still the borderman failed to speak, but his silence was not an affirmative.

"You said you loved me," she cried wildly. "You said you loved me, yet you didn't kill that monster!"

The borderman, moving quickly like a startled Indian, went out of the door.

★   ★   ★   ★   ★   ★

Once more Jonathan Zane entered the gloomy, quiet aisles of the forest with his soft, tireless tread hardly stirring the leaves.

It was late in the afternoon when he had long left Two Islands behind, and arrived at the scene of Mordaunt's death. Satisfied with the distance he had traversed, he crawled into a thicket to rest.

Daybreak found him again on the trail. He made a short cut over the ridges and by the time the mist had lifted from the valley he was within stalking distance of the glade. He approached this in the familiar, slow, cautious manner, and halted behind the big rock from which he and Wetzel had leaped. The wood was solemnly quiet. No twittering of birds could be heard. The only sign of life was a gaunt timber-wolf slinking away amid the foliage. Under the big tree the savage who had been killed as he would have murdered Helen, lay a crumpled mass where he had fallen. Two dead Indians were in the center of the glade, and on the other side were three more bloody, lifeless forms. Wetzel was not there, nor Legget, nor Brandt.

"I reckoned so," muttered Jonathan as he studied the scene. The grass had been trampled, the trees barked, the bushes crushed aside.

Jonathan went out of the glade a short distance, and, circling it, began to look for Wetzel's trail. He found it, and near the light footprints of his comrade were the great, broad moccasin tracks of the outlaw. Further searching disclosed the fact that Brandt must have traveled in line with the others.

With the certainty that Wetzel had killed three of the Indians, and, in some wonderful manner characteristic of him, routed the outlaws of whom he was now in pursuit, Jonathan's smoldering emotion burst forth into full flame. Love for his old comrade, deadly hatred of the outlaws, and passionate thirst for their blood, rioted in his heart.

Like a lynx scenting its quarry, the borderman started on the trail, tireless and unswervable. The traces left by the fleeing outlaws and their pursuer were plain to Jonathan. It was not necessary for him to stop. Legget and Brandt, seeking to escape the implacable Nemesis, were traveling with all possible speed, regardless of the broad trail such hurried movements left behind. They knew full well it would be difficult to throw this wolf off the scent; understood that if any attempt was made to ambush the trail, they must cope with woodcraft keener than an Indian's. Flying in desperation, they hoped to reach the rocky retreat, where, like foxes in their burrows, they believed themselves safe.

When the sun sloped low toward the western horizon, lengthening Jonathan's shadow, he slackened pace. He was entering the rocky, rugged country which marked the approach to the distant Alleghenies. From the top of a ridge he took his bearings, deciding that he was within a few miles of Legget's hiding-place.

At the foot of this ridge, where a murmuring brook sped softly over its bed, he halted. Here a number of horses had forded the brook. They were iron-shod, which indicated almost to a certainty, that they were stolen horses, and in the hands of Indians.

Jonathan saw where the trail of the steeds was merged into that of the outlaws. He suspected that the Indians and Legget had held a short council. As he advanced the borderman found only the faintest impression of Wetzel's trail. Legget and Brandt no longer left any token of their course. They were riding the horses.

All the borderman cared to know was if Wetzel still pursued. He passed on swiftly up a hill, through a wood of birches where the trail showed on a line of broken ferns, then out upon a low ridge where patches of grass grew sparsely. Here he saw in this last ground no indication of his comrade's trail; nothing was to be seen save the imprints of the horses' hoofs. Jonathan halted behind the nearest underbrush. This sudden move on the part of Wetzel was token that, suspecting an ambush, he had made a detour somewhere, probably in the grove of birches.

All the while his eyes searched the long, barren reach ahead. No thicket, fallen tree, or splintered rocks, such as Indians utilized for an ambush, could be seen. Indians always sought the densely matted underbrush, a windfall, or rocky retreat and there awaited a pursuer. It was one of the borderman's tricks of woodcraft that he could recognize such places.

Far beyond the sandy ridge Jonathan came to a sloping, wooded hillside, upon which were scattered big rocks, some mossy and lichen-covered, and one, a giant boulder, with a crown of ferns and laurel gracing its flat surface. It was such a place as the savages would select for ambush. He knew, however, that if an Indian had hidden himself there Wetzel would have discovered him. When opposite the rock Jonathan saw a broken fern hanging over the edge. The heavy trail of the horses ran close beside it.

Then with that thoroughness of search which made the borderman what he was, Jonathan leaped upon the rock. There, lying in the midst of the ferns, lay an Indian with sullen, somber face set in the repose of death. In his side was a small bullet hole.

Jonathan examined the savage's rifle. It had been discharged. The rock, the broken fern, the dead Indian, the discharged rifle, told the story of that woodland tragedy.

Wetzel had discovered the ambush. Leaving the trail, he had tricked the redskin into firing, then getting a glimpse of the Indian's red body through the sights of his fatal weapon, the deed was done.

With greater caution Jonathan advanced once more. Not far beyond the rock he found Wetzel's trail. The afternoon was drawing to a close. He could not travel much farther, yet he kept on, hoping to overtake his comrade before darkness set in. From time to time he whistled; but got no answering signal.

When the tracks of the horses were nearly hidden by the gathering dusk, Jonathan decided to halt for the night. He whistled one more note, louder and clearer, and awaited the result with strained ears. The deep silence of the wilderness prevailed, suddenly to be broken by a faint, far-away, melancholy call of the hermit-thrush. It was the answering signal the borderman had hoped to hear.

Not many moments elapsed before he heard another call, low, and near at hand, to which he replied. The bushes parted noiselessly on his left, and the tall form of Wetzel appeared silently out of the gloom.

The two gripped hands in silence.

"Hev you any meat?" Wetzel asked, and as Jonathan handed him his knapsack, he continued, "I was kinder lookin' fer you. Did you get out all right with the lass?"

"Nary a scratch."

The giant borderman grunted his satisfaction.

"How'd Legget and Brandt get away?" asked Jonathan.

"Cut an' run like scared bucks. Never got a hand on either of 'em."

"How many redskins did they meet back here a spell?"

"They was seven; but now there are only six, an' all snug in Legget's place by this time."

"I reckon we're near his den."

"We're not far off."

Night soon closing down upon the bordermen found them wrapped in slumber, as if no deadly foes were near at hand. The soft night wind sighed dismally among the bare trees. A few bright stars twinkled overhead. In the darkness of the forest the bordermen were at home.

CHAPTER XXII

In Legget's rude log cabin a fire burned low, lightening the forms of the two border outlaws, and showing in the background the dark forms of Indians sitting motionless on the floor. Their dusky eyes emitted a baleful glint, seemingly a reflection of their savage souls caught by the firelight. Legget wore a look of ferocity and sullen fear strangely blended. Brandt's face was hard and haggard, his lips set, his gray eyes smoldering.

"Safe?" he hissed. "Safe you say? You'll see that it's the same now as on the other night, when those border-tigers jumped us and we ran like cowards. I'd have fought it out here, but for you."

"Thet man Wetzel is ravin' mad, I tell you," growled Legget. "I reckon I've stood my ground enough to know I ain't no coward. But this fellar's crazy. He hed the Injuns slashin' each other like a pack of wolves round a buck."

"He's no more mad than you or I," declared Brandt. "I know all about him. His moaning in the woods, and wild yells are only tricks. He knows the Indian nature, and he makes their very superstition and religion aid him in his fighting. I told you what he'd do. Didn't I beg you to kill Zane when we had a chance? Wetzel would never have taken our trail alone. Now they've beat me out of the girl, and as sure as death will round us up here."

"You don't believe they'll rush us here?" asked Legget.

"They're too keen to take foolish chances, but something will be done we don't expect. Zane was a prisoner here; he had a good look at this place, and you can gamble he'll remember."

"Zane must hev gone back to Fort Henry with the girl."

"Mark what I say, he'll come back!"

"Wal, we kin hold this place against all the men Eb Zane may put out."

"He won't send a man," snapped Brandt passionately. "Remember this, Legget, we're not to fight against soldiers, settlers, or hunters; but bordermen—understand—bordermen! Such as have been developed right here on this bloody frontier, and nowhere else on earth. They haven't fear in them. Both are fleet as deer in the woods. They can't be seen or trailed. They can snuff a candle with a rifle ball in the dark. I've seen Zane do it three times at a hundred yards. And Wetzel! He wouldn't waste powder on practicing. They can't be ambushed, or shaken off a track; they take the scent like buzzards, and have eyes like eagles."

"We kin slip out of here under cover of night," suggested Legget.

"Well, what then? That's all they want. They'd be on us again by sunset. No! we've got to stand our ground and fight. We'll stay as long as we can; but they'll rout us out somehow, be sure of that. And if one of us pokes his nose out to the daylight, it will be shot off."

"You're sore, an' you've lost your nerve," said Legget harshly. "Sore at me 'cause I got sweet on the girl. Ho! ho!"

Brandt shot a glance at Legget which boded no good. His strong hands clenched in an action betraying the reckless rage in his heart. Then he carefully removed his hunting coat, and examined his wound. He retied the bandage, muttering gloomily, "I'm so weak as to be light-headed. If this cut opens again, it's all day for me."

After that the inmates of the hut were quiet. The huge outlaw bowed his shaggy head for a while, and then threw himself on a pile of hemlock boughs. Brandt was not long in seeking rest. Soon both were fast asleep. Two of the savages passed out with cat-like step, leaving the door open. The fire had burned low, leaving a bed of dead coals. Outside in the dark a waterfall splashed softly.

The darkest hour came, and passed, and paled slowly to gray. Birds began to twitter. Through the door of the cabin the light of day streamed in. The two Indian sentinels were building a fire on the stone hearth. One by one the other savages got up, stretched and yawned, and began the business of the day by cooking their breakfast. It was, apparently, every one for himself.

Legget arose, shook himself like a shaggy dog, and was starting for the door when one of the sentinels stopped him. Brandt, who was now awake, saw the action, and smiled.

In a few moments Indians and outlaws were eating for breakfast roasted strips of venison, with corn meal baked brown, which served as bread. It was a somber, silent group.

Presently the shrill neigh of a horse startled them. Following it, the whip-like crack of a rifle stung and split the morning air. Hard on this came an Indian's long, wailing death-cry.

"Hah!" exclaimed Brandt.

Legget remained immovable. One of the savages peered out through a little port-hole at the rear of the hut. The others continued their meal.

"Whistler'll come in presently to tell us who's doin' thet shootin'," said Legget. "He's a keen Injun."

"He's not very keen now," replied Brandt, with bitter certainty. "He's what the settlers call a good Indian, which is to say, dead!"

Legget scowled at his lieutenant.

"I'll go an' see," he replied and seized his rifle.

He opened the door, when another rifle-shot rang out. A bullet whistled in the air, grazing the outlaw's shoulder, and imbedded itself in the heavy door-frame.

Legget leaped back with a curse.

"Close shave!" said Brandt coolly. "That bullet came, probably, straight down from the top of the cliff. Jack Zane's there. Wetzel is lower down watching the outlet. We're trapped."

"Trapped," shouted Legget with an angry leer. "We kin live here longer'n the bordermen kin. We've meat on hand, an' a good spring in the back of the hut. How'er we trapped?"

"We won't live twenty-four hours," declared Brandt.

"Why?"

"Because we'll be routed out. They'll find some way to do it, and we'll never have another chance to fight in the open, as we had the other night when they came after the girl. From now on there'll be no sleep, no time to eat, the nameless fear of an unseen foe who can't be shaken off, marching by night, hiding and starving by day, until! I'd rather be back in Fort Henry at Colonel Zane's mercy."

Legget turned a ghastly face toward Brandt. "Look a here. You're takin' a lot of glee in sayin' these things. I believe you've lost your nerve, or the lettin' out of a little blood hes made you wobbly. We've Injuns here, an' ought to be a match fer two men."

Brandt gazed at him with a derisive smile.

"We kin go out an' fight these fellars," continued Legget. "We might try their own game, hidin' an' crawlin' through the woods."

"We two would have to go it alone. If you still had your trusty, trained band of experienced Indians, I'd say that would be just the thing. But Ashbow and the Chippewa are dead; so are the others. This bunch of redskins here may do to steal a few horses; but they don't amount to much against Zane and Wetzel. Besides, they'll cut and run presently, for they're scared and suspicious. Look at the chief; ask him."

The savage Brandt indicated was a big Indian just coming into manhood. His swarthy face still retained some of the frankness and simplicity of youth.

"Chief," said Legget in the Indian tongue. "The great paleface hunter, Deathwind, lies hid in the woods."

"Last night the Shawnee heard the wind of death mourn through the trees," replied the chief gloomily.

"See! What did I say?" cried Brandt. "The superstitious fool! He would begin his death-chant almost without a fight. We can't count on the redskins. What's to be done?"

The outlaw threw himself upon the bed of boughs, and Legget sat down with his rifle across his knees. The Indians maintained the same stoical composure. The moments dragged by into hours.

"Ugh!" suddenly exclaimed the Indian at the end of the hut.

Legget ran to him, and acting upon a motion of the Indian's hand, looked out through the little port-hole.

The sun was high. He saw four of the horses grazing by the brook; then gazed scrutinizingly from the steep waterfall, along the green-stained cliff to the dark narrow cleft in the rocks. Here was the only outlet from the inclosure. He failed to discover anything unusual.

The Indian grunted again, and pointed upward.

"Smoke! There's smoke risin' above the trees," cried Legget. "Brandt, come here. What's thet mean?"

Brandt hurried, looked out. His face paled, his lower jaw protruded, quivered, and then was shut hard. He walked away, put his foot on a bench and began to lace his leggings.

"Wal?" demanded Legget.

"The game's up! Get ready to run and be shot at," cried Brandt with a hiss of passion.

Almost as he spoke the roof of the hut shook under a heavy blow.

"What's thet?" No one replied. Legget glanced from Brandt's cold, determined face to the uneasy savages. They were restless, and handling their weapons. The chief strode across the floor with stealthy steps.

"Thud!"

A repetition of the first blow caused the Indians to jump, and drew a fierce imprecation from their outlaw leader.

Brandt eyed him narrowly. "It's coming to you, Legget. They are shooting arrows of fire into the roof from the cliff. Zane is doin' that. He can make a bow and draw one, too. We're to be burned out. Now, damn you! take your medicine! I wanted you to kill him when you had the chance. If you had done so we'd never have come to this. Burned out, do you get that? Burned out!"

"Fire!'" exclaimed Legget. He sat down as if the strength had left his legs.

The Indians circled around the room like caged tigers.

"Ugh!" The chief suddenly reached up and touched the birch-bark roof of the hut.

His action brought the attention of all to a faint crackling of burning wood.

"It's caught all right," cried Brandt in a voice which cut the air like a blow from a knife.

"I'll not be smoked like a ham, fer all these tricky bordermen," roared Legget. Drawing his knife he hacked at the heavy buckskin hinges of the rude door. When it dropped free he measured it against the open space. Sheathing the blade, he grasped his rifle in his right hand and swung the door on his left arm. Heavy though it was he carried it easily. The roughly hewn planks afforded a capital shield for all except the lower portion of his legs and feet. He went out of the hut with the screen of wood between himself and the cliff, calling for the Indians to follow. They gathered behind him, breathing hard, clutching their weapons, and seemingly almost crazed by excitement.

Brandt, with no thought of joining this foolhardy attempt to escape from the inclosure, ran to the little port-hole that he might see the outcome. Legget and his five redskins were running toward the narrow outlet in the gorge. The awkward and futile efforts of the Indians to remain behind the shield were almost pitiful. They crowded each other for favorable positions, but, struggle as they might, one or two were always exposed to the cliff. Suddenly one, pushed to the rear, stopped simultaneously with the crack of a rifle, threw up his arms and fell. Another report, differing from the first, rang out. A savage staggered from behind the speeding group with his hand at his side. Then he dropped into the brook.

Evidently Legget grasped this as a golden opportunity, for he threw aside the heavy shield and sprang forward, closely followed by his red-skinned allies. Immediately they came near the cliff, where the trail ran into the gorge, a violent shaking of the dry ferns overhead made manifest the activity of some heavy body. Next instant a huge yellow figure, not unlike a leaping catamount, plunged down with a roar so terrible as to sound inhuman. Legget, Indians, and newcomer rolled along the declivity toward the brook in an indistinguishable mass.

Two of the savages shook themselves free, and bounded to their feet nimbly as cats, but Legget and the other redskin became engaged in a terrific combat. It was a wrestling whirl, so fierce and rapid as to render blows ineffectual. The leaves scattered as if in a whirlwind. Legget's fury must have been awful, to judge from his hoarse screams; the Indians' fear maddening, as could be told by their shrieks. The two savages ran wildly about the combatants, one trying to level a rifle, the other to get in a blow with a tomahawk. But the movements of the trio, locked in deadly embrace, were too swift.

Above all the noise of the contest rose that strange, thrilling roar.

"Wetzel!" muttered Brandt, with a chill, creeping shudder as he gazed upon the strife with fascinated eyes.

"Bang!" Again from the cliff came that heavy bellow.

The savage with the rifle shrunk back as if stung, and without a cry fell limply in a heap. His companion, uttering a frightened cry, fled from the glen.

The struggle seemed too deadly, too terrible, to last long. The Indian and the outlaw were at a disadvantage. They could not strike freely. The whirling conflict grew more fearful. During one second the huge, brown, bearish figure of Legget appeared on top; then the dark-bodied, half-naked savage, spotted like a hyena, and finally the lithe, powerful, tiger-shape of the borderman.

Finally Legget wrenched himself free at the same instant that the bloody-stained Indian rolled, writhing in convulsions, away from Wetzel. The outlaw dashed with desperate speed up the trail, and disappeared in the gorge. The borderman sped toward the cliff, leaped on a projecting ledge, grasped an overhanging branch, and pulled himself up. He was out of sight almost as quickly as Legget.

"After his rifle," Brandt muttered, and then realized that he had watched the encounter without any idea of aiding his comrade. He consoled himself with the knowledge that such an attempt would have been useless. From the moment the borderman sprang upon Legget, until he scaled the cliff, his movements had been incredibly swift. It would have been hardly possible to cover him with a rifle, and the outlaw grimly understood that he needed to be careful of that charge in his weapon.

"By Heavens, Wetzel's a wonder!" cried Brandt in unwilling admiration. "Now he'll go after Legget and the redskin, while Zane stays here to get me. Well, he'll succeed, most likely, but I'll never quit. What's this?"

He felt something slippery and warm on his hand. It was blood running from the inside of his sleeve. A slight pain made itself felt in his side. Upon examination he found, to his dismay, that his wound had reopened. With a desperate curse he pulled a linsey jacket off a peg, tore it into strips, and bound up the injury as tightly as possible.

Then he grasped his rifle, and watched the cliff and the gorge with flaring eyes. Suddenly he found it difficult to breathe; his throat was parched, his eyes smarted. Then the odor of wood-smoke brought him to a realization that the cabin was burning. It was only now he understood that the room was full of blue clouds. He sank into the corner, a wolf at bay.

Not many moments passed before the outlaw understood that he could not withstand the increasing heat and stifling vapor of the room. Pieces of burning birch dropped from the roof. The crackling above grew into a steady roar.

"I've got to run for it," he gasped. Death awaited him outside the door, but that was more acceptable than death by fire. Yet to face the final moment when he desired with all his soul to live, required almost super-human courage. Sweating, panting, he glared around. "God! Is there no other way?" he cried in agony. At this moment he saw an ax on the floor.

Seizing it he attacked the wall of the cabin. Beyond this partition was a hut which had been used for a stable. Half a dozen strokes of the ax opened a hole large enough for him to pass through. With his rifle, and a piece of venison which hung near, he literally fell through the hole, where he lay choking, almost fainting. After a time he crawled across the floor to a door. Outside was a dense laurel thicket, into which he crawled.

The crackling and roaring of the fire grew louder. He could see the column of yellow and black smoke. Once fairly under way, the flames rapidly consumed the pitch-pine logs. In an hour Legget's cabins were a heap of ashes.

The afternoon waned. Brandt lay watchful, slowly recovering his strength. He felt secure under this cover, and only prayed for night to come. As the shadows began to creep down the sides of the cliffs, he indulged in hope. If he could slip out in the dark he had a good chance to elude the borderman. In the passionate desire to escape, he had forgotten his fatalistic words to Legget. He reasoned that he could not be trailed until daylight; that a long night's march would put him far in the lead, and there was just a possibility of Zane's having gone away with Wetzel.

When darkness had set in he slipped out of the covert and began his journey for life. Within a few yards he reached the brook. He had only to follow its course in order to find the outlet to the glen. Moreover, its rush and gurgle over the stones would drown any slight noise he might make.

Slowly, patiently he crawled, stopping every moment to listen. What a long time he was in coming to the mossy stones over which the brook dashed through the gorge! But he reached them at last. Here if anywhere Zane would wait for him.

With teeth clenched desperately, and an inward tightening of his chest, for at any moment he expected to see the red flame of a rifle, he slipped cautiously over the mossy stones. Finally his hands touched the dewy grass, and a breath of cool wind fanned his hot cheek. He had succeeded in reaching the open. Crawling some rods farther on, he lay still a while and listened. The solemn wilderness calm was unbroken. Rising, he peered about. Behind loomed the black hill with its narrow cleft just discernible. Facing the north star, he went silently out into the darkness.

CHAPTER XXIII

At daylight Jonathan Zane rolled from his snug bed of leaves under the side of a log, and with the flint, steel and punk he always carried, began building a fire. His actions were far from being hurried. They were deliberate, and seemed strange on the part of a man whose stern face suggested some dark business to be done. When his little fire had been made, he warmed some slices of venison which had already been cooked, and thus satisfied his hunger. Carefully extinguishing the fire and looking to the priming of his rifle, he was ready for the trail.

He stood near the edge of the cliff from which he could command a view of the glen. The black, smoldering ruins of the burned cabins defaced a picturesque scene.

"Brandt must have lit out last night, for I could have seen even a rabbit hidin' in that laurel patch. He's gone, an' it's what I wanted," thought the borderman.

He made his way slowly around the edge of the inclosure and clambered down on the splintered cliff at the end of the gorge. A wide, well-trodden trail extended into the forest below. Jonathan gave scarcely a glance to the beaten path before him; but bent keen eyes to the north, and carefully scrutinized the mossy stones along the brook. Upon a little sand bar running out from the bank he found the light imprint of a hand.

"It was a black night. He'd have to travel by the stars, an' north's the only safe direction for him," muttered the borderman.

On the bank above he found oblong indentations in the grass, barely perceptible, but owing to the peculiar position of the blades of grass, easy for him to follow.

"He'd better have learned to walk light as an Injun before he took to outlawin'," said the borderman in disdain. Then he returned to the gorge and entered the inclosure. At the foot of the little rise of ground where Wetzel had leaped upon his quarry, was one of the dead Indians. Another lay partly submerged in the brown water.

Jonathan carried the weapons of the savages to a dry place under a projecting ledge in the cliff. Passing on down the glen, he stopped a moment where the cabins had stood. Not a log remained. The horses, with the exception of two, were tethered in the copse of laurel. He recognized Colonel Zane's thoroughbred, and Betty's pony. He cut them loose, positive they would not stray from the glen, and might easily be secured at another time.

He set out upon the trail of Brandt with a long, swinging stride. To him the outcome of that pursuit was but a question of time. The consciousness of superior endurance, speed, and craft spoke in his every movement. The consciousness of being in right, a factor so powerfully potent for victory, spoke in the intrepid front with which he faced the north.

It was a gloomy November day. Gray, steely clouds drifted overhead. The wind wailed through the bare trees, sending dead leaves scurrying and rustling over the brown earth.

The borderman advanced with a step that covered glade and glen, forest and field, with astonishing swiftness. Long since he had seen that Brandt was holding to the lowland. This did not strike him as singular until for the third time he found the trail lead a short distance up the side of a ridge, then descend, seeking a level. With this discovery came the certainty that Brandt's pace was lessening. He had set out with a hunter's stride, but it had begun to shorten. The outlaw had shirked the hills, and shifted from his northern course. Why? The man was weakening; he could not climb; he was favoring a wound.

What seemed more serious for the outlaw, was the fact that he had left a good trail, and entered the low, wild land north of the Ohio. Even the Indians seldom penetrated this tangled belt of laurel and thorn. Owing to the dry season the swamps were shallow, which was another factor against Brandt. No doubt he had hoped to hide his trail by wading, and here it showed up like the track of a bison.

Jonathan kept steadily on, knowing the farther Brandt penetrated into this wilderness the worse off he would be. The outlaw dared not take to the river until below Fort Henry, which was distant many a weary mile. The trail grew more ragged as the afternoon wore away. When twilight rendered further tracking impossible, the borderman built a fire in a sheltered place, ate his supper, and went to sleep.

In the dim, gray morning light he awoke, fancying he had been startled by a distant rifle shot. He roasted his strips of venison carefully, and ate with a hungry hunter's appreciation, yet sparingly, as befitted a borderman who knew how to keep up his strength upon a long trail.

Hardly had he traveled a mile when Brandt's footprints covered another's. Nothing surprised the borderman; but he had expected this least of all. A hasty examination convinced him that Legget and his Indian ally had fled this way with Wetzel in pursuit.

The morning passed slowly. The borderman kept to the trail like a hound. The afternoon wore on. Over sandy reaches thick with willows, and through long, matted, dried-out cranberry marshes and copses of prickly thorn, the borderman hung to his purpose. His legs seemed never to lose their spring, but his chest began to heave, his head bent, and his face shone with sweat.

At dusk he tired. Crawling into a dry thicket, he ate his scanty meal and fell asleep. When he awoke it was gray daylight. He was wet and chilled. Again he kindled a fire, and sat over it while cooking breakfast.

Suddenly he was brought to his feet by the sound of a rifle shot; then two others followed in rapid succession. Though they were faint, and far away to the west, Jonathan recognized the first, which could have come only from Wetzel's weapon, and he felt reasonably certain of the third, which was Brandt's. There might have been, he reflected grimly, a good reason for Legget's not shooting. However, he knew that Wetzel had rounded up the fugitives, and again he set out.

It was another dismal day, such a one as would be fitting for a dark deed of border justice. A cold, drizzly rain blew from the northwest. Jonathan wrapped a piece of oil-skin around his rifle-breech, and faced the downfall. Soon he was wet to the skin. He kept on, but his free stride had shortened. Even upon his iron muscles this soggy, sticky ground had begun to tell.

The morning passed but the storm did not; the air grew colder and darker. The short afternoon would afford him little time, especially as the rain and running rills of water were obliterating the trail.

In the midst of a dense forest of great cottonwoods and sycamores he came upon a little pond, hidden among the bushes, and shrouded in a windy, wet gloom. Jonathan recognized the place. He had been there in winter hunting bears when all the swamp-land was locked by ice.

The borderman searched along the banks for a time, then went back to the trail, patiently following it. Around the pond it led to the side of a great, shelving rock. He saw an Indian leaning against this, and was about to throw forward his rifle when the strange, fixed, position of the savage told of the tragedy. A wound extended from his shoulder to his waist. Near by on the ground lay Legget. He, too, was dead. His gigantic frame weltered in blood. His big feet were wide apart; his arms spread, and from the middle of his chest protruded the haft of a knife.

The level space surrounding the bodies showed evidence of a desperate struggle. A bush had been rolled upon and crushed by heavy bodies. On the ground was blood as on the stones and leaves. The blade Legget still clutched was red, and the wrist of the hand which held it showed a dark, discolored band, where it had felt the relentless grasp of Wetzel's steel grip. The dead man's buckskin coat was cut into ribbons. On his broad face a demoniacal expression had set in eternal rigidity; the animal terror of death was frozen in his wide staring eyes. The outlaw chief had died as he had lived, desperately.

Jonathan found Wetzel's trail leading directly toward the river, and soon understood that the borderman was on the track of Brandt. The borderman had surprised the worn, starved, sleepy fugitives in the gray, misty dawn. The Indian, doubtless, was the sentinel, and had fallen asleep at his post never to awaken. Legget and Brandt must have discharged their weapons ineffectually. Zane could not understand why his comrade had missed Brandt at a few rods' distance. Perhaps he had wounded the younger outlaw; but certainly he had escaped while Wetzel had closed in on Legget to meet the hardest battle of his career.

While going over his version of the attack, Jonathan followed Brandt's trail, as had Wetzel, to where it ended in the river. The old borderman had continued on down stream along the sandy shore. The outlaw remained in the water to hide his trail.

At one point Wetzel turned north. This move puzzled Jonathan, as did also the peculiar tracks. It was more perplexing because not far below Zane discovered where the fugitive had left the water to get around a ledge of rock.

The trail was approaching Fort Henry. Jonathan kept on down the river until arriving at the head of the island which lay opposite the settlement. Still no traces of Wetzel! Here Zane lost Brandt's trail completely. He waded the first channel, which was shallow and narrow, and hurried across the island. Walking out upon a sand-bar he signaled with his well-known Indian cry. Almost immediately came an answering shout.

While waiting he glanced at the sand, and there, pointing straight toward the fort, he found Brandt's straggling trail!

CHAPTER XXIV

Colonel zane paced to and fro on the porch. His genial smile had not returned; he was grave and somber. Information had just reached him that Jonathan had hailed from the island, and that one of the settlers had started across the river in a boat.

Betty came out accompanied by Mrs. Zane.

"What's this I hear?" asked Betty, flashing an anxious glance toward the river. "Has Jack really come in?"

"Yes," replied the colonel, pointing to a throng of men on the river bank.

"Now there'll be trouble," said Mrs. Zane nervously. "I wish with all my heart Brandt had not thrown himself, as he called it, on your mercy."

"So do I," declared Colonel Zane.

"What will be done?" she asked. "There! that's Jack! Silas has hold of his arm."

"He's lame. He has been hurt," replied her husband.

A little procession of men and boys followed the borderman from the river, and from the cabins appeared the settlers and their wives. But there was no excitement except among the children. The crowd filed into the colonel's yard behind Jonathan and Silas.

Colonel Zane silently greeted his brother with an iron grip of the hand which was more expressive than words. No unusual sight was it to see the borderman wet, ragged, bloody, worn with long marches, hollow-eyed and gloomy; yet he had never before presented such an appearance at Fort Henry. Betty ran forward, and, though she clasped his arm, shrank back. There was that in the borderman's presence to cause fear.

"Wetzel?" Jonathan cried sharply.

The colonel raised both hands, palms open, and returned his brother's keen glance. Then he spoke. "Lew hasn't come in. He chased Brandt across the river. That's all I know."

"Brandt's here, then?" hissed the borderman.

The colonel nodded gloomily.

"Where?"

"In the long room over the fort. I locked him in there."

"Why did he come here?"

Colonel Zane shrugged his shoulders. "It's beyond me. He said he'd rather place himself in my hands than be run down by Wetzel or you. He didn't crawl; I'll say that for him. He just said, 'I'm your prisoner.' He's in pretty bad shape; barked over the temple, lame in one foot, cut under the arm, starved and worn out."

"Take me to him," said the borderman, and he threw his rifle on a bench.

"Very well. Come along," replied the colonel. He frowned at those following them. "Here, you women, clear out!" But they did not obey him.

It was a sober-faced group that marched in through the big stockade gate, under the huge, bulging front of the fort, and up the rough stairway. Colonel Zane removed a heavy bar from before a door, and thrust it open with his foot. The long guard-room brilliantly lighted by sunshine coming through the port-holes, was empty save for a ragged man lying on a bench.

The noise aroused him; he sat up, and then slowly labored to his feet. It was the same flaring, wild-eyed Brandt, only fiercer and more haggard. He wore a bloody bandage round his head. When he saw the borderman he backed, with involuntary, instinctive action, against the wall, yet showed no fear.

In the dark glance Jonathan shot at Brandt shone a pitiless implacability; no scorn, nor hate, nor passion, but something which, had it not been so terrible, might have been justice.

"I think Wetzel was hurt in the fight with Legget," said Jonathan deliberately, "an' ask if you know?"

"I believe he was," replied Brandt readily. "I was asleep when he jumped us, and was awakened by the Indian's yell. Wetzel must have taken a snap shot at me as I was getting up, which accounts, probably, for my being alive. I fell, but did not lose consciousness. I heard Wetzel and Legget fighting, and at last struggled to my feet.

Although dizzy and bewildered, I could see to shoot; but missed. For a long time, it seemed to me, I watched that terrible fight, and then ran, finally reaching the river, where I recovered somewhat."

"Did you see Wetzel again?"

"Once, about a quarter of a mile behind me. He was staggering along on my trail."

At this juncture there was a commotion among the settlers crowding behind Colonel Zane and Jonathan, and Helen Sheppard appeared, white, with her big eyes strangely dilated.

"Oh!" she cried breathlessly, clasping both hands around Jonathan's arm. "I'm not too late? You're not going to—"

"Helen, this is no place for you," said Colonel Zane sternly. "This is business for men. You must not interfere."

Helen gazed at him, at Brandt, and then up at the borderman. She did not loose his arm.

"Outside some one told me you intended to shoot him. Is it true?"

Colonel Zane evaded the searching gaze of those strained, brilliant eyes. Nor did he answer.

As Helen stepped slowly back a hush fell upon the crowd. The whispering, the nervous coughing, and shuffling of feet, ceased.

In those around her Helen saw the spirit of the border. Colonel Zane and Silas wore the same look, cold, hard, almost brutal. The women were strangely grave. Nellie Douns' sweet face seemed changed; there was pity, even suffering on it, but no relenting. Even Betty's face, always so warm, piquant, and wholesome, had taken on a shade of doubt, of gloom, of something almost sullen, which blighted its dark beauty. What hurt Helen most cruelly was the borderman's glittering eyes.

She fought against a shuddering weakness which threatened to overcome her.

"Whose prisoner is Brandt?" she asked of Colonel Zane.

"He gave himself up to me, naturally, as I am in authority here," replied the colonel. "But that signifies little. I can do no less than abide by Jonathan's decree, which, after all, is the decree of the border."

"And that is?"

"Death to outlaws and renegades."

"But cannot you spare him?" implored Helen. "I know he is a bad man; but he might become a better one. It seems like murder to me. To kill him in cold blood, wounded, suffering as he is, when he claimed your mercy. Oh! it is dreadful!"

The usually kind-hearted colonel, soft as wax in the hands of a girl, was now colder and harder than flint.

"It is useless," he replied curtly. "I am sorry for you. We all understand your feelings, that yours are not the principles of the border. If you had lived long here you could appreciate what these outlaws and renegades have done to us. This man is a hardened criminal; he is a thief, a murderer."

"He did not kill Mordaunt," replied Helen quickly. "I saw him draw first and attack Brandt."

"No matter. Come, Helen, cease. No more of this," Colonel Zane cried with impatience.

"But I will not!" exclaimed Helen, with ringing voice and flashing eye. She turned to her girl friends and besought them to intercede for the outlaw. But Nell only looked sorrowfully on, while Betty met her appealing glance with a fire in her eyes that was no dim reflection of her brother's.

"Then I must make my appeal to you," said Helen, facing the borderman. There could be no mistaking how she regarded him. Respect, honor and love breathed from every line of her beautiful face.

"Why do you want him to go free?" demanded Jonathan. "You told me to kill him."

"Oh, I know. But I was not in my right mind. Listen to me, please. He must have been very different once; perhaps had sisters. For their sake give him another chance. I know he has a better nature. I feared him, hated him, scorned him, as if he were a snake, yet he saved me from that monster Legget!"

"For himself!"

"Well, yes, I can't deny that. But he could have ruined me, wrecked me, yet he did not. At least, he meant marriage by me. He said if I would marry him he would flee over the border and be an honest man."

"Have you no other reason?"

"Yes." Helen's bosom swelled and a glory shone in her splendid eyes. "The other reason is, my own happiness!"

Plain to all, if not through her words, from the light in her eyes, that she could not love a man who was a party to what she considered injustice.

The borderman's white face became flaming red.

It was difficult to refuse this glorious girl any sacrifice she demanded for the sake of the love so openly avowed.

Sweetly and pityingly she turned to Brandt: "Will not you help me?"

"Lass, if it were for me you were asking my life I'd swear it yours for always, and I'd be a man," he replied with bitterness; "but not to save my soul would I ask anything of him."

The giant passions, hate and jealousy, flamed in his gray eyes.

"If I persuade them to release you, will you go away, leave this country, and never come back?"

"I'll promise that, lass, and honestly," he replied.

She wheeled toward Jonathan, and now the rosy color chased the pallor from her cheeks.

"Jack, do you remember when we parted at my home; when you left on this terrible trail, now ended, thank God! Do you remember what an ordeal that was for me? Must I go through it again?"

Bewitchingly sweet she was then, with the girlish charm of coquetry almost lost in the deeper, stranger power of the woman.

The borderman drew his breath sharply; then he wrapped his long arms closely round her. She, understanding that victory was hers, sank weeping upon his breast. For a moment he bowed his face over her, and when he lifted it the dark and terrible gloom had gone.

"Eb, let him go, an' at once," ordered Jonathan. "Give him a rifle, some meat, an' a canoe, for he can't travel, an' turn him loose. Only be quick about it, because if Wetzel comes in, God himself couldn't save the outlaw."

It was an indescribable glance that Brandt cast upon the tearful face of the girl who had saved his life. But without a word he followed Colonel Zane from the room.

The crowd slowly filed down the steps. Betty and Nell lingered behind, their eyes beaming through happy tears. Jonathan, long so cold, showed evidence of becoming as quick and passionate a lover as he had been a borderman. At least, Helen had to release herself from his embrace, and it was a blushing, tear stained face she turned to her friends.

When they reached the stockade gate Colonel Zane was hurrying toward the river with a bag in one hand, and a rifle and a paddle in the other. Brandt limped along after him, the two disappearing over the river bank.

Betty, Nell, and the lovers went to the edge of the bluff.

They saw Colonel Zane choose a canoe from among a number on the beach. He launched it, deposited the bag in the bottom, handed the rifle and paddle to Brandt, and wheeled about.

The outlaw stepped aboard, and, pushing off slowly, drifted down and out toward mid-stream. When about fifty yards from shore he gave a quick glance around, and ceased paddling. His face gleamed white, and his eyes glinted like bits of steel in the sun.

Suddenly he grasped the rifle, and, leveling it with the swiftness of thought, fired at Jonathan.

The borderman saw the act, even from the beginning, and must have read the outlaw's motive, for as the weapon flashed he dropped flat on the bank. The bullet sang harmlessly over him, imbedding itself in the stockade fence with a distinct thud.

The girls were so numb with horror that they could not even scream.

Colonel Zane swore lustily. "Where's my gun? Get me a gun. Oh! What did I tell you?"

"Look!" cried Jonathan as he rose to his feet.

Upon the sand-bar opposite stood a tall, dark, familiar figure.

"By all that's holy, Wetzel!" exclaimed Colonel Zane.

They saw the giant borderman raise a long, black rifle, which wavered and fell, and rose again. A little puff of white smoke leaped out, accompanied by a clear, stinging report.

Brandt dropped the paddle he had hurriedly begun plying after his traitor's act. His white face was turned toward the shore as it sank forward to rest at last upon the gunwale of the canoe. Then his body slowly settled, as if seeking repose. His hand trailed outside in the water, drooping inert and lifeless. The little craft drifted down stream.

"You see, Helen, it had to be," said Colonel Zane gently. "What a dastard! A long shot, Jack! Fate itself must have glanced down the sights of Wetzel's rifle."

CHAPTER XXV

A YEAR ROLLED round; once again Indian summer veiled the golden fields and forests in a soft, smoky haze. Once more from the opal-blue sky of autumn nights, shone the great white stars, and nature seemed wrapped in a melancholy hush.

November the third was the anniversary of a memorable event on the frontier—the marriage of the younger borderman.

Colonel Zane gave it the name of "Independence Day," and arranged a holiday, a feast and dance where all the settlement might meet in joyful thankfulness for the first year of freedom on the border.

With the wiping out of Legget's fierce band, the yoke of the renegades and outlaws was thrown off forever. Simon Girty migrated to Canada and lived with a few Indians who remained true to him. His confederates slowly sank into oblivion. The Shawnee tribe sullenly retreated westward, far into the interior of Ohio; the Delawares buried the war hatchet, and smoked the pipe of peace they had ever before refused. For them the dark, mysterious, fatal wind had ceased to moan along the trails, or sigh through tree-tops over lonely Indian camp-fires.

The beautiful Ohio valley had been wrested from the savages and from those parasites who for years had hung around the necks of the red men.

This day was the happiest of Colonel Zane's life. The task he had set himself, and which he had hardly ever hoped to see completed, was ended. The West had been won. What Boone achieved in Kentucky he had accomplished in Ohio and West Virginia.

The feast was spread on the colonel's lawn. Every man, woman and child in the settlement was there. Isaac Zane, with his Indian wife and child, had come from the far-off Huron town. Pioneers from Yellow Creek and eastward to Fort Pitt attended. The spirit of the occasion manifested itself in such joyousness as had never before been experienced in Fort Henry. The great feast was equal to the event. Choice cuts of beef and venison, savory viands, wonderful loaves of bread and great plump pies, sweet cider and old wine, delighted the merry party.

"Friends, neighbors, dear ones," said Colonel Zane, "my heart is almost too full for speech. This occasion, commemorating the day of our freedom on the border, is the beginning of the reward for stern labor, hardship, silenced hearths of long, relentless years. I did not think I'd live to see it. The seed we have sown has taken root; in years to come, perhaps, a great people will grow up on these farms we call our homes. And as we hope those coming afterward will remember us, we should stop a moment to think of the heroes who have gone before. Many there arc whose names will never be written on the roll of fame, whose graves will be unmarked in history. But we who worked, fought, bled beside them, who saw them die for those they left behind, will render them all justice, honor and love. To them we give the victory. They were true; then let us, who begin to enjoy the freedom, happiness and prosperity they won with their lives, likewise be true in memory of them, in deed to ourselves, and in grace to God."

By no means the least of the pleasant features of this pleasant day was the fact that three couples blushingly presented themselves before the colonel, and confided to him their sudden conclusions in regard to the felicitousness of the moment. The happy colonel raced around until he discovered Jim Douns, the minister, and there amid the merry throng he gave the brides away, being the first to kiss them.

It was late in the afternoon when the villagers dispersed to their homes and left the colonel to his own circle. With his strong, dark face beaming, he mounted the old porch step.

"Where are my Zane babies?" he asked. "Ah! here you are! Did anybody ever see anything to beat that? Four wonderful babies! Mother, here's your Daniel—if you'd only named him Eb! Silas, come for Silas junior, bad boy that he is. Isaac, take your Indian princess; ah! little Myeerah with the dusky face. Woe be to him who looks into those eyes when you come to age. Jack, here's little

Jonathan, the last of the bordermen; he, too, has beautiful eyes, big like his mother's. Ah! well, I don't believe I have left a wish, un-less—"

"Unless?" suggested Betty with her sweet smile.

"It might be—" he said and looked at her.

Betty's warm cheek was close to his as she whispered: "Dear Eb!" The rest only the colonel heard.

"Well! By all that's glorious!" he exclaimed, and attempted to seize her; but with burning face Betty fled.

★ ★ ★ ★ ★ ★

"Jack, dear, how the leaves are falling!" exclaimed Helen. "See them floating and whirling. It reminds me of the day I lay a prisoner in the forest glade praying, waiting for you."

The borderman was silent.

They passed down the sandy lane under the colored maple trees, to a new cottage on the hillside.

"I am perfectly happy to-day," continued Helen. "Everybody seems to be content, except you. For the first time in weeks I see that shade on your face, that look in your eyes. Jack, you do not regret the new life?"

"My love, no, a thousand times no," he answered, smiling down into her eyes. They were changing, shadowing with thought, bright as in other days, and with an added beauty. The wilful spirit had been softened by love.

"Ah, I know, you miss the old friend."

The yellow thicket on the slope opened to let out a tall, dark man who came down with lithe and springy stride.

"Jack, it's Wetzel!" said Helen softly.

No words were spoken as the comrades gripped hands.

"Let me see the boy?" asked Wetzel, turning to Helen.

Little Jonathan blinked up at the grave borderman with great round eyes, and pulled with friendly, chubby fingers at the fringed buckskin coat.

"When you're a man the forest trails will be corn fields," muttered Wetzel.

The bordermen strolled together up the brown hillside, and wandered along the river bluff. The air was cool; in the west the ruddy light darkened behind bold hills; a blue mist streaming in the valley shaded into gray as twilight fell.

FICTION

FLATLAND: A ROMANCE OF MANY DIMENSIONS, Edwin A. Abbott. (0-486-27263-X)

PRIDE AND PREJUDICE, Jane Austen. (0-486-28473-5)

CIVIL WAR SHORT STORIES AND POEMS, Edited by Bob Blaisdell. (0-486-48226-X)

THE DECAMERON: Selected Tales, Giovanni Boccaccio. Edited by Bob Blaisdell. (0-486-41113-3)

JANE EYRE, Charlotte Brontë. (0-486-42449-9)

WUTHERING HEIGHTS, Emily Brontë. (0-486-29256-8)

THE THIRTY-NINE STEPS, John Buchan. (0-486-28201-5)

ALICE'S ADVENTURES IN WONDERLAND, Lewis Carroll. (0-486-27543-4)

MY ÁNTONIA, Willa Cather. (0-486-28240-6)

THE AWAKENING, Kate Chopin. (0-486-27786-0)

HEART OF DARKNESS, Joseph Conrad. (0-486-26464-5)

LORD JIM, Joseph Conrad. (0-486-40650-4)

THE RED BADGE OF COURAGE, Stephen Crane. (0-486-26465-3)

THE WORLD'S GREATEST SHORT STORIES, Edited by James Daley. (0-486-44716-2)

A CHRISTMAS CAROL, Charles Dickens. (0-486-26865-9)

GREAT EXPECTATIONS, Charles Dickens. (0-486-41586-4)

A TALE OF TWO CITIES, Charles Dickens. (0-486-40651-2)

CRIME AND PUNISHMENT, Fyodor Dostoyevsky. Translated by Constance Garnett. (0-486-41587-2)

THE ADVENTURES OF SHERLOCK HOLMES, Sir Arthur Conan Doyle. (0-486-47491-7)

THE HOUND OF THE BASKERVILLES, Sir Arthur Conan Doyle. (0-486-28214-7)

BLAKE: PROPHET AGAINST EMPIRE, David V. Erdman. (0-486-26719-9)

WHERE ANGELS FEAR TO TREAD, E. M. Forster. (0-486-27791-7)

BEOWULF, Translated by R. K. Gordon. (0-486-27264-8)

THE RETURN OF THE NATIVE, Thomas Hardy. (0-486-43165-7)

THE SCARLET LETTER, Nathaniel Hawthorne. (0-486-28048-9)

SIDDHARTHA, Hermann Hesse. (0-486-40653-9)

THE ODYSSEY, Homer. (0-486-40654-7)

THE TURN OF THE SCREW, Henry James. (0-486-26684-2)

DUBLINERS, James Joyce. (0-486-26870-5)

FICTION

THE METAMORPHOSIS AND OTHER STORIES, Franz Kafka. (0-486-29030-1)

SONS AND LOVERS, D. H. Lawrence. (0-486-42121-X)

THE CALL OF THE WILD, Jack London. (0-486-26472-6)

GREAT AMERICAN SHORT STORIES, Edited by Paul Negri. (0-486-42119-8)

THE GOLD-BUG AND OTHER TALES, Edgar Allan Poe. (0-486-26875-6)

ANTHEM, Ayn Rand. (0-486-49277-X)

FRANKENSTEIN, Mary Shelley. (0-486-28211-2)

THE JUNGLE, Upton Sinclair. (0-486-41923-1)

THREE LIVES, Gertrude Stein. (0-486-28059-4)

THE STRANGE CASE OF DR. JEKYLL AND MR. HYDE, Robert Louis Stevenson. (0-486-26688-5)

DRACULA, Bram Stoker. (0-486-41109-5)

UNCLE TOM'S CABIN, Harriet Beecher Stowe. (0-486-44028-1)

ADVENTURES OF HUCKLEBERRY FINN, Mark Twain. (0-486-28061-6)

THE ADVENTURES OF TOM SAWYER, Mark Twain. (0-486-40077-8)

CANDIDE, Voltaire. Edited by Francois-Marie Arouet. (0-486-26689-3)

THE COUNTRY OF THE BLIND: and Other Science-Fiction Stories, H. G. Wells. Edited by Martin Gardner. (0-486-48289-8)

THE WAR OF THE WORLDS, H. G. Wells. (0-486-29506-0)

ETHAN FROME, Edith Wharton. (0-486-26690-7)

THE PICTURE OF DORIAN GRAY, Oscar Wilde. (0-486-27807-7)

MONDAY OR TUESDAY: Eight Stories, Virginia Woolf. (0-486-29453-6)

PLAYS

THE ORESTEIA TRILOGY: Agamemnon, the Libation-Bearers and the Furies, Aeschylus. (0-486-29242-8)

EVERYMAN, Anonymous. (0-486-28726-2)

THE BIRDS, Aristophanes. (0-486-40886-8)

LYSISTRATA, Aristophanes. (0-486-28225-2)

THE CHERRY ORCHARD, Anton Chekhov. (0-486-26682-6)

THE SEA GULL, Anton Chekhov. (0-486-40656-3)

MEDEA, Euripides. (0-486-27548-5)

FAUST, PART ONE, Johann Wolfgang von Goethe. (0-486-28046-2)

THE INSPECTOR GENERAL, Nikolai Gogol. (0-486-28500-6)

SHE STOOPS TO CONQUER, Oliver Goldsmith. (0-486-26867-5)

GHOSTS, Henrik Ibsen. (0-486-29852-3)

A DOLL'S HOUSE, Henrik Ibsen. (0-486-27062-9)

HEDDA GABLER, Henrik Ibsen. (0-486-26469-6)

DR. FAUSTUS, Christopher Marlowe. (0-486-28208-2)

TARTUFFE, Molière. (0-486-41117-6)

BEYOND THE HORIZON, Eugene O'Neill. (0-486-29085-9)

THE EMPEROR JONES, Eugene O'Neill. (0-486-29268-1)

CYRANO DE BERGERAC, Edmond Rostand. (0-486-41119-2)

MEASURE FOR MEASURE: Unabridged, William Shakespeare. (0-486-40889-2)

FOUR GREAT TRAGEDIES: Hamlet, Macbeth, Othello, and Romeo and Juliet, William Shakespeare. (0-486-44083-4)

THE COMEDY OF ERRORS, William Shakespeare. (0-486-42461-8)

HENRY V, William Shakespeare. (0-486-42887-7)

MUCH ADO ABOUT NOTHING, William Shakespeare. (0-486-28272-4)

FIVE GREAT COMEDIES: Much Ado About Nothing, Twelfth Night, A Midsummer Night's Dream, As You Like It and The Merry Wives of Windsor, William Shakespeare. (0-486-44086-9)

OTHELLO, William Shakespeare. (0-486-29097-2)

AS YOU LIKE IT, William Shakespeare. (0-486-40432-3)

ROMEO AND JULIET, William Shakespeare. (0-486-27557-4)

A MIDSUMMER NIGHT'S DREAM, William Shakespeare. (0-486-27067-X)

THE MERCHANT OF VENICE, William Shakespeare. (0-486-28492-1)

HAMLET, William Shakespeare. (0-486-27278-8)

RICHARD III, William Shakespeare. (0-486-28747-5)

NONFICTION

POETICS, Aristotle. (0-486-29577-X)

MEDITATIONS, Marcus Aurelius. (0-486-29823-X)

THE WAY OF PERFECTION, St. Teresa of Avila. Edited and Translated by
E. Allison Peers. (0-486-48451-3)

THE DEVIL'S DICTIONARY, Ambrose Bierce. (0-486-27542-6)

GREAT SPEECHES OF THE 20TH CENTURY, Edited by Bob Blaisdell.
(0-486-47467-4)

THE COMMUNIST MANIFESTO AND OTHER REVOLUTIONARY WRITINGS:
Marx, Marat, Paine, Mao Tse-Tung, Gandhi and Others, Edited by Bob Blaisdell.
(0-486-42465-0)

INFAMOUS SPEECHES: From Robespierre to Osama bin Laden, Edited by Bob
Blaisdell. (0-486-47849-1)

GREAT ENGLISH ESSAYS: From Bacon to Chesterton, Edited by Bob Blaisdell.
(0-486-44082-6)

GREEK AND ROMAN ORATORY, Edited by Bob Blaisdell. (0-486-49622-8)

THE UNITED STATES CONSTITUTION: The Full Text with Supplementary
Materials, Edited and with supplementary materials by Bob Blaisdell.
(0-486-47166-7)

GREAT SPEECHES BY NATIVE AMERICANS, Edited by Bob Blaisdell.
(0-486-41122-2)

GREAT SPEECHES BY AFRICAN AMERICANS: Frederick Douglass, Sojourner
Truth, Dr. Martin Luther King, Jr., Barack Obama, and Others, Edited by
James Daley. (0-486-44761-8)

GREAT SPEECHES BY AMERICAN WOMEN, Edited by James Daley.
(0-486-46141-6)

HISTORY'S GREATEST SPEECHES, Edited by James Daley. (0-486-49739-9)

GREAT INAUGURAL ADDRESSES, Edited by James Daley. (0-486-44577-1)

GREAT SPEECHES ON GAY RIGHTS, Edited by James Daley. (0-486-47512-3)

ON THE ORIGIN OF SPECIES: By Means of Natural Selection, Charles Darwin.
(0-486-45006-6)

NARRATIVE OF THE LIFE OF FREDERICK DOUGLASS, Frederick Douglass.
(0-486-28499-9)

THE SOULS OF BLACK FOLK, W. E. B. Du Bois. (0-486-28041-1)

NATURE AND OTHER ESSAYS, Ralph Waldo Emerson. (0-486-46947-6)

SELF-RELIANCE AND OTHER ESSAYS, Ralph Waldo Emerson. (0-486-27790-9)

THE LIFE OF OLAUDAH EQUIANO, Olaudah Equiano. (0-486-40661-X)

WIT AND WISDOM FROM POOR RICHARD'S ALMANACK, Benjamin Franklin.
(0-486-40891-4)

THE AUTOBIOGRAPHY OF BENJAMIN FRANKLIN, Benjamin Franklin.
(0-486-29073-5)

PLAYS

THE ORESTEIA TRILOGY: Agamemnon, the Libation-Bearers and the Furies, Aeschylus. (0-486-29242-8)

EVERYMAN, Anonymous. (0-486-28726-2)

THE BIRDS, Aristophanes. (0-486-40886-8)

LYSISTRATA, Aristophanes. (0-486-28225-2)

THE CHERRY ORCHARD, Anton Chekhov. (0-486-26682-6)

THE SEA GULL, Anton Chekhov. (0-486-40656-3)

MEDEA, Euripides. (0-486-27548-5)

FAUST, PART ONE, Johann Wolfgang von Goethe. (0-486-28046-2)

THE INSPECTOR GENERAL, Nikolai Gogol. (0-486-28500-6)

SHE STOOPS TO CONQUER, Oliver Goldsmith. (0-486-26867-5)

GHOSTS, Henrik Ibsen. (0-486-29852-3)

A DOLL'S HOUSE, Henrik Ibsen. (0-486-27062-9)

HEDDA GABLER, Henrik Ibsen. (0-486-26469-6)

DR. FAUSTUS, Christopher Marlowe. (0-486-28208-2)

TARTUFFE, Molière. (0-486-41117-6)

BEYOND THE HORIZON, Eugene O'Neill. (0-486-29085-9)

THE EMPEROR JONES, Eugene O'Neill. (0-486-29268-1)

CYRANO DE BERGERAC, Edmond Rostand. (0-486-41119-2)

MEASURE FOR MEASURE: Unabridged, William Shakespeare. (0-486-40889-2)

FOUR GREAT TRAGEDIES: Hamlet, Macbeth, Othello, and Romeo and Juliet, William Shakespeare. (0-486-44083-4)

THE COMEDY OF ERRORS, William Shakespeare. (0-486-42461-8)

HENRY V, William Shakespeare. (0-486-42887-7)

MUCH ADO ABOUT NOTHING, William Shakespeare. (0-486-28272-4)

FIVE GREAT COMEDIES: Much Ado About Nothing, Twelfth Night, A Midsummer Night's Dream, As You Like It and The Merry Wives of Windsor, William Shakespeare. (0-486-44086-9)

OTHELLO, William Shakespeare. (0-486-29097-2)

AS YOU LIKE IT, William Shakespeare. (0-486-40432-3)

ROMEO AND JULIET, William Shakespeare. (0-486-27557-4)

A MIDSUMMER NIGHT'S DREAM, William Shakespeare. (0-486-27067-X)

THE MERCHANT OF VENICE, William Shakespeare. (0-486-28492-1)

HAMLET, William Shakespeare. (0-486-27278-8)

RICHARD III, William Shakespeare. (0-486-28747-5)

DOVER THRIFT EDITIONS

PLAYS

THE TAMING OF THE SHREW, William Shakespeare. (0-486-29765-9)

MACBETH, William Shakespeare. (0-486-27802-6)

KING LEAR, William Shakespeare. (0-486-28058-6)

FOUR GREAT HISTORIES: Henry IV Part I, Henry IV Part II, Henry V, and Richard III, William Shakespeare. (0-486-44629-8)

THE TEMPEST, William Shakespeare. (0-486-40658-X)

JULIUS CAESAR, William Shakespeare. (0-486-26876-4)

TWELFTH NIGHT; OR, WHAT YOU WILL, William Shakespeare. (0-486-29290-8)

HEARTBREAK HOUSE, George Bernard Shaw. (0-486-29291-6)

PYGMALION, George Bernard Shaw. (0-486-28222-8)

ARMS AND THE MAN, George Bernard Shaw. (0-486-26476-9)

OEDIPUS REX, Sophocles. (0-486-26877-2)

ANTIGONE, Sophocles. (0-486-27804-2)

FIVE GREAT GREEK TRAGEDIES, Sophocles, Euripides and Aeschylus. (0-486-43620-9)

THE FATHER, August Strindberg. (0-486-43217-3)

THE PLAYBOY OF THE WESTERN WORLD AND RIDERS TO THE SEA, J. M. Synge. (0-486-27562-0)

TWELVE CLASSIC ONE-ACT PLAYS, Edited by Mary Carolyn Waldrep. (0-486-47490-9)

LADY WINDERMERE'S FAN, Oscar Wilde. (0-486-40078-6)

AN IDEAL HUSBAND, Oscar Wilde. (0-486-41423-X)

THE IMPORTANCE OF BEING EARNEST, Oscar Wilde. (0-486-26478-5)